Advance Praise
The Grateful V

'Twisty, thrilling and visceral, and one of the finest historical crime novels of recent years. *The Grateful Water* does for Dublin what Dickens did for London. Adelman is a superb storyteller, and her debut novel is a clever, lively and gripping, page turner.'
    —Niamh Boyce, author of *The Herbalist* and *Her Kind*

'*The Grateful Water* combines the pace and intrigue of a mystery with a beautifully rendered setting that gives life to the concerns, travails, and tragedies of women often overlooked by history. Juliana Adelman brings 1860s Dublin expertly to life, not only through the Liffey and her waterways, but also through a rich cast of characters whose dreams, adversities and relationships make the past so vivid on the page. A hugely accomplished debut from a talented new writer.'
    —Rosemary Hennigan, author of *The Favourite*

'Juliana Adelman superbly evokes the squalor and grandeur of nineteenth-century Dublin with a powerful story that is intricate, absorbing, and beautifully told. I was gripped from the very first page.'
    —Andrew Hughes, author of *The Coroner's Daughter*
    and *Emma Disappeared*

'Juliana Adelman brings a clear eye to nineteenth-century Dublin with all its character, poverty, stink and middle-class hypocrisy. Detective Peakin is a wonderful creation, a wry, complicated man of his time, keeping his private desperation in. Adelman's writing is crisp and unsentimental yet rich in sensory details of the sights, smells and sounds of the thronged city.'

—Laura McKenna, author of *Words to Shape My Name*

THE
GRATEFUL
WATER

THE GRATEFUL WATER
First published in 2024 by
New Island Books
Glenshesk House
10 Richview Office Park
Clonskeagh
Dublin D14 V8C4
Republic of Ireland
newisland.ie

Print ISBN: 978-1-84840-924-8
eBook ISBN: 978-1-84840-925-5

British Library Cataloguing in Publication Data. A CIP catalogue record for this book is available from the British Library.

Set in 14 on 16.3pt Mrs Eaves
Typeset by JVR Creative India
Edited by Susan McKeever, susanmckeever.biz
Cover design by Luke Bird, lukebird.co.uk
Printed by L&C Printing Group, Poland, lcprinting.eu

The paper used in this book comes from the wood pulp of sustainably managed forests.

New Island received financial assistance from The Arts Council (An Chomhairle Ealaíon), Dublin, Ireland.

New Island Books is a member of Publishing Ireland.

10 9 8 7 6 5 4 3 2 1

THE GRATEFUL WATER

JULIANA ADELMAN

NEW ISLAND

For my mother, Lydia Rogers

Part I

The river slid, in her greasy way, towards the port. She picked up Dublin's rubbish and dropped it again like a child with too many toys. Here a rotting basket, there a rusted birdcage. Cats and dogs and parakeets, pigs' blood and cows' shit, the contents of ash pits, privies and new-fangled water closets. The grateful water received them all and carried them to the sea.

When you stood beside her on Richmond Bridge and turned east, you saw spare houses of brick running down the quays to Carlisle Bridge. The houses faced the Liffey like a dismal receiving line. They would have turned their backs on her if they could have. Instead, they watched through closed windows as Dubliners with sensitive noses fled to villas in the suburbs. The old houses filled up with doctors and solicitors, fancy ribbon sellers, portmanteau makers and dealers in hygienic plumbing. Warm sunlight flattered the houses, but a dull day drew your eye to crumbled corners and dirty plaster. Tenement families gathered in lanes behind the houses where the light was thin and the air was thick.

One night, unremarkable except for the heat, a woman approached the river. She listened to the wet slap against the bridge. She held her silent bundle over the water, shame and guilt wound tight in plain cloth. She dropped it and listened as it fell, one hand gripping the stone rail.

Chapter One

Rose

4th August, 1866

When Denis didn't arrive at the expected hour, Rose allowed herself another teacupful of gin. She'd taken the first bottle from Mrs Kennedy's house a few months ago, expecting to get caught. Cook kept on top of the wine, the whiskey, the brandy. Rose saw her counting them and making up her orders. Maybe no one drank the gin. Just in case, she returned the bottle filled with water.

Denis's boots sounded on the stairs as she ran her tongue around the inside of the cup. She took a biscuit from her skirt, put it in her mouth and chewed. The stitches swam a little on the shirt she was mending. She had drunk the gin too fast. Her lip was numb when she licked it for crumbs.

'I'm sorry for being so late.' Denis was breathing fast and loud, like he'd been hurrying.

'Well, don't come crying to me if your bath's gone cold,' Rose said. She felt him watching her from the doorway. He would be thinking about her hair, about running a hand over it. He would be wanting to kiss her. She kept her head down as he crossed the room and stood beside her. She focused on keeping her hands steady and the stitches straight.

'Something strange happened. I thought I saw something in the river.' His hand was on the back of the chair, she heard it brush the fabric. She wanted to please him, to lean into his touch, but she couldn't. He left her hair alone.

'There's no end to the tricks this heat does be playin' on the eye. You can see the air move.' Sweat prickled the back of her neck. The window was open, but there was no breeze, not even a tickle.

'No, that wasn't it. It wasn't an illusion. It was a baby in the river. Stuck in the mud, under the bridge. I had to fetch the police.'

Rose stopped sewing as she made sense of his words. She thought of Anne, pale and miserable when she'd left Mrs Kennedy's. The gin made her mouth dry and her face hot. She felt his expectation on her neck as warm as the sun through the window. He clicked the coins in his pockets together.

'You never could leave a thing be,' she said, and pulled another stitch tight. She pictured the baby swaddled in dirty sheets.

'You think I should have left it there? A poor babba in that sewer of a river?' She heard him straining to keep his voice level, always trying to avoid angering her. His caution made her furious.

'Once you seen what it was, of course not.' She raised her eyes and swallowed a sigh. 'I'm just saying that every other person on the bridge passed it by without a second glance. It was only you was the fool who had to go down into the river. I suppose you've ruined your boots.' She tried to smile and wondered if he could smell the gin off her like she could smell the pig off him.

Denis frowned. 'I think you and Detective Peakin would get on well. He didn't seem delighted to find it either.'

Rose shrugged. 'All the policemen do be at these days is stalking Fenians and sniffing out nuisances. Your reward for snoopin' is a tub of cold water. Your foolish wife expected you before seven.' She straightened her back and picked up the sewing again to show that the conversation was over.

His lips brushed her cheek and she wrinkled her nose at the familiar animal odours. She caught the tang of blood and felt her pulse rise. The usual scenes began to appear in her mind, but the gin helped them to slip by a little faster. She took a breath through her mouth. It was absurd to still think of the birth, to return to her terror again and again. Denis stepped away.

'I'll wash up now.'

She heard him upstairs, entering the bedroom and undressing. A drawer screeched as he pulled it open, water splashed when he climbed into the bath. She pictured the solid, slippery flesh of him. She got up to make the tea.

Rose spread the table with things that his money had bought her. She smoothed the new serviettes, straightened the shiny plated cutlery stamped with the name of some English city. She heard the bedroom door open and smelled the lemon soap that Denis thought removed the other smells.

'The table's pretty, love,' Denis called as he sat down. Rose was in the kitchen. Even though the doors to the front room were open, she pretended she couldn't hear.

She was hungry. She loaded the plate with more ham, added what was left of the cheese and the loaf. Dropping the food onto the table, she turned back to the kitchen. She wondered would he bring up the maid again. He'd come home last week with notions about hiring a girl to ruin the washing and burn the dinner. They would sit like lord and lady, he said, waiting to be served. She'd refused, but Denis wouldn't let it go. Just like he wouldn't let their baby go. She was the one who'd suffered and bled but it was Denis who still mooned over the tiny stranger who'd almost killed her. She rattled the sideboard for teacups, banging the glass door closed and making the plates jump. She heard him startle in his chair.

'How was your day?' he ventured.

'Desperate quiet. Cook made marmalade. She said I can take a jar tomorrow when it's set.'

'No one else sick? And is Mrs Kennedy's niece recovered now?'

'Please God.' Rose wondered what Anne was doing. Probably reading to Mrs Kennedy from the newspaper.

'I don't like the thought of you in there, shut up with some sickness in the house.'

'There's no one sick now, Denis. Don't be fussing. And your day? How was the shop?' Denis looked at her but didn't press any further.

'Quiet enough. Customers are waiting until there's fresh from the market. I'll have to salt up the unsold pork tomorrow. So it doesn't taint. The beef will serve for another day.' Rose nodded and relaxed a little. She liked that Denis spoke to her as if she was another butcher, another man.

'And have you the floor sparkling and the walls whitewashed?' Rose asked. 'With that cholera case in the port, the inspector is sure to come this week.' Mrs Kennedy was insisting on keeping the curtains drawn and the windows shut against the miasma.

'Yes I heard that.' He wasn't listening to her now.

Rose gulped her tea and watched as Denis reached to serve himself. He cut a thick wedge of bread and applied a slab of butter to it. Rose didn't bother to chide him for his gluttony. She tried to think of another thing to say. She put a piece of ham on her plate.

'The coroner came as well. To see the body. Said there'll be a postmortem and then if they find anything strange an inquest. I'll have to give evidence.' He chewed.

'Anything strange?'

'Well, signs of violence or the like. Infanticide was what the detective thought. The coroner seemed to agree.'

'The police is no better than the newspapers. Everything's a sensation or a horror.'

'What else could it be, though?' They didn't look at each other then, both thinking the same thing. It could be like theirs. Though he'd gone away in a coffin, been buried properly and mourned.

'An accident or something else. Didn't need to be murder.'

'I guess the doctor will know. Anyway, I hope the poor creature didn't suffer too much.'

'I hope the poor mother didn't suffer too much. And now they'll be looking for her. People will be whispering and all.'

Denis kept his eyes on his plate. He didn't like what she'd said. She hadn't been able to stop herself. She wanted to stir him up a little. Her good, calm husband, so much less spiteful than herself. The lines in his forehead meant he was trying to decide if he would risk the argument, the possibility of raised voices.

'I hope I haven't done wrong.' He sunk back in his chair, ran his hand over his beard. 'I didn't like to think of the body rotting there. Or being swept out to sea. It's a human being. At least it should be buried like any other Christian.'

They finished their meal in silence. He left her washing up and went out to the yard to clean his boots. She knew he would pump the water and bring it up to the kitchen like an offering, hoping that she would let him back into the bedroom. So she dried the dishes and went up without even a second cup of tea. She'd just closed the door when she heard him downstairs. She stood holding the handle, listening for his steps. But when she heard the creak of the settee, she released her breath and went to undress.

Chapter Two

Anne

May 1865

Anne Mulhall stood in the small garden where everything was ripening. The clematis buds had swelled and pinkened until it looked like if you touched one it would burst. Soon, the petals on each bloom would spread slightly and curl into sharp little points, like the beaks of baby birds. After they opened, they lost much of their charm. Even a small vine would produce hundreds of identical blooms, falling over one another, vying for attention.

Anne's mother, in the years before she'd been confined to bed, had stuffed the tiny square behind the house with plants. Even on the morning she'd taken ill, she'd been sowing seeds. The headache had overcome her and the plants hadn't paused to wait for her to recover. They continued growing in all directions: tulips reached up through spreading mats of geranium and nasturtium. Climbing roses tumbled over one another, thorny whips of stems swaying in the slightest breeze. And without her tender attention, weeds threatened to overtake everything else.

The garden reminded Anne that time was passing while, inside the house, days ran into one another. The week was punctuated by meals and turns at nursing. No one went to Mass and her father stopped giving dancing lessons. She wasn't sure how they were paying Maggie at all. There was no music, no confident *thunk thunk thunk* of the teacher followed by the student's timid *pat pat pat*. Anne missed the music and thought that her mother did too. Silence didn't suit the house. Where there had once been laughter and the thunder of careless feet, there was now only tiptoes and whispers.

Anne's father was breakfasting in the dining room, Ellen beside him. They froze as Anne entered. Her father leaned back from the table, away from Ellen.

'Morning, Nan,' he said. 'How's the garden?'

'She'll be sorry to see the dandelions and clovers springing up in all the beds. I thought I might tidy things a little this afternoon.'

Mr Mulhall dropped his gaze and then looked at Ellen instead of Anne. Anne knew they thought her mother was dying, but they never said anything directly. Instead, they said things like 'at a low ebb' and 'sinking'. As if she was a body of water. Anne knew they were wrong: if she could just make it until June, then she would recover. The air would lose its chill, the winds would drop and most of the flowers would be out. She couldn't die while everything else was coming to life.

'I'm sure she would appreciate that,' Ellen said. 'I'm so clumsy with plants, I'd be just as likely to pull out some prize specimen as a weed.' She smiled. Mr Mulhall's eyes flicked between the two of them and he smoothed his moustache with his fingers.

Anne wanted to say that Ellen seemed to be clumsy with anything she didn't like to do. Or that she seemed quite able to fuss around her father like he was a prize specimen. But instead she said nothing because no one in the house ever said anything of consequence now that her mother was ill. As though when her mother took to her bed and her sister moved to England they all agreed to continue playing their parts.

'Will you have your porridge with us? I'll ring for Maggie.'

'I've eaten already, thank you.'

Anne had always found sleeping difficult once the days began to stretch. Now she lay awake listening for her mother's ragged breathing or for her to call out. It was a relief to see the sun seep between the curtains, give up the effort and get out of bed.

'Well, maybe you can tempt your mother with something.'

'There's more of the beef tea I made, just ask Maggie.' Ellen's voice reminded Anne of the chirpy little robin that scolded her from the garden wall. 'But make sure she doesn't salt it. I've spoken to her about the salt but she doesn't listen to me at all.'

'Thank you, Ellen. I'll see what I can do.'

Anne fled upstairs without visiting the kitchen, knowing there was no point in bringing anything without seeing how the patient was feeling. Ellen had met Anne's mother through charity work and she prided herself on her nursing skills. Anne's mother thought Ellen would make a nice companion for Anne now that Frances had married and moved away. Over these past two months she'd been devoted to Mrs Mulhall, helping to feed and wash and dress her as she grew weaker. Anne knew she should be grateful for her help. Aunt Julia hadn't even visited, though Father wrote to her. Frances was in London, confined with her first child. No one dared to trouble her. So Ellen came more often and stayed later until one day she stopped going home. She moved into the room Anne once shared with Frances though she was rarely there when Anne woke.

Her mother was sitting up with her arms crossed over the covers. Someone had already opened the curtains. The May sunlight was less generous with her than the garden. Her hair looked brittle, and the skin on her face papery. Anne had become fearful of touching her, as though she might crumble.

'It's me,' Anne said, stepping into the room. 'I've been out in the garden. The lilac is glorious today. I think it smells sweeter when the air is a little cold.'

'Oh lovely. Tell me all about it.'

She went through the beds one wall at a time, naming the plants she could remember and how close they were to blooming. Mrs Mulhall closed her eyes and Anne knew she was picturing everything: the tulips, green except for a tiny tip of pink; the giant bumblebee bouncing around in the lavender.

'Oh and the clematis. It's just about to open. In a few weeks you'll be well enough to see for yourself. When it's a little warmer. Father can carry an armchair out to the garden.'

'Yes, that will be nice. Will you read me Frances's letter once more?'

So Anne read the 'news' that was now more than two weeks old. A few days ago they had tut-tutted over Frances having the nursery papered blue because she was so certain she was carrying a boy. Mrs Mulhall stayed silent and Anne stopped to see if she was awake.

'I'm listening. I'm just a bit tired this morning. But you can stop reading now and tell me a story. Something you remember. I like to hear how you remember things.'

'Do you recall when Frances and I became consumed by fairies?'

Her eyes stayed closed but she smiled.

'I do. I think I read you a picture book and you decided that you could see them everywhere, just at the corner of your eye.'

'Yes and we built that little house underneath the lilac tree out of sticks and we decorated the roof with moss and tiny little flowers. Then Frances got the idea that the bumblebees were just fairies in disguise and she must have a fairy to live in her house. She was positively shocked when it stung her. How could something so small and furry cause such pain?'

Mrs Mulhall squeezed Anne's hand while she carried on recounting the rest of the day and how they'd had to promise Frances apple fritters for tea to get her to stop crying. That was the end of playing fairies.

'Nan, will you fetch me a few flowers from the garden? Even if they're just buds. A clematis maybe. I'd like to feel them in my hands. Not too many. Two or three will do.'

'Of course I will. And maybe I'll bring up some porridge and honey at the same time? Father says you haven't eaten today.'

'That would be nice. And no more of Ellen's beef tea, if you please. Don't tell her, she means well and I'm sure it's good for me. But it's about as tasty as sucking on rusted nails.'

Anne laughed and made sure that her mother was tucked comfortably into the bed. When she got downstairs, Mr Mulhall and Ellen had disappeared somewhere. 'Out for a bit of air,' Maggie said when Anne went into the kitchen for the scissors. While she was in the garden she decided to pull a few weeds. More time passed than she'd intended and it was almost eleven when she mounted the stairs again with a tray.

Anne knocked at the door before pushing it open with her back, careful not to spill the porridge or the vase of rapidly wilting clematis buds surrounding one very green tulip. She'd felt bad picking it, it seemed like it couldn't possibly turn red and open now.

Mrs Mulhall didn't reply, her eyes were closed. She looked beautiful and, Anne thought, maybe a bit recovered. She'd loosened her hair and it was spread across the pillow. She was smiling a little in her sleep. Her cheeks were flushed pink. Anne put the tray down on the dresser and went to sit beside her to see if she could wake her gently. She reached out and felt Mrs Mulhall's forehead. The fever seemed to have receded. She was sleeping so soundly that Anne decided to lie down on the bed beside her.

When she woke the room was crowded. Maggie was whispering 'She's gone, Anne,' and trying to pull her away. Her mother's mouth had fallen open and the space between her parted lips was black. Ellen was wailing while Mr Mulhall leaned against the doorframe, holding a parcel of butcher's meat that he must have gone out to get. A bit of blood had soaked through the paper and he'd let it smudge the wall. For a moment he didn't move, just stood watching. Then he put his arms around Ellen to comfort her.

Chapter Three

Peakin

5th August, 1866

Detective Martin Peakin woke because he couldn't feel his fingers. With great care, he moved the pillow under Peggi's heavy head and withdrew his arm. She stirred, but didn't wake. He brushed a strand of hair from her face.

He cursed himself as he disentangled his body from the damp sheet and reached for his pocket watch on the night stand. It wasn't there, and neither was the night stand because he wasn't at home. He stood and surveyed the room for his clothing. Peggi sighed and rolled over. His eyes adjusted to the dark, and he saw his folded clothes piled on the room's only chair. He groped for the watch in his trousers. Three o'clock; still enough time to get home to bed.

He checked his billfold to see what Peggi had left. She robbed him by silent agreement, just enough to satisfy her pride. He'd been quite happy with Eliza's company but one evening he arrived at Mrs Wilson's and there was Peggi instead. 'Off to reform herself, isn't she?' Peggi said when he asked. His disappointment was absurd. Most men visited houses of ill fame to escape the constancy of marriage. But Peakin preferred constancy and he believed he would make the transition to the marriage bed gladly.

She'd taken an extra shilling but the single pound note from his wages was still there. He found a sixpence and left it on the chair. He would have to forgo chops this week to ensure he could pay his rent. He tiptoed from the room, down the stairs and out the front door. It was always too warm in Mrs Wilson's, so he was surprised when the air on the street failed to cool his face. No breeze, no rain.

The streets were almost silent. He heard the cry of a drunk, the exhalations of a horse in a yard nearby, the deep lowing of cows that needed to be milked. The city's equivalent of Peggi's snores. As he walked, he thought about the baby boy, alone in the cool room waiting for the postmortem. He tried to imagine a woman killing it. His mind conjured first Eliza and then his sister but the images disturbed him, so he blinked to make them disappear. He wondered if the woman had been mad. Puerperal mania, they called it.

He peered down into the river as he crossed over Sackville Bridge. The weak light of the few gas lamps made the water as black as oil. Dublin's own River Styx. He walked faster.

Another door, this one locked. Once more on tiptoe, this time up the stairs. Inside his bedroom, he stopped himself from collapsing onto the bed with the resulting groan of springs that would wake Mrs Malone. He took off the clothes he'd just put on, climbed in with the curtains open, and slept until the sunlight woke him.

The two rooms he rented at the top of Mrs Malone's house suited him absolutely. The bedroom's window overlooked a tiny yard (which had only a privy and no pigs) whereas the parlour's looked down onto the square and across to the Castle Hotel. With both windows open, the ventilating breeze wasn't sweet but he had smelled worse. Now the heat was driving him mad. After a day of sweating in the streets, he returned to his rooms to sweat out the night. He promised himself that on Sunday he would take the train out to Bray and do a bit of entomologising. The thought of the sea air almost cooled him.

Kate knocked at the door and entered, carrying his breakfast tray. Her hair made its usual efforts to escape from her white cap as she swung the tray without regard for the safety of its contents.

'Morning, sir,' she said.

'Good morning, Kate. Here, let me take that from you.'

'Not at all, sir. I've brung it this far and I wouldn't want Mrs Malone thinking I was shirking me duties and letting a gentleman serve his own breakfast.'

Peakin watched Kate wobble her way to the small table, the china rattling like the teeth of a man dragged from icy water. He sighed with relief when the tray landed. He studied the benefit of his six shillings weekly board: porridge (made with more water than milk and not enough salt), a few slices of apple (brown at one edge and wrinkled at the other), tea (the leaves on their third drawing). In truth he was not sure that any wife would have tolerated this existence, never mind the wife he'd chosen. He imagined Isobel in the room, her sharp gaze taking the measure of everything. Would she have set herself to work and made the rooms homely? Mending curtains and painting furniture? He'd never know since she'd decided not to marry him after all.

'How do you like this heat?'

Kate studied him with contempt. She pushed the cap back on her head. She sniffed.

'Imagine you complaining of the heat. You just try dragging skirts around after you. My legs is stuck together with sweat.'

Peakin tried not to picture this, to imagine the slip and suck of them.

'I think rain might be coming,' he suggested.

'Humph. There wasn't none of them clouds around the moon last night. I wouldn't be getting your hopes up. Seems only a week ago you was complaining the weather wouldn't dry up.'

'I was, Kate. I like it a little more even. Not too hot and not too cold, not too wet and not too dry.'

'Do you need me for anything this morning, sir?' She chewed on a strand of hair.

'No, you're free to go. Thank you.'

'I'll just fetch the pot as I'm here.'

'I'll empty it myself, Kate, there's no need.'

'And what does Mrs Malone be paying me for? It's not for prancing about and making conversation, that's for certain,' and she went to fetch the bowl filled with his piss and shit. It was all he could do to keep from blushing.

'Thank you, Kate,' he called after her. 'Remind Mrs Malone I won't be taking any tea this evening.'

She grunted in reply. Mrs Malone's stratagem for increasing her income was to provide him with meals he hadn't asked for and then demand payment: a kind of genteel blackmail. She never asked about his absent wife but he sensed her steady collection of useful titbits to be brandished whenever she required them. She was the one who handed over his post.

He turned to his breakfast and the newspapers. More Fenian arrests. A threatened cholera epidemic. Cattle plague. Disorder marched on, even in the heat. Perhaps especially in the heat.

There was nothing to do but to get the postmortem over with. He folded the newspaper and placed it on the table that served for a desk. Next to the desk, his net leaned against the wall. On the desk was his microscope, which Kate was not allowed to dust or polish, a box of pins and his specimen box and notebooks. He'd learned not to leave any specimens out in the open. He'd returned one day to find that Kate had taken them to the ash pit and begun searching his rooms for an infestation. 'How was I to know you was keepin' 'em on purpose?' Kate wailed after he spoke sharp words. And it was true, how was she to know?

Peakin walked past Exchequer Court and to the barracks where the body was. He'd already sent a boy for Dr Mapother and he hoped the doctor would be quick. Taking charge of an infanticide did not seem a likely route to promotion. Neither did a slow churn of recovering stolen property in pawnshops. He could not understand why Inspector Ryan hadn't assigned him to the Fenian division. Hadn't he proven himself enough times in his eighteen years on the force? Hadn't he excelled at all the examinations he'd been set? Every evening, when he submitted his report to the inspector, he hoped for some indication of a future change in his fortunes. One that might involve a salary of £156 per annum and some rooms more suited to matrimony than Mrs Malone's. And every evening he worried that the inspector might announce that he knew that Isobel had called it off. That she wasn't going to marry Peakin and then he would have to return to the barracks. Peakin still hoped that she might change her mind, write to say they could set another date. He'd had no word in more than a month.

The baby lay on the table in a dark room that had once acted as an extra meat store, at the north side of the square of barracks buildings. The room had been cleared of signs of butchering before Peakin adapted it for postmortems.

By Peakin's own calculation, the body had not been in the water very long, perhaps a day or two. The river, ever full of an abundance of decaying matter, would have hastened decomposition. If Mr Doyle had passed by the next day, or just a few hours later in the evening, then it might have sunk invisibly into the mud. But alas, here it was. Retrieved in time for fresh violence to be done.

Peakin did not approve of postmortems. When he died in mysterious circumstances, he wished for no dissection to be performed on his body; let the murderer escape unpunished but leave his body intact. There was something indecent in it, the poking and prodding and destruction of flesh. And to what end? Doctors couldn't tell you what was wrong with you in life. In death, they became even more impotent. He had yet to hear a doctor tell him something he couldn't have surmised by close examination of the corpse. Why cut a man open when there were finger-mark bruises on his neck and all the signs of strangulation? Or a blow to his head that had cracked his skull? Yet the medical profession had convinced their brothers in the legal profession (and doctors and lawyers were often in the one family) that a postmortem was a necessary step when determining the cause of unexpected death. Mapother was not the worst kind of doctor, but Peakin shuddered at the gruesome things he would do to this infant in the name of science.

'Sorry for disturbing your rest,' Peakin said to the body. Soaking in the water had made the baby appear plump and healthy, if you could ignore the streaks of mud and the smell. There was no sign of any injury.

Having reassured himself that everything was ready, Peakin walked to the gate to meet the doctor who was already waiting.

'Very hot this weather, isn't it Peakin?'

'It is indeed, Dr Mapother. Most unusual, even for August.'

'In India, there's no relief from the heat! As hot at midnight as it is here at noon on a summer's day. But the body adapts. One stops feeling the heat the same way, the appetite returns. Wonderful machine, the body. I'm studying adaptations to heat with Dr Murray in Calcutta. We compare details from the postmortems we perform, the diameters of blood vessels and such.'

'Thank you for coming,' Peakin said, hoping to put an end to the doctor's medical lecture.

'I'm sorry it could not be sooner, but Mrs Mapother disapproves of rushing out during breakfast.' He smiled at Peakin, who had learned to mirror such expressions on his face with no reciprocal feeling in his heart. 'And how is your fiancée, detective? Any improvement in her mother? I'm sure you're very eager for her to join you in Dublin.'

'No improvement. I think it will be some months yet before she can leave Wicklow.' Peakin held the door open and the doctor stepped into the room.

Peakin watched from a polite distance as the doctor took the tools out of his bag and spread them on the table. He'd seen more human dissections than a medical student and was certain he could perform the steps himself. Some tools resembled those of a butcher: a bone saw, some kind of hatchet, a large knife. But the real work was performed by an array of delicate scalpels, scissors and tweezers.

He'd arranged the basin of water that Mapother would need to 'float' the lungs and another for washing his hands. Mapother accepted these with a nod.

Peakin's eyes found the corners of the ceiling, the piles of dust on the floor, as the doctor began his examination. He smelled river mud and the various gases given off during the process of decomposition. He didn't like to think what the effects of breathing them in might be. He pictured particles colonising his body like the spores from a fungus. He tried not to take any deep breaths. Mapother grunted and sighed.

'Perhaps this little one died of its own accord,' Mapother said.

'It's possible.' Peakin could only hope.

'I regret that I'll have to cut him open to be sure.'

Once again Peakin's eyes roamed the room, coming to rest on the cobwebs draping the window. He tried to turn the sounds of the doctor's tools meeting flesh into something else in his mind but the smell made it impossible. He felt a surge of unprofessional nausea as he recalled his visit to Peggi. Here was the plausible result of such a congress despite the care he took not to spend himself inside her. He knew that if he looked at the table he would see Mapother's hands pawing over the tiny body.

'There's no burning on the inside of the oesophagus or in the stomach.' Peakin pretended to look at what Mapother was now holding out to him. It was only meat, after all. The same as one might find inside of any living animal. The heat was affecting him, everything seemed to glisten or slip, to rot and fester.

'So he wasn't poisoned.'

'Exactly. And I don't see any other injury. Now we just have to see about these lungs.'

He would remove the tiny life-giving organs now and 'float' them in the dish of water. If the lungs sank, the doctors claimed, it meant that they had never inflated. The baby had been born dead. No murder, just concealment of birth. Peakin waited.

'Ah,' said Dr Mapother, 'as I expected.'

Chapter Four

Anne

August 1865

Exactly three months after Anne's mother died, her father married Ellen and they announced that Anne would go to live with her Aunt Julia. She returned from a walk and found them sitting in the parlour with the fire blazing. Ellen was a thin little whisper of a woman who always complained that she could feel a draught or sat rubbing her hands together as though she'd just come in from the cold. She was leaning against Anne's father with her feet tucked up under her skirts. Her shoes, small like a little girl's, had been kicked off and lay on the floor. Her shawl was draped over the back of a chair and her bonnet lay on the seat of another. For a dainty person she took up a lot of space. When she spoke, she tried to sound like a mother speaking to a child, though she was barely older than Anne.

'Darling, your father and I have been talking and we're certain you'll feel more comfortable with your aunt.' She smiled and placed one of her tiny hands across her middle, which was when Anne knew she was with child.

'Ellen's right, Nan,' her father agreed, 'there will be much more to keep you occupied. We're not really able for dinner parties and such. The kinds of things to occupy a young woman. And she has a very nice piano. Much better than ours.' He smiled a lizard smile. Anne had a feeling like she was in a doll's house and the child who owned it was simply picking it up and sliding out the dolls she no longer wanted. First her mother, replaced with Ellen. Now Anne, to be replaced by a sweet little baby doll instead.

'Whatever you think is best.' Anne excused herself and went to bed without eating, hoping to fall asleep before the nightly chorus of whispers and groans began.

And that was that. Anne did not rage or cry or throw things. She let her father and Ellen turn her out with no whimper of discontent. Maybe it was a just punishment, she thought, for the refusal of four suitors on no grounds other than that she didn't like them. This fresh tragedy refilled her wells of sorrow, allowed her to wallow in grief for her mother, gave her permission to mourn for herself.

When the day of her departure arrived, Anne wandered through the rooms of her home, laying her hands on objects that had once been dear. The pink porcelain rabbit with its ear glued back on because Frances had dropped it. The piano with ivory keys worn faintly hollow by her mother's fingers. Three crooked lace doilies that she'd been so proud of, aged nine. Books of fairy tales with broken spines. Chintz curtains whose roses once were bright red, almost garish, when her parents hung them together. In the end she took only a little box of mementos and six dresses: four of her own and two of her mother's.

Mr Mulhall helped the driver load Anne's cases into the cab and then offered her a hand to climb in. Anne almost turned for a final look at the house but she was afraid she would see Ellen in the window and this would make her cry. They didn't speak on the journey over, shy of what might spill out if the fragile silence was broken. Anne longed for her father to shout. She'd even written lines for him in her head. He would say that Anne was a grown woman of twenty-three years who had to refused to marry and resisted a kindly suggestion of retiring to a convent to pursue a vocation. Anne could not just remain in *his* house, sulking about and making her stepmother most uncomfortable. But he kept his mouth closed and so Anne's retorts stayed in her head.

He rapped on the door of Number 27 Mountjoy Square and a maid with a puckered face opened it, beckoning them over the threshold. Mr Mulhall stepped lightly into the house, depositing the cases on the floor. He turned and joined the maid who was staring at Anne, waiting on the step.

'The mistress is expecting you,' the maid said, as though that might draw her in. Anne found she could not move. 'She's in the drawing room,' the maid tried again. 'Down the hall and the first door on the right. I'll bring the cases up for you.'

A scowl began to form on her father's face and Anne forced her feet up the last step, onto the tiled hall. The maid pulled the door behind, hooshing her the last few inches with her arm. The house smelled familiar, a mixture of lavender and shoe polish. The drawing room was less gloomy and cavernous than Anne remembered but Aunt Julia was still a tower of black crêpe. Mr Mulhall now looked uncomfortable, brushing invisible specks of dust from his hat and sleeves. Aunt Julia was as tall as he was and had much more presence.

'Good afternoon, Anne, Charles. Tell me, the journey wasn't too terrible? My driver finds it so difficult to navigate those lanes around Townsend Street. I hear there's been some cholera cases. I hope it's no one you know.' She shivered at the imagined horrors of their shabby street.

'It was fine, thank you, Julia.' Mr Mulhall made a little bow and Anne tried to arrange her features in a friendly way. Aunt Julia gestured for them to sit down. She was so like Anne's mother in appearance that Anne had to fight the urge to embrace her.

'I'm very sorry for your loss. But after all she was sick for so long that I'm sure it was a relief for everyone in the end.' Perhaps she didn't intend to be cruel or was only oblivious to the way that her words might wound. Anne's mother never spoke about the nature of their differences but Anne guessed at them. Some secret shame surrounded her parents' marriage, something more than the fact that Mr Mulhall's occupation as a dancing master placed him outside the golden circle of acceptable husbands. Her aunt's words offered no comfort, indicated no softness or sympathy.

'Thank you, Aunt Julia,' Anne said, studying the dark swirls of the carpet.

'When I asked your father how you spent your time he told me that you still played the piano so I've had it tuned.'

'Thank you, that was kind.'

'I thought you might play sometimes for my amusement. Or the amusement of my guests. Your position here is to be useful. I have no time for idlers, everything in this house runs smoothly and efficiently. I'm sure you will want to make yourself helpful.' She faced Anne's father as though it wasn't Anne she was speaking to.

'I'll be pleased to help in any way you see fit.'

A servant came in with tea and the three sipped in silence. The threatened rain arrived and the house began to shudder and squeak around them. The sounds of rain drew more attention to the quiet. Even when Anne's cousins had lived there, the house had been almost silent. On visits with their mother, Anne and Frances would be told to go and play with

Emily and Caroline who would say things like 'Don't bang
the door' or 'We must keep our voices low.' They whispered
to each other and Anne remembered always leaning in to
catch what they were saying. As a child, she'd pictured a
sleeping ogre in the pantry or the basement that everyone
was trying not to wake. When she grew older she understood
the ogre was Aunt Julia. When they stood on the step and
turned towards home, Anne's mother would say, 'Well, that
was lovely, wasn't it girls?' when Anne knew rightly she was
glad to leave.

'And how are Emily and Caroline?' Anne asked, thinking
that her cousins were a safe topic of conversation.

'Very well. I suppose they haven't written to you in a while.
They're so very busy. Caroline and Anthony have taken over
the estate in Galway and Emily and James are in Bray.'

Mr Mulhall sat, smiling. Anne imagined he was thinking
of how pleasant his house would be now, no daughters left to
remind him of his dead wife. Just pretty little Ellen and no
need for modesty. She felt an urge to scream, high and shrill
and window-rattling. Anne pictured the look of horror on
Aunt Julia's face, her father fumbling his teacup in surprise.
She suppressed the smile pulling at her lips.

'I'm so glad to hear that.'

Aunt Julia gave a sharp nod but her lips remained parallel
lines of forbearance.

'Shall I have Johanna show you up? Your father and I
have a few things to discuss.'

'Yes, of course. Thank you.'

'You may like to rest or change. Dinner is at six.'

Anne stood and obeyed. Her father surprised her with
an embrace. He squeezed her against him, smoothed down
the hair at the back of her head and whispered into her ear,
'I love you, Nan, you'll be happy here, I'm sure. It's just for

a while. Until things are more settled. We'll visit you.' He loosened his arms and Anne pulled away before she could sob. She sensed that tears were very much unwanted in this house. Aunt Julia rang a bell. The maid returned and Anne followed her up the stairs. The room was dark even with the curtains open, the wallpaper a heavy pattern. The maid lit the lamps though it was scarcely three in the afternoon and full daylight. There was a scent of damp suggesting a leak.

'I set the fire but the mistress said not to light it till you came. I'll do it now.'

'Thank you.'

Anne unpacked her dresses and put them in the wardrobe, where there was a whiff of camphor. Then she lay on the bed and tried to think of all the ways that this was better than staying on in Townsend Street.

Chapter Five

Denis

6th August, 1866

In the newspaper reports Denis had read, an inquest always seemed a simple and business-like affair. Witnesses deposed. The jury returned a verdict. An investigation was either closed or opened.

He'd never considered that an inquest had a smell and a taste. This inquest smelled of river water and tasted of tainted pork. Someone had added lashings of carbolic acid on top. The carbolic acid dried the back of his throat, demanding that Denis keep swallowing great gulps of fetid air.

Denis surveyed the small room at the back of the police barracks. He recognised it as a disused meat store and felt uneasy, as though the inquest was an act of desecration. A cloth covered the body but there was no mistaking what it was. He wished that someone would remove the cloth, so he would stop picturing his own son beneath it. He dug his hands into his pockets, pushing away the memory of the doll-sized coffin that he'd carried to Glasnevin alone. So light that he almost believed it was empty. He wondered would this baby get a coffin, would anyone gather flowers to place inside.

He turned to the jurors, huddled like crows in their black suits with their hands behind their backs. Denis wondered how hard they were trying not to put their hands over their mouths to stop the sweet rot from entering.

So many dark-suited men made Denis a little nervous and he reminded himself that he was not under suspicion. The heat hadn't let up and even the thick stone walls couldn't keep the room cool. Denis's shirt stuck to a spot between his shoulders where no movement could dislodge it. When he sniffed he thought he could smell pig's blood in his beard.

He'd found the body but now he stood impotent, a spectator to the process of justice. He thought about Rose again. About how she'd seemed angry at him, almost, for finding it. Poking his nose in. He'd thought he was helping, rescuing the baby's soul.

The inquest opened with his deposition.

The coroner called 'Mr Denis Doyle' and Denis stood and deposed. He hadn't been sure what to leave in and what to leave out. The finding of the body now seemed so inconsequential compared to the enormous task of finding a murderer.

'I was on my way to order more salt at Thomas Maguire's provision shop. It was a particularly lovely evening and I stopped on Richmond Bridge, as I was crossing, to see the view down the river.'

'Are you in a habit of taking in the view?' The coroner asked, a slight smile suggesting disbelief. Denis stared, uncertain what was implied in the question. 'There was no other reason for your stopping?'

Denis felt there was an accusation in the question. 'No, I can think of no other reason,' he said.

'Nothing alerted you to the body other than your sight of it?'

'No, I didn't see anyone on the river bed, if that's what you mean. Sometimes there are children there under the bridge, they pick through the rubbish, but there was no one that day. It was hot. The smell was considerable.'

'But the smell didn't bother you. And you're sure you weren't expecting to see anything?'

'Well, most people would tell you a butcher doesn't mind a smell,' Denis smiled but the coroner remained stony. 'I'm not sure I understand your meaning,' he continued. 'I had no reason to expect to see anything.'

Denis saw impatience beginning to crease Peakin's face. The coroner cleared his throat and moved on. Denis described his descent down the ladder, his quest for the police. The coroner praised him for his quick thinking but the tone was of an adult praising a child, Denis thought. Just to remind him who was in charge.

The coroner examined Peakin next. He was brief, confirming much of Denis's testimony. He became animated when he began to discuss tides and the river's flow. He seemed taken by the idea that the body might have moved from some other spot. He declared that the only item found with the body was the cloth in which it was wrapped.

When Dr Mapother rose to speak, Denis noticed Peakin straighten up. The doctor explained that the infant was less than one week old, possibly only a day old, and that something called a flotation test suggested that it was born alive. Denis flinched at the descriptions of the postmortem. Mapother said that he'd found no marks of violence on the body. This, he said, suggested smothering. At this, Denis was surprised to see Peakin rise to his feet.

'Coroner. Dr Mapother. If I may? I'm not sure if you are aware of the most recent science on the lung flotation test.' Denis saw a curl to the doctor's lips but the coroner looked most displeased.

'Detective, really. You cannot be suggesting—'

Dr Mapother stood and Denis wondered what kind of altercation he might be about to witness. Something interesting perhaps to tell Rose later on. But the doctor wasn't angry at all.

'Let him speak, I have no objection.'

'Thank you, Dr Mapother.' Detective Peakin nodded. The coroner sighed.

Denis soon lost interest as the detective began to quote scientific authorities on how various forms of decay could introduce air pockets into the lungs. As far as he could tell, the detective was suggesting that no one had killed the infant after all. Dr Mapother presented counter evidence and the two men seemed to be enjoying themselves. Denis wondered at how little information could be prised from a human body. Perhaps the body of an infant had nothing to tell of a life barely lived. By contrast, the bodies of animals revealed so much. He often found traces of old injuries, where the flesh had built little hardened walls to contain them. There were the signs of disease and age, the different textures of fat, meat and sinew.

The argument came to naught. Dr Mapother declared his opinion that it was infant murder and the coroner agreed. Peakin looked disappointed but not surprised. The inquest proceeded quickly then. The jurors asked Denis and Peakin each a few further questions and then they questioned the policeman who had assisted Peakin. A few other people who worked in the buildings near to the river had been summoned but they had nothing to say as they had seen nothing and heard nothing. The jury declared its verdict.

'A baby boy, having been found in the River Liffey on the 4th of August, was a victim of infant murder by an unknown hand.'

There was a murmur of affirmation.

Infant murder. The murderer was probably somewhere in the city, perhaps enjoying her breakfast. Was she thinking of what she had done? Of the tiny corpse she'd discarded? Denis thought of ways to murder a baby. Some women tried to murder it when it was inside them. Took pills, fell down the stairs. He'd always wondered if Rose had maybe … but he pushed the thought away. He noticed Peakin approaching him.

'Thank you,' Peakin said.

'I didn't think I had much choice,' Denis replied, trying to lighten his voice a little.

'Well, if you hadn't seen the body and fetched the police the chances are the river would have washed it away or covered it over and it never would have been found.'

'Yes, it was a bit of luck.'

Chapter Six

Anne

September 1865

Despite her father's suggestion that she visit, Anne did not return to Townsend Street. She pictured Ellen growing as plump and content as a house cat, prowling the rooms for pieces of family memorabilia she could send to the pawnshop. She imagined the preparations being made for the baby's arrival, the remnants of her childhood swept from the house or repurposed in anticipation of its new resident. Anne passed her few rescued mementos through her hands like a string of rosary beads: prize rosettes from musical competitions, letters from her sister, a handful of pressed flowers, scraps of fabric saved from cherished dresses outgrown. The diary that she'd pocketed from her mother's dressing table still emitted wisps of her mother's scent. She took delicate sniffs, as though a gulp would swallow it forever, taking her happy childhood with it.

Anne tried to settle into her aunt's routine. They moved from room to room for meals as if performing achingly slow Stations of the Cross (the parlour for breakfast, the dining room for luncheon and dinner, the sitting room for tea). She tiptoed around during her aunt's afternoon naps, reading books in her uncle's study or taking short walks alone. She read to her in the drawing room or played the piano while her aunt pretended to listen. Worst of all were the parties which were, her aunt repeatedly told her, for Anne's benefit. The names changed but the guests were always the same: a gaunt spinster cousin, a couple of fat widows who drank too much sherry, a bachelor lawyer with bad breath, a widowed dispensary doctor. Anne was never sure if Aunt Julia enjoyed them but she knew their not-so-secret purpose: a half-hearted search for someone to take Anne as wife or governess. Anne was a burden to be shifted on somewhere else.

Anne met Dr Matthias J. Kelly at one of these parties. She wandered the room, lips pulled into a smile, pretending she couldn't feel her aunt watching. When she first saw him, she thought he'd turned up by mistake. Too young and too handsome. He'd gotten the wrong address maybe. People often confused the east and west sides of the square. Aunt Julia's preferred guests were always shabbier than herself and easily impressed. Their mouths fell open a little when they stepped inside the house and their eyes lingered on the furnishings that glowed in the dim gaslighting. They knew nothing of the mildewed wallpaper lurking behind the curtains and seemed immune to the stable smell lingering around the sofas. Anne felt the men running their eyes over her, imagining that she might be the key to unlocking a treasure chest. But nothing that glittered in Aunt Julia's house was gold and none of it belonged to Anne. Dr Kelly didn't admire the marble fireplaces or the ugly green landscapes, he just smiled, said 'How do you do?' and kissed Anne's hand.

That night Dr Pratt appeared for his second visit: an ominous signal of intent. Anne amused herself at dinner by counting the crumbs that stuck in his beard. There were fourteen. One of them stayed there for all of the dessert course before he removed it by wiping his face. He caught Anne undefended in the drawing room. His thin, clammy fingers rested on her bare arm and he loomed over her. She could smell the bear's grease in his hair and the dinner on his breath.

'Your aunt has given me to understand that you enjoy seaside walks.'

The pink tip of his tongue flicked against the side of his mouth, searching for another crumb. Oh the words seemed innocent enough, but Anne recognised them as the start of a negotiation. She pictured his withered body pressing against her on the marital bed. Perhaps even the very bed where his first wife had died. He watched her, waiting.

'I find it is rather too windy for my liking these days,' she said, and took a step back, but the doctor did not release his hand from her arm. She wanted to pull her arm away to see what he would do but she simply leaned back a little.

'I'm sure there are other lovely places if you would care to—'

'Excuse me please, Dr Pratt, I promised my aunt that I would play the piano and it's long past eight o'clock now.' His grip loosened, she turned, he let go.

Anne sat down at the piano bench and Dr Kelly sat down next to her. He moved in close, leaving just the width of a hand between them.

'Mrs Kennedy mentioned you might play something. Do you sing?'

'Not usually.'

'Let's sing "The Last Rose of Summer".' As he spoke he leaned closer, so that the words warmed the side of her face, her ear, her neck. His breath was sweet with brandy and he smelled of something clean and sharp.

'I don't know that one,' she lied. His arm brushed against hers and he left it there long enough for her to feel the warmth of his body under the sleeve. His face was clean-shaven and his hair fell into his eyes. For just a second he pressed his suited shoulder against her bare one as he reached across to pick up her sheet music.

'You don't know the music of the great Tom Moore? You've lived a life without romance.' She must have blushed because he added, 'Well, a musician such as yourself must be more choosy than mere enthusiasts like me.'

'My aunt prefers me not to sing. She finds that singing interrupts conversation.' She could hear the blood rushing in her ears, her breath going in and out.

'Well, we cannot displease the great lady, can we?' He winked. He leafed through the pages of music and picked something from Mendelssohn's *Songs Without Words*. When he got up from the bench she felt the loss of his heat, like a door had been opened and a draught let in. Anne glimpsed him over her sheet music as he made his rounds of the room, flirting with each woman in turn. Distracted, she thumped the keys and Aunt Julia stared until she lowered her eyes and pretended to watch her fingers.

An hour later, the party reached its natural end: the time where some people are too loud and others have fallen silent. Dr Pratt and a spinster cousin (closer to his age than Anne) were drinking too much claret and laughing riotously. He'd been watching Anne across the room. He would turn up for a more intimate dinner where she could find no excuse to walk away. She felt a hand on her back and found her aunt standing beside her.

'Anne, I'd like you to meet someone.' She'd hooked Dr Kelly by the arm. A wrinkling at the edges of his eyes betrayed amusement. 'This is Dr Matthias J. Kelly. A very promising surgeon. A cousin of your uncle Hugh, God rest him. Once or twice removed. Dr Kelly, Miss Anne Mulhall.'

'Very pleased to meet you, madam.'

'And you.' Anne let him take her hand and kiss it, pressing her skin with warm lips. The kiss seemed to spread its warmth over her entire body. She'd been careful not to drink too much yet her hands were heavy and her tongue was thick.

'I know that Dr Kelly is also interested in music,' her aunt continued.

'In truth, Mrs Kennedy, Anne and I have already met because I intruded upon her piano playing.'

'Oh! I see.' Anne saw her eyes narrow a little, dismayed that something had escaped her notice. She saw Dr Kelly sense her aunt's displeasure and move quickly to smooth things over.

'I apologise for my forwardness, I couldn't help myself when I saw that she was going to play. It's so rare that one hears real music on such a fine piano as you have, Mrs Kennedy. Miss Mulhall is very talented.'

Aunt Julia smiled, the storm clouds skidding past without dropping rain.

'Dr Kelly is very generous in his praise,' Anne added, lest her aunt find her immodest.

'He is. My girls played beautifully when they were younger. But now, of course, they are too preoccupied with the joys of motherhood. No time for idleness or indulgence of any kind.' Her face suggested just how idle and indulgent she believed Anne to be.

'I'm sure. Well, it is lucky for us and for Miss Mulhall that you've kept the instrument in such careful condition. Perhaps she can teach your grandchildren when they visit.'

Later, Anne would recall that she fell in love that instant. Compliments made no impression on her, men dropped them like dust from their cuffs. No, it wasn't the compliments. It was how, with impeccable manners, Dr

Kelly wrong-footed her aunt. The look on Aunt Julia's face as she'd strained to produce the expected smile. Anne felt certain that he enjoyed the mild torment as much as she did. For the first time since her mother died, someone was interested in her and only her. He was on her side.

Dr Kelly sought her out to wish her goodbye. He handed her his calling card.

'I hope that we might see one another again.'

'Thank you, Dr Kelly.'

'Please call me Matthias.'

'Yes, alright.' She made herself look into his face and not down at her feet or at a point beyond his ear. She forced out a little laugh in an attempt to convey indifference and wound up sounding like a giddy fool.

Anne hid the card in her sheet music. Every time she sat down at the piano she could sense it there, like an ember threatening to erupt into flames. It was Tuesday before she took it out. His name was printed so thickly that you could read it with your fingers. Beneath his name it said, *Surgeon and accoucheur, member R.C.S.I.* There was no address. She turned the card over and saw that he'd scrawled '*Walk with me at the Rotunda Gardens on Thursday, 2 p.m.*' on the back.

Chapter Seven

Peakin

7th August, 1866

Sweat gathered under Peakin's moustache and dripped down the edges of his lips. He blotted first his mouth and then his forehead. He listened to the scratching of pens as the other men prepared reports. The window of the office was open but no breeze disturbed his papers and the room filled with a masculine fug comprised of perspiration, hair oil and disappointment. Between strokes of his pen he snuck glances at his fellow detectives and wondered who the inspector had in mind for promotion. Could it be Fiddler? The magistrate awarded him ten shillings after he'd returned a haul of stolen cutlery to the Elephant Warehouse. He was looking very sure of himself these days.

'The superintendent wants this taken care of quickly and with discretion,' the inspector said after drill. 'The magistrates look well on having these kinds of cases resolved.' He never actually mentioned anything about a promotion but Peakin could hope. The woman responsible probably hadn't gone far. The logical place to begin was the workhouses.

At the South Dublin Union, the matron led him to a receiving room where the seats of the chairs had been polished by the bony rear ends of thousands of paupers. She wore her dress high and tight on her throat so that it forced out a flap of wizened neck skin that hung like a hen's wattle. The wattle swayed in a mesmerising way as she *tsk-tsked* at the terrible news of the infanticide and informed him that none of her female charges had left recently.

'None have left us with a newborn child. On that point I can reassure you. In fact, there have been no births in over a week, none that I know of, and nothing escapes my notice.'

'Nonetheless, may I have a look at the register? In case there are any names I recognise from informants?' There were no names from informants but Peakin felt he shouldn't take the woman's word for anything. Certainty made him suspicious. She opened out the register without hesitation. His eyes scanned neat columns of names and dates, the warp and weft of human misery. He found himself looking out for Eliza's name among the others. She'd been proud that she could read *and* write, had written him a little note once to prove it. *My dearest Martin*, it said, *How shall we fuck today? Kind regards, Elizabeth Mooney*. She'd added so many flourishes to her signature that the 'M' for Mooney looked like a drawing of a woman with her hair in curlers. He wished now that he'd kept the note. The matron shifted in her chair and sighed.

'In truth, detective, there's a few girls in here that I'd be expecting nothing better from.' She sniffed and pulled at the edges of her pinafore. 'But they're all still with us for now. There's some arrived in the last few days and you're welcome to speak with them, but the women consist of two widows well past childbirth, a waif of no more than twelve years and another woman come with a whole family including an infant of six months.'

'Thank you, I don't think I'll need to speak with them.' Peakin stood, but she wasn't finished. She wanted to give her opinions on the nature of the crime, of course.

'I'm glad the police are taking infanticide seriously. Better late than never. A disgusting crime that no amount of desperation can excuse. To think that someone would kill their own living child with their own hands.' The matron clucked and shook her head. The wattle shivered. 'And the punishments should be greater. Just think of all the charity they can avail themselves of! There is simply no need.'

'I'm sure many agree with you.' Peakin let her believe he was one of them. He decided not to opine on the subject of giving infants watered-down milk or separating children from their siblings under the pretence of moral improvement. Before she could lecture him further, Peakin bid her good day. 'I can find my own way out,' he said as she began to rise.

'Nonsense, I'll conduct you. I'll need to open the doors.'

She bustled after him down the corridors. He could hear the sounds of children reciting in a schoolroom somewhere. Would they be learning something that could keep their own children from washing up here? Sums and letters. How to be quiet and do as they were told. Never to be a bother to anyone. She unlocked the bolts that kept the unworthy paupers out and the chastened paupers in. Peakin felt her eyes on him as he turned up James's Street.

He headed over the river. As he crossed Richmond Bridge he studied the water below, wondering what other unfortunate souls it contained. He pictured the riverbed lined with corpses, their arms waving gently with the ebb and flow of the tide. Of course he knew that most of what rotted along the bottom was of animal or vegetable origin. The human bodies ended up as floating, bloated messes that were almost invariably pulled out. Still, when the sun was at a certain angle and you could see under the water, Peakin always imagined he might look down to see a face staring up at him.

The North Dublin Workhouse was nestled among other institutions dedicated to solving the city's problems with rational geometry and heavy stone. Peakin felt mankind set far too much faith in right angles and straight lines. Behind the façade of the workhouse were the same blocks of rooms around square yards, mirrored on the male and female sides, as could be found at the neighbouring asylum or the nearby prison. This matron, much younger than her Southside counterpart, wore her glossy chestnut hair in a severe parting that drew attention to her thick eyebrows. The effect made an impression but was not flattering. Peakin found himself staring at them rather than her eyes. She repeated the same refrain: no suspect females had arrived or left in recent days. Two births, but mother and baby were alive and accounted for. Instead, she was eager to draw Peakin's attention to other matters entirely.

'There is a most unbearable stench coming from the dairies in the lane behind. We have written to the Corporation but they have done nothing at all.'

'Tsk tsk.' Peakin shook his head and prepared to leave.

'I must insist that you come to see for yourself. Perhaps if a policeman were to write to them …'

'I'm afraid I have further inquiries to attend to.' But despite his efforts, Peakin found himself marched down a laneway in which he could confirm there was a considerable odour, as well as all the sounds of a large barnyard. He made many promises that he did not plan to keep until she was satisfied.

His suit felt uncomfortably damp as he turned towards Exchequer Court. He considered going home to change into a fresh shirt but remembered that he had only one clean one left. After he'd stopped paying Mrs Malone for laundry, he'd been forced to sweet-talk Kate into bringing him extra water and soap to wash his clothes himself.

Needless to say, they were washed less frequently than he might like. He sighed and decided to tolerate the sweat. Instead, he made a round of the pawnshops on his beat to check up on the constables. Finding nothing untoward, he continued on to headquarters.

As he walked, he vacillated between frustration and satisfaction. On the one hand, there was not much left to do before the case might be closed. On the other hand, there had been the vague promise of advancement or at least a few shillings. The inspector often hinted at such inducements and Peakin knew better than to trust that they would materialise. They would not be forthcoming if there was no one called to account.

In Exchequer Court, Peakin presented himself to the inspector. As always, he braced himself for questions about Isobel. In the first month after his permission to marry was granted the questions were incessant, but recently they'd dried up. Perhaps the inspector had decided that there was something wrong with Peakin's invisible wife. Deformed or an incurable melancholic. He'd noticed the way a room went quiet when he entered it and he wasn't vain enough to suppose that it was respect that slowed their tongues.

'Too bad,' the inspector said as he half-listened to Peakin's report on the workhouses. The inspector did not stand but continued leafing through reports on his desk. Perhaps there had been significant events in the Fenian conspiracy line. Peakin moved a little closer, glanced down at the desk. The inspector scratched at his beard, gathered the pages together into a stack and snapped, 'What next?'

'I've sent Constable Delaney for some maps. Perhaps some knowledge of the river and the drains might help.'

'Very good. Remember, swift and discreet. I'll expect a report in the morning.'

'I'm sure I should have something by then.'

'We need only to satisfy the coroner. If you find nothing then we can return you to your beat. That's what you want, isn't it?'

'Yes, certainly,' Peakin lied. He wondered if any of the other acting sergeants had a sniff of whatever was occupying the inspector. He could ask Fiddler. But then he would have to admit that he didn't know himself.

He returned to the office to stew. Most of the other men were gone now. Only the clerk remained, rustling and fluttering with his paperwork. Two huge flies bumbled around the room like drunks who'd forgotten the way home. They collided with desks and walls and windows until one rested in front of Peakin, silently rubbing its legs. Peakin swatted and missed. The clerk jumped.

Peakin opened his notebook and wished he was at his microscope instead. The newspaper reports of an inquest sometimes brought witnesses forward but this time they only attracted attention from more newspapers. Peakin was not surprised. Every kind of crime showed its own pattern and characteristics, like the wings of an insect revealing its species. No matter how the papers fretted over infanticide as though it were a signal of fresh moral decline, Peakin didn't believe it. Where there were people, there was fucking and where there was fucking, there would soon be unwanted offspring.

Infanticide was like a red burnet moth, he thought. It appeared exotic with its black wings and red spots, but it was common enough. Peakin didn't believe that women should vote or own property. But neither did he believe that unwanted babies were the fault of the women who birthed them. He swatted again at the fly. This time he felt its body burst under the notebook. He turned it over and examined the streak of blood. He took a small bottle of rubbing alcohol from his breast pocket, soaked the end of his handkerchief in it and cleaned the notebook and then his hands. He pulled at the end of his moustache and began his report.

Dead infant discovered by Denis Doyle in the River Liffey, next to Richmond Bridge, approx. 6.30 p.m. on 4th of August.

Body retrieved by Peakin and men, approx. 7 p.m. on 4th of August.

Postmortem by Dr Mapother set the date of death as 1st or 2nd of August and cause of death as infant murder by suffocation.

Constable Delaney had obtained a map of the drains and, on his own initiative, copied some tide charts from the Custom House. Peakin marvelled at the precision with which the engineers mapped the little flows of filth through sewers and drains, rivers and rivulets, the highs and lows of tides. Yet they could do nothing to clean the river. Would people throw babies into a clean river? Probably they would.

The charts just confirmed what Peakin already knew. If someone dropped the baby in the river overnight, they'd probably done it very close to where it was found. It might have been washed down from near to Kingsbridge Station, but if it had come from the countryside, it would have taken much longer to arrive and the body would have been more decayed. The baby had probably been wrapped in the cloth it was found with. The cloth was nothing special, just a cotton sheet such as almost anyone might get hold of.

Only three citizens of Dublin wrote in to offer 'information'. No one presented themselves at Exchequer Court. He considered these letters to be the idle amusement of a few gossips. They gave names of young women they had seen 'enlarged' but, as none of these names was the same, Peakin discounted this evidence. He kept the letters. If he grew desperate he could call on the letter writers. He continued his list.

Body deposited somewhere between Kingsbridge Station and Richmond Bridge.

Cannot determine how the body was brought there. No witnesses to the body's deposit.

He might have written down his own suspicion, in keeping with all previous cases of infanticide he had dealt with, that the woman herself had most likely walked from somewhere less than a mile away.

Recovered from the scene: body, unclothed but intact; pieces of cloth found near the body.

He washed the cloth, looking for some kind of distinctive characteristic: a lace edge or a bit of embroidery that might tell him where it had come from. It was good linen cambric, not cheap imported calico. He'd rubbed his fingers over it, trying to imagine what had happened. The cloth was torn from something larger. Maybe the woman was a servant, and tore it from her employer's worn sheets? Or was the cloth something you might buy from a rag and bone dealer? Had she chosen it with care, wrapped the body in tender regret? He would never know. He added *No distinguishing features* and continued writing.

Witnesses: None.

Investigation: Matrons of the North and South Union Workhouses questioned. No information obtained.

He sighed. He had nothing else. He would send Constable Delaney to question businesses and households near the bridge – maybe they would turn something up. But as he put down his pen he conceded that he would not find the woman – he was sure it was a woman – unless someone came forward and made accusations.

Part II

At dawn, a mist gathered on the river like a muslin shroud pulled over her. The shroud was made of her own nightly exhalations. The mist rose with the sun, higher and higher, until it began to spill over the quay walls. The men of the Corporation, headed to City Hall, wrinkled their noses as the smell of death seeped in through invisible gaps in their snug carriages. They gathered their force of sanitary sergeants and set them to stalk the vapours where they bubbled into fever nests in the Coombe, in Denzille Street, in Ormond Square. The sergeants pounded two miles of Dublin streets and lanes and alleys. On North Earl Street, Rose watched from the upstairs window as they pushed their way into the tenement yards one by one, searching for overflowing privies and crowded pigsties.

Chapter Eight

Anne

October 1865

Dr Pratt had come to call on Anne but he'd spoken hardly a word to her over the interminable dinner. Anne bent her head to her plate, cutting her food into tiny portions and pushing it around to give the impression of having eaten something. Cook had outdone herself with service *à la russe* and the dishes seemed like they would never end. Brown soup, stuffed pigeon, stew of mutton, cod surrounded by cubes of turnip, wilted asparagus drowned in mayonnaise, creamed spinach, a plate of fruit and nuts. Finally, the arrival of a cake glistening in syrup signalled that the end was near. Dr Pratt gamely cleared his plate with each dish but he stared at the fat slice of cake that Johanna served him with trepidation.

'This is Cook's specialty, Dr Pratt. An orange cake.'

'I hardly know how I could manage another mouthful.'

Her aunt and the doctor seemed to remember her presence then and both of them looked across the table. Was she supposed to have a view on whether Dr Pratt had stuffed himself?

'The cake looks beautiful. I don't recall when I've had a dinner like this before.'

Aunt Julia wanted Dr Pratt to know what kind of household she ran. She wanted him to tell everyone about her generosity and the half dozen different sets of plates and silver cutlery that had passed through his hands in the course of the meal. Anne wanted to know when he would leave.

After the cake there was the inevitable coffee in the sitting room.

'I will leave you young people to chat,' Aunt Julia said before excusing herself. The room was cold and empty, the fire low. Johanna had no doubt been too busy with all the dishes to remember to heap it up. The afternoon light was grey and dull. Dr Pratt, crumpled into his chair, reminded her of a daddy long legs that you might find in an unswept corner. She felt suddenly sorry for him. Alone with his children, no one to care for him aside from servants. He shifted on his seat, put down his coffee without drinking from it.

'I wondered, or Mrs Kennedy suggested, that, perhaps, if you were not otherwise engaged, that you might consider accompanying me to the concert in the Antient Concert Rooms in a fortnight.'

'Thank you, Dr Pratt. But I must decline. My first duty is to my aunt and she usually requires my company in the evening.'

'It was Mrs Kennedy who suggested it.'

'I think you have got an idea—'

'I know that a young woman such as yourself might not wish to take on children. It can be difficult to be a stepmother, of course. But I do believe that there are things that I might offer. That if you were to permit me—'

Her hand flew to cover her open mouth. Surely he wouldn't come to that so quickly?

'Please. Don't say anything more. I have nothing to offer you, or any other gentleman.'

'It's not a question of that. Your financial circumstances are not—'

'You've misunderstood. I have nothing I wish to offer you. I am not free.'

'Not free? But you appear … and Mrs Kennedy made it clear that—'

'My aunt, I fear, has given you the wrong impression.'

Her heart pounded. How could she not have seen the trap that had been laid for her? He had settled things with her aunt over dinner and now she'd been left alone with him so that he could propose. She stared at her hands. Would he leave? Had she humiliated him? What would her aunt say? She'd implied that she was engaged which was a lie. He raised himself from the chair but she did not dare to look up.

'I do believe that I have a touch of indigestion after so full a meal. I think I'll take my leave. Please thank Mrs Kennedy for me.'

She stood and watched him, his shoulders slumped. She couldn't bring herself to apologise, though she was sorry. She was an ungrateful woman, unmarriageable even. She wanted what her parents once had. Dr Pratt, the same as all the others, was offering an alliance of two lonely people. How could that be anything other than twice as cold? She heard Johanna in the hall, the whoosh of air and the shuddering of furniture as the door closed after him.

After Dr Pratt, her aunt gave up on the miscellany of widowers and bachelors. She began dropping hints about convents, about friends who were seeking a governess who could play piano. But Anne could tell that her aunt had lost her enthusiasm for now. She withdrew a little further, rarely asking Anne to accompany her on rounds of visiting. She was occupied with various other problems. Her grandchildren gave her daughters unexpected trouble. Her son-in-law wanted to sell more of the Galway estate and she did not agree. The old laundress in Mountjoy Square was retiring and needed to be replaced. She made it clear to Anne that her burdens were many. Anne tried to take up as little space as possible.

At first, Anne did nothing to hide her meetings with Matthias or the letters they exchanged. They were cousins, of a sort, after all. Her aunt said nothing and so she assumed that she approved. But when Cook asked after 'her gentleman' with a suggestive smirk, Anne became more careful. She wanted no interference from anyone. Matthias, far from objecting, seemed to relish the secrecy: sending letters to and from the post office and meeting in isolated places where they might not see anyone at all. One evening over a tea of cold ham her aunt said, as though continuing a conversation that had not begun: 'You know that he has no money. Your cousin, if we could call him that. Not two pence to rub together.' Anne pretended to be surprised by the comment, replied that they'd not been spending so much time together and that she didn't understand what money had to do with anything. Her aunt only gave her a long look over her medicinal glass of sherry and sighed.

Their first meeting had been innocent enough. She hated how she kept tilting her head to the side like a doll and smiling at everything he said.

'You're very quiet,' he said, more than once.

Arm in arm, they circled the Rotunda Gardens until Anne felt dizzy.

As the meetings became more secretive they also became more urgent. At first, she refused to kiss him. Then, once she permitted kissing, he wanted to caress her. He would beg her to sit in his lap and once she acquiesced she would feel his hands seeking other inroads. She was both ashamed and thrilled by the feeling this produced in her, the almost painful throb of desire in places she had never spoken of out loud.

One fine October day they sat on a bench in Prospect Cemetery holding hands. The air was so clear and bright that she could see the edges of everything: individual leaves and the marks on every headstone. She decided now was the time to make their courtship official. She knew that Matthias was courting her. He declared his love over and over while she withheld any declarations of her own.

'If you would just call to the house, I know Aunt Julia would be happy to invite you for tea. She prefers any company to mine.'

'I would love nothing more,' Matthias said, sounding unconvinced.

'Then come tomorrow. We've no callers tomorrow.'

'Don't be silly. Think of how bored we'll be. Your aunt looming over us like a spectre, the maid bringing fresh tea every fifteen minutes. And think of the questions,' Matthias sat up ramrod straight and pushed out his lips in an imitation of her aunt. 'Dr Kelly, do tell us, how many patients have you seen this quarter? And what about that position in the hospital? Surely you can't be satisfied on such a very *small* income.' Anne laughed.

'Would that be so awful?'

'Well, what if she decided that my visit was some kind of declaration of intent? What if she decided that we couldn't meet like this? That we needed a chaperone? Then I wouldn't be able to do this,' and he pulled Anne against him. He bent his head to kiss the skin along the neckline of her dress. Then he sent his fingers probing along the same edge, slipping one inside her bodice, stretching for her nipple. He'd never been so bold in public before. A sigh of pleasure escaped her lips before she pushed his hand away.

'We'd need a blind chaperone,' she said. He laughed and kissed her deeply while he tried to slip a hand up her skirt. Anne agreed that of course they were better, much better, like this.

Matthias walked her towards home along the canal. As they made their formal goodbyes at the corner of the Circular Road, she felt her mood drop. The excitement for the week was over. Now began another round of waiting for his letters and fretting that they might never come. Another week of visiting the post office with imaginary letters to Frances or her father and wondering if the clerk recognised her from last week. Another week of avoiding any conversation with Cook and ignoring her knowing glances.

Luckily Cook was not in the kitchen as Anne entered from the yard and climbed the back stairs to her room. She glanced at the clock. Just after four. She'd been gone longer than she'd planned. Aunt Julia would be up from her nap. Anne fabricated visits to school friends to hide her meetings with Matthias. She tried to picture how she might have filled the hours if she'd gone to Lizzy's or Maria's or Charlotte's instead. Maybe if she offered to read to her aunt then she wouldn't ask too many questions.

She listened to the steps in the hall but it wasn't her aunt and it wasn't Johanna. She opened the door to look out and a young woman in a maid's apron stood looking up and down as though lost. She spoke before Anne could ask her business.

'Begging your pardon. Are you Miss Mulhall? You're wanted in the sitting room. By the mistress.'

Anne remembered now that her aunt had mentioned something about replacing the woman in the laundry. She'd been stooped and her reddened hands were almost painful to look at.

'Are you the new laundress?'

'Well, I believe laundry is only part of me duties. Rose Doyle, miss.'

The woman was unusually pretty and Anne thought that Johanna and Cook wouldn't like her. Though laundry was taxing and hot work that could roughen a woman in months.

'I see. Did my aunt tell you the nature of my summons? It isn't a Doctor Pratt is it?'

'There's a caller. I think it's your da.'

'And is Ellen, I mean Mrs Mulhall, with him?' She held her breath.

'No, miss, it's just him on his own. They're waitin' on ya.'

'I see. I'll come down with you now straight away. Am I presentable?'

'I'll just straighten the hair, miss. There's a bit of a breeze out there.'

Anne tried to sit still while the new servant guided her head this way and that, twisting and pinning until she was satisfied. She'd never had her hair fixed by a laundress and she studied her reflection as she worked. The woman must be close to her own age. A neat figure, blonde curls and dark blue eyes. Her hands were less rough than Johanna's.

'Thank you, Rose, I look just as though I was sitting in a drawing room all afternoon.'

'Weren't you, miss?' Anne caught the servant's quick smile in the mirror. 'Cook told me you have a beau. That you were out meetin' someone.'

'I was meeting a friend. My cousin. I don't have a beau.'

'Cook must have it wrong then.'

'You won't tell my aunt.' Anne surprised herself when the words came out as a command and not a question.

'Of course not. It weren't none of me business anyway. And mind yourself. Men are slippery creatures, full of wants.'

Anne felt she knew plenty about men's wants. She saw the way her father stared at Ellen even during the months when she'd been nursing her mother. He took every chance to touch her, brushing her hand as he passed her in the hall. Worse, she knew her mother had seen it too. The doctor said she'd died of an inflammatory fever but it was the broken heart that finished her.

When Anne entered the parlour everyone fell silent, so that she was sure Father and Aunt Julia had been arguing about her. Or perhaps he'd been asking for money. He'd visited once since her move to Mountjoy Square. There was no repeat of the warm embrace or the kind words. They sat like strangers forced together in a train compartment, making pleasant sounds and enduring one another's company for the journey. He hadn't asked Anne to visit. Ellen was too busy with the house, things weren't quite ready, or Ellen was too tired with the pregnancy. This visit was undeclared and unexpected. Anne wondered what would happen if her mother had left her a hidden fortune. Or if her father wanted her to return home? Could she refuse?

'You look well, Anne.' He didn't stand, just accepted her kiss on his cheek.

'And you, Father.' She sat down between them and waited.

'You see, Anne, there are some financial matters I must attend to. And, well ...' His voice trailed off. She felt her hopes deflate. Had she really expected that he'd come to fetch her? Aunt Julia continued what he'd begun.

'Your father has asked me to take you as my ward indefinitely. He will give me the little money your mother left for you. To manage until you are settled. It seems his new life is rather more expensive than he gambled.'

Her father didn't even wince at the insult, just gave a little shrug.

'I think it's for the best. Your stepmother is certain you'll be happier here when the baby comes.' Anne kept her face still and clasped her hands together. He flashed the same appeasing smile he'd given her when she caught Ellen reaching for his hand at the wake. She wanted to send the tea tray tumbling into his lap.

'Of course,' she said.

After he left Anne went to change for dinner. Her aunt stopped her on the stairs.

'He's a disgrace, that man. I'm sorry to say that, I know he's your father, but he has treated you poorly and I'm sorry.'

Anne was surprised by the sudden flush of kindness but then her aunt added, 'It's hardly a surprise that he failed to find you a suitable husband.'

Chapter Nine

Denis

8th August, 1866

Denis rose before dawn. Market day. The best beasts would be sold before six. He padded through the silent house. As he let himself out through the shop there was already a crust of light on the horizon and a steady beat of footfall on the road. At the top of Sackville Street he turned up Great Britain Street and swerved his way to the Circular Road. He could smell and hear the market before he could see it. A great sea of cattle and sheep spread before him, the tide of animals contained by sticks of steel railings. Little clouds of pipe smoke, like a hundred tiny chimneys, showed where the men were.

He plunged into the roaring mass. There was a buzz of flies, drawn to the shit, and a flutter of birds, drawn to the flies. Denis enjoyed the frenetic energy of the market and the scent of the fields that seemed to cling to it in the early hours. Soon the scent of defecation and sweating men in unwashed suits would overwhelm the last shreds of country breeze.

James Lyons beckoned from his shed, inviting Denis to run his hands over a selected heifer.

'I've been keepin' her aside for you. Just the right size.'
Denis felt her haunches. Her sides twitched. She flicked
her tail and fluttered her heavy eyelashes in defence against
the flies.

'Clean bill of health?' Denis pulled open her mouth to
inspect the teeth and tongue, looked into her eyes. 'Price?'

'Thought you'd like her. Let's say seventy-two shillings.'

'Mr Lyons, after so many years you still take me for a fool.
I'll give you sixty-five and no more. It's not good business to
bankrupt a loyal customer.'

They haggled enjoyably for a few minutes until the price
was agreed and the dealer moved on to other news.

'I hear you fished a baby out of the river a few days ago.'

'I found it, that's true. But the detective recovered it.'

'Nearly fell over when I recognised your name in the
paper. Terrible thing to see. Although it's rampant in
London, I believe. The Thames is full of them, and they
leave them in gutters and privies you know. Mrs Doyle wasn't
with you, I hope?'

'No, no. I was on my own.'

'Not a kind of thing you'd want a woman seeing. Mind
you, the streets are full of things no woman should see.
And how is she anyway? Your wife, I mean? I look forward
to the day when you're coming here with a little Doyle on
your shoulders.'

'She's fine, just fine. I'll tell her you were asking,' Denis
turned up the corners of his mouth. 'Good day, Mr Lyons.'

The sun drove away the shadows and any hope of a breeze.
Denis felt a little faint. Inside the City Arms Hotel he
sucked down his pint along with the greasy slithering eggs.
He watched the barmaids scuttling between tables, trying
to avoid the same handling that was being delivered to the

cattle in their pens. He tossed coins on the bar and didn't wait for his change, he wanted to get back to the shop. Rose would be up. She wasn't at Mrs Kennedy's today.

He'd stopped hoping that she would give up the house job. It would be for a few months, she'd said, just until they find someone else. Rose's mother had left the house's laundry because she was too old and stiff. Denis tried to convince Rose that there was no family reputation to maintain by taking up her mother's job. After years of service that reddened her hands and bent her back, the woman gave Rose's mother a few shillings and an earful on her last day. What was there to show gratitude for? But he knew Rose needed to be busy and, maybe for a little while, away from him. He'd hoped she would miss him and come running back to the shop. But she just spent more and more time there over the months. There was always some reason, some extra duty that Mrs Kennedy had found for her. He didn't like her spending the night there, even if Mrs Kennedy's niece had been so ill. She was needed at home.

When he reached North Earl Street, Rose had already pulled up the shutter and was behind the counter. He could see her through the glass, busy getting things in order. He watched her for a moment, wishing that he could walk through the door and find himself back in time, to the weeks after his wedding.

'How was the market?' she asked, without raising her eyes from the meat she was laying out. She picked up a cloth to wipe her hands. She was always wiping her hands now, they were red raw from soap. 'There's the last of the beef, we can sell it off today.'

'Yes, the usual vultures will be in looking for deals. The market was fine, Lyons's drover'll be down later to put her in the shed. He sends his regards.'

'Mmm.' Denis went around the counter, stepped in behind her and put his hands on her waist. She squared up like a fighter waiting for a blow as he kissed her on the neck. 'Denis, please. The shade's up. You're makin' a holy show.'

'And who would fault me for kissing my lovely wife?' He felt her raise her shoulders, just a tiny bit, as if stopping herself from brushing him off completely. She was so careful, he almost wanted her to push him away. He dropped his hands and turned towards the door, 'I'll be down in a minute. I'll just change the shirt.'

Rose and Denis settled into the familiar dance of the married couple tending the shop. It was a busy morning. As Denis had suspected, plenty of customers came in to see what they could buy up. They sniffed and prodded the meat, searching for reasons to pay less. Denis was in the midst of a negotiation when a man arrived with a slab of papers in his hand. His thin moustache and narrow shoulders gave the impression of a boy wearing his father's suit. He held his papers in two hands in front of him, as though he were about to read a speech, and demanded to see the proprietor.

'I'm he,' said Denis, wiping his hands on his apron.

'I'm here asking for support for a new society. The Society for the Protection of Infant Life. Here's the prospectus. We've the Queen herself as patron and any number of clergymen of all denominations.' He lifted a leaflet from his pile and held it out to Denis. He touched his cap to appear obliging.

Denis started at the phrase 'infant life'. He was conscious of Rose's glance in his direction.

'Support how?'

'By a small contribution to help us suppress the horrible act of infant murder. I've been to the other businessmen on the street and they've all given me a shilling or more.' The young man shifted on his feet and looked down at his papers for further inspiration.

'Is this because of that inquest was just in all the papers?' He wondered if the man knew about his own small role in all of that.

'Our founder, Mr Mills, suggested that you might be of particular value to our endeavours.' The man leaned against the counter, making himself more comfortable as he launched into his pitch. 'This seems an opportune moment. In England baby farmers and lascivious women resort to the basest crimes. We can stop the same horrors becoming commonplace here.' His voice grew louder and customers in the shop began to listen. Denis gave the man a few coins and took his notice so that he could get back to work. He placed the paper on the counter in the back room of the shop.

'What was he about?' Rose asked when the customers began to clear.

'Some new society for infant life wanting money.'

'And did you give him some?'

'I did.'

'For handing you a piece of paper for the fire? You're very soft, Denis. There'll be a queue out the door tomorrow.'

'It seemed like it might be a good cause. I won't give them another penny without asking you first.'

Rose rolled her eyes and smiled. The thoughtless gesture filled Denis with hope.

'I'll go up to make the dinner, it's quiet enough in here now.' She began to untie the apron and Denis leaned in, about to kiss her cheek. She froze and he pulled back.

'I won't be long. I'll close a little early if it's slow.'

A half hour crawled by until Denis drew the blind and put away the unsold meat. It was still too early to go upstairs, he would be in Rose's way.

He picked up the notice from the counter and began to read.

Society for the Protection of Infant Life

At a meeting at the Lord Mayor's Mansion on August the 1st 1866, it was proposed to found a Society for the Protection of Infant Life on the model recently inaugurated in England. The following gentlemen and ladies were in attendance:

The Lord Mayor

Alderman Harwood

Alderman Grey & Mrs Grey

Alderman Sweeney

Councillor Grant & Mrs Grant

The Misses Eddington

Lady Carmichael

Mrs Julia Kennedy

The Rt. Honourable Archbishop of Dublin, Richard Trench

Those present agreed on the following:

That the aim of this society is to advocate for all causes that would further the protection of infant life in this country.

That measures such as the education of mothers on home hygiene and infant feeding are of crucial importance but do nothing to prevent the evil of infant murder.

That the present system of baby farming or nursing degrades the value of infants and tempts both men and women of low virtue into the abandonment of their offspring.

That many of these so-called nurseries are conducted by women of ill-repute, without care for the health of their charges and without any inspection.

That the mis-placed sympathy of judges and the police prevents the deterrence of infant murder due to leniency in conviction and sentencing.

It was resolved that:

Membership in the society will cost 1 guinea annually.

Associate membership will cost 6 shillings annually.

Donations to be sought for the purpose of setting up an inspectorate of nursing establishments and the printing of educational literature.

Next meeting to be held on September the 1st at the Lord Mayor's Mansion.

Denis placed the leaflet in his pocket. He felt it would be wrong to throw it into the ash pit. He recalled a case the previous year when police searched a house belonging to a young woman and her father. They found a baby's hands hidden in a hollow behind a picture on the wall. Denis thought again of the tiny hands of his own dead son, the perfect restful face and smooth skin.

When he got upstairs he put the leaflet in the bottom drawer of the sideboard. He closed the drawer as Rose came in.

'Ah there you are, I'll wet the tea,' she said.

After the meal, it was still bright.

'Let's go for a walk,' Denis offered. They never walked out together anymore, not since her pregnancy, when they'd paced the streets in nervous anticipation. After the birth, he'd been so filled with grief he hadn't known how to behave. She hadn't wanted him near and he'd left her be. He was still leaving her be. How much longer could he wait?

'It's very warm. Aren't you tired?'

'No, I'm not. We can head up Sackville Street and towards the park. If we don't make it that far at least there's a view from uphill.'

'Alright.' She took a shawl that Denis knew she didn't need and they went out through the yard and the back gate. Rose frowned at the flies ornamenting the piles of bones and heaps of manure. 'There's a smell Denis, I thought I said to you about the inspector. If you're not careful that Dr Connolly will write to the Corporation again.'

'I've done my best Rose, but I can't get rid of it until Friday. Nobody wants to keep a pile in the heat.'

Everyone had warned him that Rose wasn't suited to be a butcher's wife. Too sensitive, they said. Too pretty. Denis dismissed them. She never complained of the stink, was never shy of work. But after the birth. Well, it was as if his business made her sick. As if *he* made her sick.

Rose let him take her arm and Denis's heart lifted. He conjured images of once again lying next to Rose, his body cupping hers.

'Tell me about this infant life society you were so eager to join,' Rose said, interrupting his thoughts.

'I haven't joined,' he said, 'unless you'd rather spend a guinea on that than the new linens.' Across the road he could see a woman pushing a baby carriage down the hill as they walked up. He wondered if Rose saw it too. He wondered if seeing baby carriages made her chest squeeze.

'That's a bit rich, isn't it?' Rose said. She didn't look at the baby carriage. 'I suppose it's a fancy club dressed up as charity.'

'They have some serious plans. An inspectorate for nurses for a start. And to make some judges pass harder sentences. Not to let the women away with transportation and the like.'

Rose went quiet. The woman across the street stopped pushing. Denis watched her lean over the carriage and poke her face in under the cover. He wondered what she was saying. He turned back to Rose, worried that she'd noticed him staring.

'That won't work,' Rose said with conviction.

'What do you mean, love? Surely no woman wants to hang. Or go to prison.'

'Does a woman who kills her newborn child sit weighing the baby's life against her own? Like she was deciding whether to buy six pieces of bacon or just the two chops for the same money? Those women are desperate and nothing else.' But he didn't agree. He wanted Rose to see it all the way he did. He wanted her to feel the way he felt. That it could never be right or fair or excusable to kill a baby at all. Those women who got themselves in trouble, there were people to help them. There were other ways.

'It put to mind that young one last year chopped her baby all to pieces and spread them 'round the house — planned to burn them bit by bit I suppose. Even her da lied and said he hadn't known the girl was pregnant, hadn't seen the baby born.' He felt the pitch of his voice changing, straining. He knew this was bothering him more than it should. What had he to do with this infanticide or with any other one? But finding the body stirred something in him and he couldn't leave it be. He felt the injustice of his own situation. The waste of it rather than the violence of it. A woman throwing her child away so lightly, as though it had no value, when a child was the one thing he valued almost more than Rose.

'That only shows my point. Desperation. Where was the man who did it to her? Nowhere to be found. And she so young.' Rose looked away. The air was hazy and there was a smell of fat from the chop houses on Great Britain Street. A few clerks hurried past, clutching their cases as they tried to catch the omnibus to the suburbs.

'Well, yes, of course,' Denis conceded, 'the man has some fault as well. The only one with no fault is the baby. Let's not argue.' Rose seemed happy to let it go and Denis filled all the silences that fell with news of the trade, the weather, the state of the river, the manure heap in the lane. He even resorted to describing the notice he'd seen of the performing elephant coming to the Theatre Royale. Only the elephant roused his wife into less perfunctory answers. He vowed to purchase tickets.

After they returned from the walk he sat smoking in the chair by the window. He didn't bother to light a lamp or read, he just listened to the sounds of Rose in the kitchen and the sounds of the street outside. He watched the smoke curl and slip beneath the window sash. He could no more grab hold of Rose than he could that smoke. She'd been disappearing. Ever since the night she'd spent at Mrs Kennedy's house it had been getting worse. She came home late and gave the same excuses: she'd been to see her mother, she'd visited a friend. And the drink. Most days he could smell it on her breath, hear it on her tongue. Did she think he hadn't noticed?

Chapter Ten

Anne

November 1865

One evening, Aunt Julia announced that she would go to spend two nights in Bray.

'Will you come?' Her fork hovered in the air as she waited for Anne's answer. Anne pictured herself at her cousin Emily's house, running to serve the demands of three adults and two children. She waited to reply until her aunt began to chew.

'No, thank you. I'll stay here. I can finish practising my new piece. It's a very loud and difficult one. This way, I won't disturb you by playing it over and over.' She could see her aunt's jaw moving as she weighed the idea. Leaving Anne meant relinquishing control over her. No one to read to her or fetch spectacles that she left upstairs. But leaving Anne also meant not having to think about her for a few days. A crease disappeared from her forehead.

'Alright then. I suppose it's only two nights. I imagine you'll be very lonely, though.'

'I'll have Rose and Johanna and Cook for company.'

'Don't go walking in some lonely place without a chaperone. And no callers. Don't think you're the lady of the house just because I'm away.'

'Of course not.'

Anne was giddy with the possibilities. She found she couldn't eat. She pushed her potato around her plate and nibbled at a piece of bread. She could see whoever she liked for as long as she wanted.

When the day came, Anne helped bundle her aunt into the carriage, piling coloured boxes onto the seats while the groom tied her trunk to the roof. There was enough luggage to last a month. The carriage had barely cleared the square when it returned abruptly, and the groom flew in, searching for a missing gift, another bottle of wine, and a loaf of Cook's best white bread. Anne waited an hour, expecting him to return with further demands.

Matthias suggested they meet at Grand Canal Basin and stroll towards the bay. Too nervous to occupy herself until the right time to take a cab, she decided to walk. The weather was fine, if a little cold. She crossed over Sackville Bridge and watched the Liffey ferries churning the dark water. Brown foam swirled and drifted behind them in frothy streams. She thought of the last carriage to overturn into the river, the horse spooked and rearing. She pictured her aunt in the carriage with all the boxes tumbling around her as the carriage plunged down and down and the water closed over them.

Anne was relieved to reach Lime Street and see Matthias ahead of her.

'There you are! Escaped from your aunt's clutches at last. I've missed you. I need to see you more.' He reached out and pulled her closer and she worried that he would kiss her right there in the street and that she would let him, like a common woman.

'I'm glad to see you, too. It's such a fine day, and no one expects me at home. Do you still fancy the walk to the sea?' She was lightheaded, filled with love for Matthias and delight in her freedom. She intended to savour every minute. She wondered if this was what her sister felt for her husband. But they'd always seemed so restrained and companionable whereas Anne felt a reckless, tumbling joy like a child running downhill faster than her feet could keep up.

'I've brought a sort of picnic.' Matthias drew two peaches from the pocket of his coat and presented them with a flourish.

'Where did you get those? They're probably covered in bruises or hard as stones.'

'They're perfect. As soft as your own cheeks. But if you don't want one, that's fine with me,' and he put them back in his pocket and huffed. Anne laughed.

Matthias took her arm and she folded into him. They seemed to walk for hours, the metal and sulphur fug of the factories receding and the houses thinning. Every grass verge smelled like a privy. At first Anne was enjoying herself, tucked warm against Matthias's silky coat. But the houses began to look run down and dreary and there were so few people about that she grew anxious. Finally, the sight of the sea rippling silver under a heavy sky lifted her mood. Clouds spilled down the hills like batter poured from a bowl and there was a kind of hush that only comes when the sea is filling the air with its own sounds. The world opened out, like Anne had been released from an unwanted embrace. Sunlight picked out the mound of Kingstown and the masts in its harbour. The beach was empty except for birds and a few people gathering oysters at the horizon. They walked along the curve of the bay where Matthias said they could take in the view. They were alone, just as he'd promised. Matthias stopped, spread his coat on the ground.

'Your coat will be ruined.'

'Don't be silly. That's what servants are for. What do you think of my picnic spot?'

'It's a beautiful view.' Anne felt a sudden certainty that he'd brought someone here before. That the spreading of the coat was a practised flourish rather than a spontaneous piece of gallantry.

'I should've brought some sherry to wash them down,' he said, biting into his peach. The peaches were just as he'd promised, soft and sweet. He threw the pits into the water and gave Anne his handkerchief to wipe her hands.

'It's a bit early in the day for a drink. I'd soon be wanting a nap,' she said.

'Well, you can lay your head in my lap and rest before we have to start back.' She considered for a moment too long. 'You've seen there's no one around.' He grinned and she relented.

Anne lay down, pulling the shawl around her as though the fabric was some kind of armour. But he only stroked her forehead as she tumbled into sleep.

When Anne woke, the clouds from the hills had crept in closer and the water had turned black with the rising tide.

'I was just thinking I should wake you. So much for pleasant conversation!' Matthias helped her up before he brushed down his coat.

'I'm sorry. I didn't realise I was so tired. You must find me very dull company.'

'Never. Watching someone sleep is more interesting than you might imagine. I'm famished, though. I think it's time we turned back.'

Anne felt disappointed and weary as they returned the way they'd come. The outing was coming to an end and she'd been expecting something. More affection, she supposed, even though she'd stopped him from kissing her in the street. They bought paper parcels of roasted chestnuts from a street seller and ate like greedy children, licking ash and salt from their fingers.

When they reached the edge of town, the clouds delivered their promise in a shower of sleet and hail so thick it blocked their view. Cab drivers stopped, pulling covers over passengers and blankets over horses. In less than a minute Anne was wringing wet and shivering. Her hair dripped icy tentacles down her back and the shawl hung heavy across her shoulders. Her skirts dragged behind her and she couldn't hold them up.

'You can't walk home like that,' Matthias said, 'you'll catch cold. I could give you some money for a cab, but there's no stand nearby. The omnibus is streets away.'

The street emptied of cars and drivers, all of them giving up on fares in favour of shelter.

'I don't know what to do,' Anne said, trying to wring the shawl out in her hands.

'Come to my house. You can dry yourself by the fire for a while before you go home.' The thought of the empty house on Mountjoy Square, the rain drumming down, made her shiver with cold and loneliness.

'Yes, alright,' she said, 'and when the cabs are back out, when the weather has passed, I can take one as far as Sackville Street and I'll still be back in time for tea.'

Matthias's house was smaller than she'd expected. The bricks were darkened and dull and the windows needed a wash. She felt a pang of disappointment. Matthias was an ordinary man living in an ordinary house and not a prince who'd come to sweep her away. He unlocked the door and led her into a dark hallway while calling out for 'Mrs Tuffy'. There was a sound of shuffling and doors closing, but Mrs Tuffy didn't appear. He brought her to the back of the house.

'It's much less grand than one might like,' Matthias said, reading her thoughts. 'But once I get my appointment at the hospital, I'll be better off. The rooms are comfortable enough.' He held open a door on the right and she saw a small sitting room.

Before Anne could become melancholy, Mrs Tuffy arrived in a bustle of grey skirts and thin hands. She made exclamations at the state of their clothes, built up the fire and brought scalding hot tea and a few soft biscuits. Matthias and Anne sat across from one another on deep blue sofas, sipping and reaching towards the fire to warm their hands. Anne forgot about the dark hallway and the dirty front windows. She wondered if she became his wife would they sit here like this in the evening, sharing tales from their day. And would he make space for her piano?

She could not relax because she was aware of Mrs Tuffy's presence, listening somewhere in the house. As if he could hear her thoughts, Matthias said: 'Mrs Tuffy is my only servant at the moment. She's going deaf, but she thinks no one has noticed.'

'She seems very competent, I'm sure.'

'Father asked me to take her on after she was widowed. He thought it would be easy work for her — I suppose a bachelor is undemanding.'

'Have you dried out at all?' Anne could see steam rising from them both. She felt warmer but no less soaked.

'Not really. I'll go and change. Perhaps Mrs Tuffy can find something dry for you.'

'Don't worry, I'll be fine. I should be going anyway.'

'But you're still dripping wet.' Together they looked down at the floor to where the edge of her skirt was leaving a half circle of dark lines on the rug. 'I'll leave you and send Mrs Tuffy in. She'll know what to do.' He stood over her and gave her the kiss she'd been expecting all day.

Mrs Tuffy declared that Anne would have to take off the dress and the stays and the petticoats. Before she could protest, the servant began to tug at her clothes and to pile them up on the racks she'd brought in. Having stripped Anne to her shift, she announced that she had nothing for Anne to wear.

'There were some old gowns of Mrs Kelly's in a press but the moths have been at them and they'd not be suitable anyhow.' Anne must have looked surprised because she added: 'Dr Kelly's mother. Used to give me any dresses she didn't want.'

'Have you anything at all? I don't mind what it is.' Anne hugged her arms tighter across her chest. Mrs Tuffy had formed an opinion of her as the kind of woman who could be left sitting in her shift. Hadn't she arrived at a single man's house without a chaperone?

'Oh don't you worry, there's no one here to see you but the master and me. Your dress will dry soon enough.'

'I would be more comfortable ... with something else.'

'I suppose I could bring a dressing gown.'

'Thank you, that would be most welcome.'

Having delivered the gown, a towel to dry her hair and a week-old *Freeman's Journal*, she left Anne alone. Anne thought she could hear Matthias come back down the stairs and enter his study. She moved closer to the fire but couldn't settle on anything in the paper. She lay down on the sofa and tried to sleep.

Her eyes had barely closed when she heard the door handle turn. She thought it might be Mrs Tuffy coming back with a hot drink and wanted her to go away. But she knew Matthias's step and the scent he gave off. She heard him pull the door behind him and cross the room. Then she felt his weight depressing the end of the sofa, his hand reaching under the gown.

Chapter Eleven

Peakin

8th August, 1866 (later in the day)

The infanticide attracted uncomfortable conversation at the entomology club meeting. Peakin and three other men gathered in the library of the Mechanics' Institute for their biweekly review of the latest scientific news. The armchairs, once rather fine, now had their fabric worn thin by a succession of self-improving elbows. The only books that weren't out of date were the collection of novels and political treatises. At a distance, though, you could imagine that every book on the shelves contained something of value. Peakin liked the feeling he got from the library, as though he were engulfed in the embrace of all the world's knowledge.

His friends consisted of Mr Hall (wealthy merchant), Dr Keeffe (wealthy surgeon) and Dr Pratt (wealthy physician). Peakin was invited to their group after he asked probing questions at a public entomological lecture. An interview ensued, in which the men determined that a precocious Peakin had been sending Darwin specimens for years. Peakin knew their feelings towards him consisted of a mixture of envy, curiosity and misplaced philanthropy. Unencumbered by the need to earn a living, the men toyed with nationalist sentiments. Peakin didn't speak about his views and the men rarely asked about his work. They spoke frequently of their own; Peakin felt their lack of curiosity reflected a slight embarrassment at keeping company with someone they considered no better than a brick layer. Each felt passionately about education for the working classes in an abstract way.

This evening, Dr Keeffe and Dr Pratt decided to once again ignore the rule against smoking in the library between 6 and 8 p.m. Without any warning they launched into a discussion of Peakin's case.

'What do you make of infanticide Peakin? I mean in a general, or rather, scientific sense?' Dr Keeffe asked, leaning back in the armchair and puffing harder on his pipe. He was smartly dressed, apparently impervious to the heat, with a small round belly upon which he placed the hand that was not holding the pipe. 'Is infanticide the result of vestigial animal instinct? A horrific way of culling the poor?'

Peakin tried not to wince. He wasn't sure which made him more uncomfortable, this cold Malthusian mathematics or the fact that he was being asked about his police work.

'Well, if it was some means of naturally selecting the chaste, then it has had surprisingly little effect on the availability of, ahem, working women.' There was a good-humoured chuckle all around as Peakin examined the worn patches on the knees of his trousers. The suit was only three years old and he'd hardly get another any time soon. He wondered if these men also nursed habits they wouldn't like to tell their wives about. Peakin had chosen Mrs Wilson's because it was discreet and clean, as respectable as a house of ill fame could be. The girls had most of their teeth because they'd never been forced to go on the mercury cure. He breathed in the comforting aroma of pipes and dusty books and imagined that this was how his friends felt most of the time: as though the world of the city's streets was a place that one knew about but could always escape from.

'I heard a paper in the academy on puerperal mania,' said Mr Hall. 'I believe it is more widespread than is generally thought.' He sat perched at the edge of his chair, spectacles slipping forward. 'As the doctor sees it, the exertion of the birth can make a woman quite mad. There are a number of them in Richmond Asylum as we speak. He's making a study of them. It's a great challenge, however, as few of them live very long. They find a way to end themselves.'

And they went on like this, each of them opining on the causes of infanticide and each of them looking for Peakin to approve their theory. Normally he would have enjoyed this kind of attention, the men acknowledging his expertise. But he shifted in his chair, trying to nudge the conversation back to beetles.

'Have any of you seen the latest issue of *The Entomologist*? The editor claims there are no naturalists in Dublin! I have half a mind ...' But the others would never know what half of Peakin's mind intended because Dr Pratt took that moment to make a surprising announcement.

'I wondered about providing some evidence, Peakin.' The chair barely contained his significant height but he always sat hunched forward as though in an attempt to make himself smaller. He tapped his pipe out onto the newspaper next to him and began to refill it.

'What evidence could that be?' Peakin asked. 'Dr Mapother has done the postmortem. I don't think there's further cause for medical men unless we turn up a woman's body. I can ask the inspector if you wish to be put on the list for postmortems.'

'Oh no, nothing like that. I gave up the postmortems some years ago and have no intention of going back. Mrs Pratt, God rest her, often complained of the smell. For days afterwards I was forced to sleep in my study. No it's only some little bit of a suggestion. It might be of no use, of course.' Dr Pratt paused and struck a match to light his pipe.

'What are you saying, sir?' Mr Hall demanded, clapping his hands, his spectacles now threatening to fall from his face and onto his lap.

'Yes, what could you possibly know? Unless you've been more craven than we've always suspected.' Dr Keeffe laughed at his own joke.

Peakin turned to Dr Pratt and hoped that his moustache covered his annoyance.

'If you've any evidence Dr Pratt, I'd prefer it in a form I can use. Some kind of official testimony.' Peakin couldn't imagine what it would be. Maybe the man had been dipping into the delights of French Street as Dr Keeffe was suggesting and overheard something? Or perhaps a female patient had asked for help.

'I think I'd prefer not. It might be only gossip. I don't know. I shouldn't have mentioned it.' Dr Pratt crossed his arms and sucked harder on his pipe, releasing smoke in a thin, tight stream. Peakin wanted this piece of information, whatever it might be. While he was considering what to ask, Dr Keeffe let out a groan.

'Well, if it's only gossip then what harm in telling us? I'm sure Peakin has heard plenty of that. He'll not make anything of it if it's only gossip. And now you've quite unfairly piqued our curiosity and are threatening to disappoint us. Out with it!' He leaned towards Dr Pratt and put a hand on his arm as though to keep him in the chair until he spoke. Dr Pratt looked around the library. Gaining no solace from *Newton's Mechanics Explained* or *The Museum of Nature*, he continued.

'You'll recall the young lady I almost attached myself to?'

Mr Hall groaned, pulled the spectacles from his nose and made a show of wiping them on his shirt.

'You mean the young lady that you mooned over for months, suffered through innumerable dinners with and bored us silly about? The one who you talked about proposing to for weeks on end and then never did? Is that the one?'

Dr Pratt blushed and puffed at his pipe.

'There's no need to be nasty, Hall.'

'Of course, you're right. Please continue.'

'Well, there's very little to say. As you so crudely pointed out, I never did ask her to marry me. I found her, perhaps, a little too forward for my tastes.' Rather than forward, Peakin presumed that he found her most unwilling to tie herself to a widower twice her age, with two children, who smelled like wooden furniture. 'Well, it's just that there was a bit of talk. You know how servants are. My groom is a nephew of the woman who cooks in her aunt's house. Apparently for months she wasn't seen and when she was, she was wrapped up, like she was ill. But the cook thinks there was something else going on. Anyway, she was bundled off to the countryside about a month ago and since then she hasn't been out.'

'Is that all?' Hall threw up his hands. 'The poor lady acquires an enthusiasm for shawls and you're going to tell Peakin that she might be no lady at all but one who engages in a most improper liaison and then becomes a murderess. And half of Dublin, the half with any sense if you ask me, went to the countryside to escape this confounded heat.' A nervous titter travelled from one man to the next. Peakin said nothing. He thought he could hear the books crackle in the silence as they all waited for more.

'I said it might be only gossip. Anyway, I won't waste any more of your time on it Peakin. I'm sure your investigation is getting along fine without me.'

'No witnesses have come forward as yet, though it is rather early. But the usual places, the workhouses and such, have turned up nothing. At this rate, there may be no resolution of any kind.'

Mr Hall and Dr Keeffe could have told Peakin the name, of course, but they all waited for it to slip from Dr Pratt's lips. The company broke up soon after. There was a feeling that something untoward had happened. No one had much appetite for entomology or for planning their next field outing. They shook hands at the door and Peakin watched the others make for the public house where he could not follow. Few other policemen bided that particular rule, but he didn't like to take any risks until the next promotion opportunity had passed. Just last month the inspector demoted a man for drunkenness. Peakin was waiting for the inspector to notice that he still had no wife to show for months of engagement. He could be asked to move back into the barracks. And it wasn't just the humiliation. He wasn't ready to admit that Isobel was never coming and that he might not find anyone to replace her. He clung to dreams of future domesticity: a wife to receive his kisses, children's hair to tousle, someone to provide for other than himself.

Peakin was lonely. He longed for even the sullen company of Peggi, but he couldn't afford another trip to Mrs Wilson's so soon. He turned Dr Pratt's gossip over in his mind as he strode towards home. On the one hand, the way that Dr Pratt overcame great reluctance seemed to suggest the strength of his suspicions. On the other hand, this woman had spurned him and he might have a reason to think ill of her. And then there was the fact that the woman was respectable and therefore an unlikely candidate for infanticide and very tricky to investigate. Such people were well-connected and could send forth a blizzard of angry correspondence. Nonetheless, the name bothered him. He recalled the stack of tattling letters that he'd received since the inquest: a woman grown fatter and then thinner again, a woman gone to the country unexpectedly, a woman seen meeting a soldier without a chaperone. Peakin disregarded all the letters though he felt obliged to keep them. But he was certain that Dr Pratt's *amour* was also named in one of those letters.

Chapter Twelve

Anne

November 1865

Anne ran towards Pearse Street, not caring how her skirt trailed in the mud or sobs contorted her face. She could smell him everywhere. He'd marked her, soiled her, an odour like day-old oysters. Not even the festering river or a fresh pile of manure could dislodge the scent from her nose. She trailed it like a mist, so that everyone could smell the shame clinging to her. She kept looking down at her dress expecting to see a bloom of blood, any sign of the violence she'd endured. The world mocked her with its indifference. Same sky, same river, same dirty streets and grey clouds. Same people absorbed in dramas of their own who did not meet her eyes. Or maybe they didn't meet her eyes because they could see what she was, with her hair flying and her hem filthy and her sleeve torn where she'd pulled her damp dress on too hastily. Whore, she thought. Whore, whore, whore.

Somehow she stumbled into a cab and directed the driver to her aunt's square. As he slowed the horses, she imagined the houses leaning forward, watching. She handed the driver his fare and left the wet woollen stink of the cab. She waited, shivering, for him to turn around and head back down Gardiner Street before she approached the house. She pictured him at the cab stand, feeding his skinny old nag and describing her to the other drivers. 'A drowned rat she was, looked like she'd gone for a swim. Paps showin' through her dress and all.' The river was at a low ebb. Fumes of decay pushed their way up the hill, so pungent that she could almost see them. Spidery fingers reaching into windows and choking all the living things they met.

On the steps she stood up straight and banged at the door until Johanna opened it, scowling and arms crossed. Her mouth opened and then closed again. She backed into the hall and let Anne pass. Anne went straight to her room and pulled the bell for Rose. Rose said what Johanna would not.

'You're a state! What happened to you? We'll have to clean that dress up. You must have walked through every patch of mud on Sackville Street! And was Mrs Kennedy's shawl dragged under a car?' Anne found she couldn't answer. She'd lost her voice. Rose didn't wait but tutted around her, taking clothes away to be washed and wrapping her in a blanket. Johanna brought boiling water up for the bath. Anne sat on the armchair and stared out at the darkening sky and the leaves blowing down from the trees.

'Thank you, Rose,' was all she could say as the servant helped her into the tub. Her teeth clacked together.

'Water's roasting,' said Rose. 'Get in there now and heat yourself up. You can't go catching your death on me while the mistress is away.'

The bath was so hot Anne felt like a boiling joint. She sank lower and lower and let herself burn. Rose fussed over her as if she was a child. Cook sent up a bowl of broth and Rose spooned it into her open mouth. Washed and dried, fed and put to bed.

When she was alone with the curtains pulled and the candle snuffed out, she lay against her pillows. She could still smell him, feel the weight of him against her. She told herself that she was angry. That she would do something. But what? All the little things he'd said over the past month or so lined up to taunt her. She'd ignored them, explained them away, nodded as though she agreed. But here they were, telling her that she was a fool.

'If everyone knew about us, that would spoil things, don't you think? Kissing cousins they'd say.'

'Of course, I can't afford a wife on my salary. No, I couldn't marry without getting the post at the Rotunda. And even then, I'd have to marry for money.'

'My family wouldn't like to think I was being distracted by an attachment. Not just now. But you'll meet them soon.'

She cursed herself for stupidity. She cursed her aunt for going to Bray. She cursed her sister for moving to England. She cursed her father for seducing Ellen. She even cursed her mother for dying and leaving her alone. She'd fallen into a trap more preposterous than the tales of seduction in *Duffy's Hibernian Magazine*. Matthias would never become a suitor. In truth, she hadn't wanted him to be one. She thought that they could just continue as they were until ... she hadn't imagined any kind of end point. She avoided thinking of the future. She admitted she thought it possible that Matthias would look to marry someone else and that would be the end. That ending, sad though it would be, had seemed a long way off. Years, perhaps. After all, he'd made it clear he needed a higher position to consider providing for a wife. She'd pictured the passion having faded for a friendly warmth. Matthias attending her concerts, the two of them with full and separate lives but always a companion to one another. Of course, she'd felt his desire and even returned it. Had she known what he would do? She should have known what he would do.

She longed for someone to soothe her like when she'd woken from a nightmare as a child, creeping down the hall to her parents' room where her mother would invite her into their bed. The sound of two people's steady breathing and someone stroking her hair. When she closed her eyes and tried to conjure the warm weight of her mother's hands, all she could remember was the light, ghastly things they'd become in her final days of illness.

The next morning, Anne searched her body for signs of what had happened, but there was only a streak of dried blood and an ache between her legs. She tried to remove Matthias from her mind just as she'd cleaned him from her skin. She made herself walk to Cranmer's where she chose a tricky piece of music. She banged the piano keys until the tips of her fingers went numb. When Aunt Julia returned the next day, she listened to her worries with as much empathy as she could muster.

'You seem distracted, Anne,' Aunt Julia said. 'You must be missing your family. Perhaps you should think of visiting them.'

Anne felt nothing but cold horror at the prospect of being shown the nursery, of witnessing her father's contentment. On Thursday, her usual day to meet Matthias, she tried to think of anything else. She pictured his card, waiting in the post office unread. She pictured him bereft and confused, alone and ashamed. She went down into the kitchen to look for Rose.

'She's not here,' said Cook. 'But if you're at such a loose end, I need a few messages done.'

'I can help you.' Anything to keep her busy. A brisk walk, the sight of other people unperturbed and going about their business.

'I need sugar and peel and brandy from the provisioner. Only from Smyth's on Abbey Street. Don't be lazy and go to that thief on Grenville.'

'Of course, I can fetch your order,' said Anne and gathered up a basket as Cook began lecturing her.

'Are you listening to me, Anne? Should I write it down?' Cook asked, hand on hip, as she explained Anne *must* ask for six pounds of sugar from an *unopened* sack and peel that had been nowhere near the sun. 'You tell him I said if I find anything unexpected in me sugar, I'll come back and bate him with the bag meself. I'll tell everyone who'll listen he's got vermin. You only need to carry one pound back that I want straight away. And the peel. He can have the rest carted over with the brandy tomorrow.'

'Yes, Cook.'

'And the peel? I've to make the Christmas cake today.'

'Yes, I can manage.'

'And no dallying or meeting any gentlemen. I need you back with the sugar and the peel.' Anne blushed. Cook looked her over and made a sound in her throat that was perhaps meant to express gratitude.

When she got close, Anne decided to pass the shop. She would just walk as far as Sackville Street for the air and the extra exercise. But once she saw it, the post office drew her like a magnet. Before she knew what she was doing, she was standing at the counter asking for any letters for Anne Mulhall and being handed an envelope with her name in Matthias's handwriting. Her hand trembled as she placed the letter in a pocket of her skirt.

The little window grates and the loud hollow sound of the floor had once been a joyful backdrop as she collected Matthias's secret letters. Now she felt sure the clerk was leering at her and all the footsteps of the other customers sounded like the rumble of thunder from a brewing storm. Still, he'd written. Probably he was ashamed and contrite. She'd tried to write her own letter, scribbled the words that she hadn't been able to scream. She composed the letter seven times and burned it seven times. She was aware of Matthias's letter as she queued in the provisioner's. She felt its weight as she walked. When she arrived home, Anne reassured Cook that she'd followed all her directions. Then she took the stairs two at a time and closed the door to her room.

She tore the envelope open. It was the same letter that he sent every week before a meeting: where he'd be, how long he'd wait. Did he really believe they could continue as they were? She didn't want to meet him. And yet. She missed the grip of his arm around her waist and the smell of his hair as he leaned his cheek against hers. She put the letter back in her skirt and went downstairs to Cook.

'I've given the wrong order for the brandy,' she said. 'I'll run right back. I won't be long.' Cook rolled her eyes and muttered something that Anne chose not to hear.

Anne almost lost her nerve on the way there. She began to list the tests she would put him through. He would have to grovel, he would have to come to the house. No more sneaking around, no more unchaperoned walks. He would have to make himself a suitor. Never mind if she didn't think she wanted marriage. What else was there that could follow what they'd done? At least she'd escape a convent or a governess position in the loathsome country house of some rich pig farmer.

When she got to the place he'd named, he wasn't there. She thought she might be early. She'd forgotten to check the time as she passed over Sackville Bridge. When he still didn't come, she wondered if she was late. Pacing the lane, she checked the address and counted up to five hundred. Still, he didn't come. She pictured him fallen from a carriage or called to an emergency or asleep on his sofa. She didn't know the time, but it had already been too long. She would have to go back. Her aunt would wonder where she'd gone. Cook would realise she wasn't at the provisioner's.

She took the letter from her skirt to check the address once more and then she noticed the post mark. Matthias had sent it before the picnic on Saturday. He must have been sending his letters in advance. He didn't want to see her after all.

Chapter Thirteen

Peakin

9th August, 1866

Peakin had nothing and so he decided to go back to the start. From the opposite side of North Earl Street he spotted 'Doyle' scrawled in white and gold lettering on a neat black shop front. He was looking for hanging carcasses but he hadn't thought of the heat. Everything was probably tucked away in dark sheds. He opened the door and fly papers trembled in the breeze. Muslin draped the meat like burial shawls. Mr Doyle looked up from his block where he was disassembling what might have once been a lamb.

'Detective Peakin. I'm surprised to see you. Have you made some progress?' He put down the hatchet and wiped his hands on his apron. Peakin took his hat in two hands, hoping that Mr Doyle wouldn't offer one for him to shake. The air tingled with the scent of iron and fat, he felt it sinking into his clothes, his hair, his skin. Sawdust stuck to his shoes, carrying with it unseen particles of filth.

'Mr Doyle. Afraid we haven't very much to go on. I thought, if you don't mind, that I could ask you a few more questions.'

'Of course. Although I don't see what use I might be. I'll just fetch my wife, she can mind the shop.'

Doyle disappeared and soon returned with a woman. Her apron was also streaked with blood and her hair was tucked under a white cap but this only drew attention to her face with its smooth, pale skin and perfect pink lips.

'Afternoon.'

'Good afternoon, Mrs Doyle. My apologies for this intrusion.' Peakin watched her lips part, revealing a tiny flash of teeth. He followed Doyle into the back room where he was offered a stool and refused.

'So you've run into a bit of a wall, Mr Peakin?' Doyle leaned against a barrel. Peakin placed one hand into his pocket.

'I wouldn't say that, no. We're making the usual inquiries, I expect we'll turn something up. When we first spoke, I assumed that it was perhaps a tragic accident, a stillbirth or such like.' Peakin thought he saw Doyle flinch.

'I see. Well, I'm as eager as you to see someone come to justice, but I told the coroner all I know.'

'Of course. But it's possible that the coroner may not have asked all that he should. He's not a detective after all. So, with your permission, I'd just like to go over a few things again. I won't keep you long.'

'Certainly, ask me what you like.'

Peakin soon discovered that Denis Doyle was a man of his word. He added nothing further to Peakin's paltry scraps of evidence. He said all the same things he'd said at the inquest, only drew them out in greater detail. Peakin found his mind drifting. What had he expected really? He pushed the name Anne Mulhall around in his head as Denis moved his lips. Maybe he was hoping that Mr Doyle knew her. That somehow if he asked him to go through it all again that something would jog loose in his brain and her name would fall out of his mouth. He watched

Mr Doyle's earnest face, the old-fashioned beard and the skin reddened from sun that made him look older than he was. He was a young man, really, younger than Peakin. His movements reminded Peakin of the tiger at Batty's circus. The creature paced carefully, keeping a wounded paw in the air. Peakin sensed that the animal's pain could be swiftly converted to murderous anger. Not that Mr Doyle seemed angry at him, just so very careful to keep his voice level and controlled. Peakin might have admired the way that he recalled details of the scene, if all the information wasn't so utterly useless to him. After about five minutes, Mrs Doyle came back in.

'Sorry to bother ye. But there's a fella out here asking after some bacon he says you owe him, Denis.'

'Oh that'll be Sean, his brother is home from England. Excuse me, Mr Peakin.'

'That's quite alright, there's nothing else—' Peakin began, but Doyle was already through the door and into the shop. The woman turned, but Peakin called her back. 'Mrs Doyle, could I have a word?'

'What is it?' There was no smile now, only a kind of rigid impatience as she held her hands in front of her.

'Your husband has told you about the inquest. What do you make of it all?' He watched as she wiped her hands on the apron and then took a cloth from a pocket and began to twist it between her fingers as though she were keen to remove every possible trace of meat.

'I don't know why you're asking me. I didn't find nothin'.' She put the cloth back in the pocket, moved her hands to her hips and frowned.

'I thought perhaps a woman might have more insight into this kind of thing. The state of mind of a woman in distress. Anything we might use to find her.'

'If you're so interested in a lady's opinion why don't you get yourself some lady police officers?' Peakin twirled the tip of his moustache. Wives of shopkeepers were always so sure of themselves. Their husbands let them keep the books and soon they forgot who was in charge. When summoned to court, they used their sharp tongues to make fools of junior police officers. The magistrates enjoyed the spectacle. Did he detect a little thickness in her voice? A drinker, probably. Most of them were.

'Why don't we indeed. I do apologise for the intrusion, I'm sure you have many things to do.' Peakin straightened his lips and tried to smile but Rose Doyle kept the corners of her mouth down as she watched him leave.

His interview with the Doyles had yielded nothing. Aside from the coincidence of two pieces of gossip which Peakin had no idea how he could pursue, he was at a loss. He had already spent the anticipated reward in his mind (he could at least look the part of Acting Inspector in a new suit). He gathered reports from all the constables who were on a beat near the river in the nights before the baby was found. Few of them had met a woman out alone and in each case, the constable assumed the woman was a drunk or a prostitute or both. He'd threatened to arrest her and she'd scurried off into a lane. Under questioning the constables tried to remember some identifying feature.

'She had a shawl over her head. Or maybe a cap.'

'She was barefoot. At least as far as I could see, it was rather dark.'

'She was missing a couple of teeth.'

'Her dress was of a plain colour. She was of ordinary height. Maybe a bit small.'

'She carried a basket and when I asked what was in it she told me to go to fuck.'

In short, each officer blended the woman he'd seen into the image of every woman he'd ever confronted on the street until they became of no distinct age or appearance.

One officer remembered a young woman with a pretty face (and all her teeth) carrying a basket. He was certain her hair was yellow. She'd spat at him when he asked her what she was doing on the street. Peakin became interested. But one of the other constables whispered to him that the man couldn't be trusted. He'd arrived from Cavan a few months ago, mooning over some lost sweetheart. He turned every beat into a search for her, imagining her face onto the face of any woman of suitable age.

Peakin sighed and counted his blessings. A body that could tell nothing other than a vague date of death, no witnesses, no evidence other than a soiled sheet. Just the accusation of Dr Pratt against Anne Mulhall. Maybe Dr Mapother was wrong and the baby died of natural causes. That flotation test was hardly reliable. He wanted to ask Dr Pratt and Dr Keeffe about it but he sensed they would dislike him questioning medical authority. He decided to go for a walk. Maybe if he went back to the scene, wandered up and down the quay, inspiration would strike him.

From Richmond Bridge he walked up into Smithfield. At the Ormond Markets he wrinkled his nose at the sulphurous air of rotting vegetable peelings and sickly sweet tallow. Lane after lane spewed filthy children, men in ragged waistcoats, barefoot women with lined faces and babies held to their hips. He plunged in and out of them until he began to feel dizzy.

Thousands of women on hundreds of streets were producing babies all year long. Twenty-seven a day, if the register of births was to be believed. Untold others died on their way. This baby might have come from anywhere. A dead cow, lolling in a cart with its tongue hanging out, reminded him that he was hungry. He headed for Sackville Street where he sat down to a pint of ale and a slab of bacon. The bacon, a few hairs clinging to the dimpled rind, reminded him of human flesh. He pushed it aside and ate the potatoes and cabbage, dousing them in liberal amounts of pepper. He wrapped the bacon in his handkerchief and tucked it in his breast pocket. He threw it to the first street cur he met on his way to Exchequer Court.

He'd no sooner sat down at one of the desks in the office when the inspector entered.

'Peakin, you'll gather why I'm here.'

'Checking up on the infanticide case?'

'Exactly.'

Peakin could feel the quiet descend as the other acting sergeants in the room moved their pens more slowly, wanting to hear every word. Waiting for clues as to where Peakin stood in the pecking order this month. He knew if he turned around he would find that all their eyes were glued to the pages in front of them.

'I'm afraid there is less information than we might desire.' The other way of putting it might be to say there was no information to speak of.

'Have you been to see the butcher? Press him for more details. Maybe the coroner didn't ask the right questions.'

'I've been. There's nothing to go on. When I went to fetch the body it was hard to see. I couldn't understand how he'd seen it if he hadn't been looking for it. But then, I can't discern why he'd want to discover a body if he had something to hide. And he's steady as an ox, repeated all the same information like he was reciting his catechism.'

'Maybe he's trying to get something over on someone? Let them know he can expose them and their dirty business? Those butchers are a bad lot.'

'I don't know. He didn't seem the vindictive type to me. Unusual wife.'

'Unusual how? Is she disfigured?'

'No, no. Very pretty, very soft for a butcher's wife. He keeps an eye on her like she's his best bit of silver plate.'

'Well, a married man knows his wife's a treasure, isn't that right, Peakin?'

'Oh yes, of course.' Too late, Peakin recognised that the inspector intended a joke. He wondered if a married man could always recognise a single one. If Isobel married him, would he watch her the way that Mr Doyle watched his wife? He wasn't sure if Isobel would relish glances filled with such obvious longing.

Something about Mrs Doyle bothered him. Shifty and distrustful. He kept passing the shop but he didn't have anything else to ask Mr Doyle. He noticed that she left early in the morning and so one day he followed to see where she was going. That was how he found himself standing in front of Number 27 Mountjoy Square, the same address Dr Pratt had given him.

Chapter Fourteen

Anne

December 1865

Matthias wrote her two letters but she put them into a drawer without opening them. The house closed around her like a fist. She went out only to fetch things for Cook or to visit the school friends she'd neglected or to march tight circles around the square for the sake of her constitution. Autumn turned decidedly to winter and there was no relief from the grey. Everything looked grubby and mean. The hours of darkness stretched and ate into the morning and the afternoon until it seemed as though the gaslights burned all day. Her gloom increased to match the gloom of the house. The only warm, bright place was the kitchen and she didn't want to linger where Cook might ask her about her 'gentleman' or she might catch the knowing glances passed between her and Johanna.

She forced herself out of her room to visit her father and Ellen. She made noises of approval at her bedroom transformed into a nursery. Ellen showed her delicate things she had crocheted with the eagerness of a school child seeking the teacher's approval. Anne told her they were very beautiful. Her father said almost nothing and then tried to persuade her to stay for dinner. 'Maggie's making your favourite,' he pleaded. Anne was curious what he thought her favourite meal might be but she said, 'No, I'm sorry, Aunt Julia is expecting me.' Every meal provided her aunt with an opportunity to remind her that she could not live off her largesse forever. If she ate too much, her aunt hinted that Cook was running back and forth to the grocer's trying to keep up with her appetite. If she ate too little, her aunt told her that the sight of her picking at her food made her feel ill. An anxious nausea lodged in her gut and she felt weak whether she gorged or starved. The days repeated in an endless loop. She needed to leave before it was too late. She decided to find herself a position.

Her newspaper advertisement read: *Respectable R.C. woman seeks position in household. Can teach French and piano. All reasonable offers considered.* She wasn't prepared for the number of replies. Too humiliating to answer were the requests from women she'd been in school with. After a number of letters back and forth, she settled her preference on the Lynches from Athlone. They were due a second child in the spring and sought a governess to replace the one that was leaving. They wrote to say that they were coming to Dublin to do some Christmas shopping and could meet Anne in the Gresham Hotel for an interview.

The day of the interview was a week before Christmas. Anne woke in the freezing dark, feeling even more sick than usual. She forced herself out of bed and through breakfast. She tried to distract herself by playing the piano until it was time to leave. She was nervous and sad.

She spotted the Lynches in the lobby at once. Mrs Lynch sat straight, the small hump of her belly protruding under the ribboned waistband of her dress. One hand toyed with the edge of the ribbon while the other held onto a boy of about four, sitting on the couch beside her. Next to the boy sat her husband, a compact man with a kind of coiled energy that suggested he might burst from the seat at any moment. Though very well dressed, they looked ill at ease. Their eyes scanned the room and did not light on anything. Either they were looking for Anne or they were simply distracted by the constant movement and activity around them. She wove through the tables towards them and hoped she wouldn't meet anyone she knew. They made their introductions and Mrs Lynch tried to stifle a yawn. Her pinched countenance suggested exhaustion. Anne spoke to their son.

'What do you think of the city? Have you ever seen so many people?'

'It's very fine. And Mummy let me have a bag of six sweets all for myself if only I would be very quiet at once.'

Mrs Lynch blushed. Anne liked her inability to disguise her feelings. Maybe the Lynches would be her salvation after all. She imagined a house where life ran more free than at Mountjoy Square. A house with smiles and singing and chatter. A house a little bit like her own home had been.

'Now is a good time to keep practising your quiet, darling. Mummy and Daddy want to talk to Miss Mulhall. She's going to come and watch over you and your little brother or sister in our house.'

'Why isn't my nurse going to watch over me? Where is she going to go? She'll have nowhere to live at all. And who will feed Mr Tom when she's gone?' The child began to squeeze his mother's hand with both of his own and Mrs Lynch looked pleadingly at her husband.

'There, there. I'm sure Miss Mulhall will feed Mr Tom,' Mr Lynch petted the boy's hair absent-mindedly. 'Mr Tom is our cat, Miss Mulhall. My son is very attached to his nursemaid. But she is not a young woman and I don't think she would be able for an infant. And anyway, she prefers to return to Cork where she has relatives.' He turned to the child, 'Did you know that Miss Mulhall is a musician? She can teach you to play the piano. Won't that be grand?'

He looked unconvinced and turned to picking at a thread on his socks. Anne found herself floundering for the most basic lines of conversation, distracted by an onset of dizziness. The heat of the lobby was making her lightheaded after the persistent cold of her aunt's house.

'Well, I wouldn't say I'm a musician. But I do play the piano. I would love to teach you. Do you have a favourite song?'

'No. I don't like singing.'

'Come now, that just isn't true,' Mrs Lynch forced out a smile and Anne could see her wondering how long it would be before she could lie down again. Her tiredness was contagious: Anne began to wilt in sympathy.

'You must be very tired,' Anne said. 'Please ask me anything you like.'

They bumbled through the usual questions. The Lynches were as inexperienced as Anne was. The nurse had been a house servant. They were comfortable country people with no airs about them and it seemed to Anne that the position would suit her very well. They agreed that she would travel down in the second week of May. When she told her aunt she only remarked that she didn't know any Lynches from Athlone and so they must be a very minor family. Anne didn't care. She was delighted with her enterprise. The Lynches agreed that she could offer piano lessons for other children on Saturday mornings. She would have money of her own.

Anne's cousins arrived a few days later and the house filled with the smells and sounds of Christmas. Her future now settled, she threw herself into the preparations with the servants. She ran back and forth on messages for Cook, who was flustered with so many extra mouths to feed and lost track of her stores. She helped Rose to trim the tree and sweep up the dropping needles. She was almost looking forward to the day and all its rituals.

On Christmas Day Anne woke feeling dizzy and nauseous. She struggled to the water closet. A whiff of drains brought up the contents of her stomach. She washed her face and returned to bed, wondering if influenza had struck. Rose woke her at eight. She'd been working late in the kitchen as Cook made a frenzy of preparations for Christmas dinner.

'It's late, miss, breakfast is almost ready for serving. Everyone is up and dressed. They'll be wanting to eat and go to Mass.' Rose urged as another wave of nausea hit, 'I'll help you, and you'll be ready in no time.'

She could hear the footsteps of excited children who were trying very hard to be good. Someone started to run down the stairs and then slowed down. Emily and Caroline raised their voices in turn. Their husbands would be sitting at the breakfast table already, no doubt arguing as they sipped the expensive coffee that Aunt Julia had sent out for specially. Anne couldn't face it. She turned her head back to the pillow and closed her eyes.

'I don't feel well, Rose. I don't think I can eat. I'll have to stay in bed. Will you tell my aunt I'm not well?' She closed her eyes as Rose pulled at the curtains, letting in a daylight as thin as watered-down milk. At the thought of milk she felt her stomach lurch again. Rose placed the back of her palm on Anne's forehead and then on her cheek. She frowned and then opened the wardrobe and took out the best dress. Anne saw Rose hold it against herself in the mirror for just a moment and then brush it down with great tenderness. Anne realised with a flush of shame that she'd never imagined anyone could be envious of her situation, of her shabby gowns.

'I think it would be best if you got up,' Rose said gently. 'It might be just a touch of indigestion, I'll get you something plain and soft for breakfast. Don't keep your aunt waiting. You know what she's like. She'll want Christmas Day to go exactly as she's planned.'

Anne did know what she was like. Aunt Julia hated and feared illness. She'd send someone to interrupt Dr Mapother's breakfast and soon have Anne locked in her room. And if the nausea was ... well she preferred not to think about it but she certainly didn't want any prodding by a doctor. Anne got out of bed and let Rose help her dress.

'Thank you, Rose. I do feel better now I'm on my feet.'

Rose rummaged in her dress and pulled out a biscuit.

'Here. Eat this. I always keep one in case I feel a little faint.'

Anne took the biscuit. It was dry on the tongue but it went down.

'You seem to always be taking care of me.' As she said it she realised how true it had become. Rose had been quietly tending her since November, her bustle a cushion between Anne and all her sorrows.

'I'll bring some more tomorrow. You can leave them in the drawer beside the bed. They never go off. If you eat one before you get out of bed it stops the stomach turnin'.'

Rose gave Anne a pointed look and the kindness in it made the sorrow rise from her chest to her throat. She wished she'd thought to buy Rose a Christmas gift.

'You've a card from somebody. Cook's boy told me to give it to you.' In her palm was an envelope. With a start,

Anne recognised Matthias's scrawl. She'd had no word in weeks. Anne allowed herself to imagine that he was desperate to apologise and see her again.

'Thank you, Rose, I'll leave it until after breakfast,' she said, closing the letter into a drawer. Anne followed Rose downstairs to where everyone was already at the breakfast table and eating. They barely looked up to nod at Anne as she entered. Emily and Caroline were busy trying to keep the children from soiling their Christmas finery before they made it as far as the church. Their husbands, James and Anthony, sat piling eggs into their mouths. Anne's stomach wrenched and she sat down. She watched the movement around her as though it was a pantomime. Rose brought her a bowl of sweet porridge sprinkled with cinnamon and she tried her best to eat it.

Everyone bustled out the door to Mass and back again. Christmas dinner was noisy and sumptuous and dull. The children opened their gifts in a flurry of shrieks and shredded paper. Aunt Julia surprised Anne with a parcel of sheet music and a tasselled woollen shawl in swirls of red paisley. Her sister sent some London magazines and a lock of the baby's hair, her father a pen and diary. Anne took the children up to bed and hoped that she might be excused for the evening but as she was leaving her aunt announced that Anne would play some Christmas songs for everyone in the drawing room when she returned. She left the children with their nurses and went into her own room to lie on the bed. The dizziness and exhaustion hadn't lifted and she thought of Rose's face. Anne knew what Rose was thinking and hoped that she was wrong. She remembered Matthias's Christmas card and decided to open it. The cover was a picture of a little robin perched on a snowy pine bough, with *Happy Christmas* in shiny green lettering above. Inside there was no Christmas greeting.

Dear Anne,
I regret that we have become estranged but I wish you well and I remember our walks with fondness as I hope you do, too.

I wished to write so that there can be no confusion about my intentions. I am engaged and we are to be married this summer. I am sure that you will pray for our happiness.
With affection,
M.

The solitude of her room now seemed more oppressive than the thought of playing the piano for everyone. She forced herself up off the bed and down the back stairs. In the drawing room, they all ignored her while she played every Christmas song too staccato.

The next morning she threw up into her chamber pot. Then she threw up every day for a week until she had to accept that something was wrong.

Chapter Fifteen

Peakin

10th August, 1866

In the eighteen years since Peakin had arrived in Dublin, Mountjoy Square had grown shabbier. A few of the houses had been converted to offices. Brass plates listed names of solicitors or barristers or doctors or dentists. A further few were empty, their curtains drawn, and drifts of street dust like tide marks gathered along their façades. Paint peeled in dreary curls from their doors. He stood on the yellowed grass of the central square, watching Number 27 and thinking about what he would say. He'd checked with Dr Pratt and this was definitely the house that Miss Mulhall lived in. The doctor reluctantly told him a few details after Peakin swore never to mention his name. In order to reassure himself of his authority, he berated a group of cab drivers loitering at the edge of the square. They sat smoking in their rickety vehicles, letting their horses piss and shit prodigiously into the road. They dispersed with a creaking rumble and a volley of curses.

He raised his hand to the knocker and felt damp spreading in the armpits of his shirt. Visiting the house under such slim pretence was a risk. He was just here to rule something out. He'd ruled out the workhouses and now he had to rule out this woman of Dr Pratt's.

'Yes?' A maid opened the door, crossed her arms and frowned. The frown drew attention to a damaged mouth, like a poorly stitched seam, and a set of eyes spaced too far apart. She was remarkably ugly and a curious choice for receiving callers. Reduced circumstances, he thought.

'My name is Martin Peakin. From G Division of the Dublin Metropolitan Police. I'm here to see Mrs Kennedy.' The maid didn't even try to stifle her surprise.

'The mistress isn't receiving no callers, not even ones can recite the alphabet.' Peakin quickly placed his foot far enough in the way of the door to prevent it slamming.

'Here's my card. Please take it to her. Tell her I'm here about some robberies there have been on the square. And here's sixpence for the trouble.' The maid frowned even more deeply but he could see the temptation of the coin was unbearable. She snatched it from his hand and the price of a chop disappeared into her pocket.

'Alri'. I'll bring her the card. But I'm making no promises.'

He withdrew the foot and the door closed in his face. The bolt turned and he cursed himself for not pushing into the hallway. He'd been left out like the coal man. He turned to study the square again. Gardiner Street ran downhill towards the river, two leaning queues of dull brick houses facing one another. Across the square, a carriage pulled into a stable lane and he had the definite feeling that someone was watching him from behind curtains. He sniffed the air, picturing the dung-heaped lanes behind the houses where he usually did his policing. The door opened again.

'Mrs Kennedy will see you now.' The arms were no longer crossed but the face was no more welcoming. 'Follow me.'

Inside, the house was very still and smelled of Condy's Fluid. All the front windows were tightly curtained. The walls of the hallway were papered in a dark, ornate pattern that reminded Peakin of the pictures where you saw either an old woman or a young woman depending on how you focused your eyes. He followed the retreating maid into a drawing room where the curtains admitted just a few shafts of daylight. The windows were firmly closed and perspiration began to gather along the back of his collar. In the light of the window sat a woman, clad entirely in black. She stood as she heard him enter.

'Mr Peakin, madam,' the maid said.

'Thank you, Johanna. Have Rose bring us some refreshment, please. I'm sure Mr Peakin is quite exhausted from his perambulations. Mr Peakin. Come sit over here. I'm afraid you'll find it very warm. There's just no relief to be had from opening windows and one never knows what kind of dangerous miasma might be coming in with the air.'

'Indeed, madam. Quite sensible in the present circumstances. I won't take up much of your time.'

'Of course. But I don't understand why you're here.' Peakin sat down on the armchair that Mrs Kennedy indicated. Black fabric fell in folds all around her and Peakin wondered if close inspection would have found her as full of dust as the upholstery. He tried to guess her age. Sixty, perhaps older. The blood weakened with age, he knew, flowing more sluggishly and making the body appear dried out. He realised now the folly of his visit. He'd imagined that Miss Mulhall would be sitting here with Mrs Kennedy, doing whatever it was that women like this did all day. She was nowhere to be seen.

'Yes, well, there have been a number of burglaries in the city of late.'

'More than the usual number? That hardly makes for news.'

'You will understand, madam, that we are eager to increase our vigilance. Beyond the usual measures of surveying the pawnshops I thought that we might gather some information from residents in affected areas.'

'I see. You haven't caught anyone so you're snooping around and hoping we might do the work for you.'

Peakin began to panic. What did he think was going to happen? How was he going to bring himself round to the topic of Miss Mulhall or the infanticide? Just as he was about to make his apologies and leave, the door pushed open.

'Oh! I'm very sorry Aunt Julia, I didn't realise you had a caller. I'll come back.' A young woman stood in the doorway, undecided about entering. She held a sheaf of papers in her hand.

'That's quite alright, Anne. This is my niece, Mr Peakin. Miss Anne Mulhall. Anne usually practises her piano at this hour.' Peakin almost sighed with relief at his luck. But then he surveyed Miss Mulhall. She was a good, plain, symmetrical kind of woman. Pleasing rather than beautiful. Not what he'd pictured, given Dr Pratt's insinuations. And of course she wouldn't look pregnant, not now.

'Pleased to meet you,' the woman said, dipping her head in a kind of half curtsy.

'Come in, Anne. This gentleman is here making inquiries about some burglaries. You haven't seen anything have you? Any suspicious individuals on the square? I mean, with people like the McEvoys putting up any number of squalid dwellings in lanes and letting out their stables, one never knows who might be suspicious. We're surrounded on all sides.' Anne moved closer. She looked as though she wanted to say something but Mrs Kennedy prattled on, naming the neighbours who had let their properties go, who had moved to England, who had broken their houses into tenements. 'You can't imagine what a grand square this once was.' She sighed and Anne took the brief opening this afforded.

'I'm afraid I can't help you, detective. But if I see anything I shall tell my aunt at once so she may report it to you. The piano can wait, I'll come back later.' And with a swift nod, she left.

After she left the door opened again and a new maid approached with a tea tray. Peakin was busy scheming about how he might bring the infanticide into the conversation just to test the waters. He wasn't sure what he was hoping for. That Mrs Kennedy would suddenly throw her hands up and begin weeping? That Anne would burst in and throw herself at his feet in confession? As a consequence, he did not recognise the maid until she placed the tea tray down. Their eyes met and he watched her recognise him in the same instant. He admired the speed with which she disguised her expression.

'Mrs Doyle! I had no idea that you were employed here! How pleasant to see you again.'

The maid allowed a glance of pure fury to cross her countenance for a second. Maybe there was something here after all. He couldn't quite put the pieces together yet.

'And you, detective.' She did a little curtsy and turned to leave. Mrs Kennedy rustled in her chair.

'But how on earth are you acquainted with my Rose? I'm sure she can't be in any trouble.'

'I've interviewed her husband, madam. In regard to the baby that was found in the river.'

'I see. Rose told me about that. Should you not be putting more resources towards that particular crime? Rose says that no one's been found. Tell him, Rose.'

'Yes, that's what Denis told me. Excuse me, madam, I'll just take these dishes away.'

She directed her formidable gaze at him and Peakin felt exposed. Mrs Doyle hurried out the door.

'You're quite correct. A very unfortunate case. Mr Doyle has been most helpful but so far we are without any suspects.'

'I see.'

Peakin thought he would sense if there was a secret hidden in the house. Instead, he felt that he was being watched and assessed. All these servants. Over a career, how much information must they have hoarded about each member of a household and all their appetites?

'An infanticide is often a very tricky case,' he said.

'I can only imagine.'

'And of course if you've heard anything that could help us we'd be most eager for any information.' Even before she opened her mouth he realised that he had overstepped. Her face contorted as though the tea was too bitter.

'Me? I'm not sure what you think I could possibly know. There's no saying what might go on in the lanes, but you can't imagine that I'm well informed on the habits of every Bridget I pass on the street. And my servants would never trade in sordid gossip.'

Mrs Kennedy moved to the edge of her seat. Peakin noted with sadness that the tea tray included a scone and a generous lump of butter. He felt saliva pooling in his mouth but he feared his welcome was coming to an end. Tiny rivulets of sweat trickled slowly down his back. He watched Mrs Kennedy's face but saw only annoyance. He pressed on.

'Then you have noticed nothing? No agitation among the servants or rumours among your circle?'

'Certainly not!'

'Of course, well I'm sure that I have taken up quite enough of your time.'

'And what about the burglaries? Which you came here to discuss? What am I to do about those? Am I to post guards about the place and stash cutlery under my pillows? Is this what you were sent to tell me?'

'No, madam. Only please report any suspicious characters you see gathering around the square. Send for the police — do not intervene yourself. Usually what shuts down one of these little gangs is information and reports. A sense that people are looking for them.' Peakin rose to take his leave. 'Thank you very much for your assistance. You can find me at Exchequer Court should you have any information.'

'On the other matter, I want you to understand that you will have no information from me because I have none to give. I am a most respectable widow. There is no untoward business here.'

'I never imagined ...'

'I'm sure you did not. I thank you for your admirable thoroughness in questioning. One only hopes that your investigations might come to some practical end. Good day.'

Peakin stood and bent at the waist, holding his hat in his hands. He allowed himself to be led down the hall and out the door. As he walked away he imagined the indignant letters that the inspector should soon receive and wondered if he'd gone too far. Or not far enough. Maybe he should have tried to question Anne. His little gamble had yielded nothing. But no, if he pressed it any more, then the indignant letters would call for his immediate resignation. And he admitted that Mrs Kennedy seemed unlikely to be deceived.

Chapter Sixteen

Anne

February 1866

May ticked closer and Anne's panic grew into a hard, nobbled thing that lived at the back of her throat. The other thing, the one that lived in her belly, continued growing as well. When she lay back on her bed, her stomach no longer dipped between her hip bones. Anne told herself that it could be some other kind of ailment. She'd heard of cancers of the womb: false pregnancies where the woman swelled and swelled but no child arrived. She tried to make herself think of solutions. She knew she could not take the position in Athlone but she didn't know what else to do. Making all the decisions for herself had led her here, exactly where she'd been warned she would end up.

Every once in a while her aunt would allow her manner to thaw a little and Anne would plan to reveal everything and beg for assistance. And then they would sit down to dinner and her aunt would say something like, 'You don't look healthy, Anne. You don't eat and yet you look a little thicker, almost. It's the wrong kind of exercise and the wrong kind of food. Dr Mapother will put you on the proper regimen, if you'd only let me ask him.' And Anne would feel the buzz of panic and reply that she was fine, that she'd always experienced fluctuations in her weight, that it was only that her stomach bothered her at the change of seasons, filling with air like risen dough.

Anne found excuses not to leave her room, dressed herself rather than ringing for Johanna or Rose. She pulled a shawl around her shoulders no matter the temperature. The performance was for herself as much as her aunt and the servants. The more she pretended that nothing was happening, the more that she could almost believe it was true. One day, no matter how she tugged, she could not lace herself into her dress. Desperate, she rang for Rose.

'I think the dress needs altered, miss. Will we try another?'

So Anne stepped out of it and into the next. The laces strained and they gave that one up, too. The room swam as silent tears filled Anne's eyes. Rose didn't comfort her, didn't ask what was wrong.

'I can fix these. Just let me fetch my stitching.'

Anne sat staring at the leaf buds on the trees in the square while Rose stitched and sighed, ripped and mended.

'Here, let's try again. I've left them a little too loose, just in case. You can wrap this underneath.' Rose held out a length of fabric and wound it around Anne's middle and then she laced her into the dress. Her waist was gone now. She looked almost masculine with her small breasts and her thick middle.

'Thank you,' she said.

Anne told Rose nothing but she leaned on her for company. Only Rose could dress her. Only Rose could draw her bath. Only Rose could accompany her outside the house. With Rose around, no one looked at Anne. They looked at Rose instead. Anne waited, thinking that a solution would present itself.

In her fantasies, Anne confronted Matthias in Sackville Street. She accused him in a loud, clear voice as a crowd gathered around. She pictured his face, hurt and reddened with embarrassment. Fruit sellers hissed their disapproval and maybe tossed a few rotten apples at him; cab drivers crossed their arms and shook their heads, whips twitching in their hands. A murmur of disgust would grow louder and Matthias would be forced to flee.

One day she dragged Rose to the confectioner's on Grafton Street to collect a message for her aunt. The air was heavy with orange water and ginger beer and a hundred other syrupy flavours. Rose stood inspecting trays of chocolate bon bons, choosing the ones that Aunt Julia liked best. Anne could hear her refusing all the shop attendant's suggestions as she stared at coloured jars and tins of chocolate powder in the window display. That was when she saw Matthias pass with a young woman on his arm. Anne held her breath, convinced they would turn into the shop. When she peeked again, they were continuing down Grafton Street. She dug her nails into her own palm. She walked out of the shop after them.

When she felt a hand on her arm, she flinched.

'Anne! I didn't know where you'd gone. Lucky that I glimpsed your frock,' Rose said.

'I'm sorry, Rose. It was so stuffy in the shop. I need a little air.'

'Alright, but not too far. Where are we going?'

'I'm not sure.' Anne sensed Rose hesitate but her eyes were locked on Matthias's back, twenty paces ahead of her. Rose linked her arm in Anne's and Anne pulled a little to hurry her along.

The streets were crowded with shoppers and carts and carriages. Anne was too busy staring ahead to mind her skirts or where she put her feet. She let Rose guide her around obstacles. People seemed to move out of Matthias's way, while they bustled and bumped up College Green and over Sackville Bridge. The bridge was crowded. The river boiled beneath them, brown and angry. Anne imagined calling his name and throwing herself from the bridge while he watched, slipping under the water and being carried out to sea.

'Ah well, so we're on the way home, anyway,' Rose said, interrupting her fantasy. She'd lost Matthias and she pulled Rose a little too sharply forward. 'What are you in such a hurry for?' Her gaze followed Anne's. 'Are we chasin' someone?'

'Yes.'

'Well, you might have said, I could be a better help then.'

'That gentleman ahead there, the one in the black topcoat and with the young lady on his arm.'

'Ah, I see him. Is that ...?' Anne didn't answer.

They turned down Moore Street. A breeze carried the smell of blood and withered cabbage from the markets. The street was full with shoppers and hawkers who got in their way. Matthias stopped at a flower seller and so Rose and Anne stopped too. Anne looked around for something to occupy her and approached an apple cart, while she tried to look sideways at what flowers he was choosing.

'Six for a penny, thirteen for tuppence, love.' The seller started holding out a selection of fruit that was soft and wrinkly. The cart reeked of cheap cider. The woman made a show of gathering up the best ones, checking them for spots, pushing them at Anne in handfuls.

'Those are soft,' Rose sniffed, glowering at the seller. 'We're not in need of any rotten fruit.' Anne ignored her and reached for her purse. The apples would give a plausible excuse for being on the street. In case he should turn and see her.

'I'll have six,' Anne said. She could feel Rose staring at her like she'd taken leave of her senses. Rose sighed and moved closer to the cart.

'I'll pick them, there's barely six good enough for cider.' And Rose began to lift apple after apple against the seller's protests. Anne glanced down the road, worried she would lose sight of them as they drifted further away.

'Those are fine, Rose. Please.' Rose went silent and accepted the apples, tying them into her handkerchief. Anne handed over the money.

She almost ran to the corner of Capel Street, pulling Rose along and not caring who jostled them. Men leered as they brushed past. Rose kept her eyes on her feet. Beyond Capel Street were only houses and a very few businesses, and no reason to hide behind if they were caught following. Anne hesitated.

'They're up ahead there,' said Rose. 'They've stopped at a house. I think it's time we was turning back.' But she followed her anyway.

As they watched, the couple stopped in front of a house with a green door. Anne realised that she wasn't going to confront him. Not today. The girl knocked and soon a servant, clearly her servant, was greeting them and bringing them inside. A huge, glittering knocker in the shape of a lion's head crowded the closed door. The house's bricks were old and dull but the windows were decorated in layers of brocade curtains held open by tasselled cords to display an abundant inner layer of muslin. Anne felt her lip curl when she noticed that the pattern on the curtains was peacocks. She was so busy staring that she didn't notice Rose turn and head for home. She hurried to catch up.

Back at Mountjoy Square, Anne retreated to her room and Rose fled to the kitchen with the apples. Just as she was about to mount the stairs Rose put her hand on Anne's arm and said in a low whisper, 'If you should be in any sort of trouble and I can help you, just ask.' Anne shook her head.

In her room she slid into despair. Seeing him filled her with a nauseating jealousy.

She reviewed all her mistakes, one by one. If only she hadn't gone to meet him at all. If only she hadn't let him kiss her or touch her. If only she hadn't gone on that picnic. If only she hadn't gone into his house. God was punishing her and by the summer, when this baby would arrive, He would have taken away what little she had left. All she could think to do was to go to England, throw herself on the mercy of Frances and her husband. She pictured herself being turned away to roam the streets. But hostile strangers would be better than the disdain of Aunt Julia, the disgust of her father. She imagined her teeth stained from snuff, pounding a piano and smiling at the garish customers of a dingy music hall while her bastard crawled between her legs. She only needed to add in a few friendly whores and a syphilitic spot and she'd be her own Hogarth print.

But even for this nightmarish vision Anne needed more money and so she would have to beg. She wrote her letter and went to find Rose. Anne could hear Johanna moving through the house, airing rooms and changing linens. In the kitchen, Cook's voice boomed and pots banged. All fell silent when she opened the door. Anne wondered if they'd been talking about her. She looked down at her waist, resisted the urge to place a hand on her belly.

'Afternoon, Miss Anne, what can I do for you?' Cook's cap drooped and she pushed it back with a dirty hand. The heat was furious. Cook stood in front of the stove, poking at things that were boiling and roasting. The air felt as solid as a loaf. Anne remembered the comfort of

Cook's onion-scented bowl of broth after the last day with
Matthias. What did she know? And if she knew, how long
before her aunt knew?

'I'm looking for Rose,' she said. Cook gestured towards
the laundry with her ladle. Flecks of whatever she was stirring
flew through the air and spattered on the floor and wall.

Anne met Rose coming out of the laundry with a pile of
washing. She stopped and smiled, a basket on her hip and a
heap of white over her shoulder. Something in Anne's face
wiped the smile away.

'Rose, I need you to deliver a message for me. To Dr
Kelly and no one else, into his hand.' She tried to sound
firm rather than hysterical. Rose's face showed no sign of
emotion or disapproval. 'The house is 32 Hatch Street.'

'I'll get Johanna to hang the sheets,' Rose said, dropping
the pile of washing on a table and reaching for the note.
Though Rose was no gossip, Anne imagined them whispering
as she passed Johanna the sheets. She caught hold of both
her hands.

'Please, Rose, I need this to be a secret. Tell no one where
you're going. Tell Dr Kelly's servant that only he can receive
the letter. Say it's personal to a patient and you must hand it
to him. And please don't get Johanna, I'll hang the washing
for you.' She felt sorry to be asking Rose for another favour,
asking her to risk Aunt Julia's displeasure on her behalf. 'If
he's not in, ask when he'll return and come right back.'

If Rose was startled by this turn of events she didn't show
it. She simply put her bonnet back on her head and set
her small frame in motion towards the garden gate. Anne
watched the gate close after her and listened to her steps fade
away. It was too late to take it back.

Chapter Seventeen

Peakin

11th August, 1866

Peakin did not sleep well. In an effort to generate a stir of the sultry air, he opened both the bedroom and the parlour window. At half past one he was disturbed by a couple of neighbours shouting the slurred epithets that signalled Friday night. The chorus of hisses and 'go the fuck to bed' directives that fell from the windows around the court seemed to egg them on.

'You're makin' a scene and wakin' the fuckin' street.'

'You started the shouting. I was only after telling you to shut yer hole.'

'A wife should be seen and not heard.'

'That's childers should be seen and not heard you fuckwit.'

'Well it shoulda been wives.'

They eventually went the fuck to bed but his ears were assaulted by an intermittent chorus of bawling and braying. A cat in heat wailed like a devil. A neighbour's dog, possibly gone rabid, policed the laneway. It whined and barked and snarled any time someone, or something, passed nearby.

Did sound travel further in the hot air? And where were the constables on their beat? Surely they should have rounded up the drunks to dry out on the station office straw. Unable to sleep, Peakin mulled and worried. His sheets felt like a hair shirt. He tried to lie still and his mind drifted to his conversation with the inspector, sifting for deeper meanings. Had the inspector been disappointed in him? When he had mentioned wives, had Peakin failed some test? Was there maybe just a hint of suspicion in his expression?

At long last, daylight began to seep into the room. Peakin could see first the end of his bed, then the wardrobe with its chipped paint and broken handle. He heard the shuffle and swish of Kate in the hall and went to retrieve his paper. The water in his wash basin was tepid and swampy. Half an hour later he was shaved, dressed in his one remaining clean shirt and sat in the parlour with the paper spread before him. He found that his infanticide was the subject of an editorial. His shoulders tensed as he scanned the columns in the *Freeman's Journal*.

'What do you make of this, Kate?' He proceeded to recite the editorial in a jeering tone. Plenty of nonsense about the chaste young maidens of Erin and the degenerate harlots of England. According to the writer, English women were getting rid of unwanted offspring just as fast as they could produce them. 'I call that a heap of shite.'

'Which part sir?' Kate moved around the room with a rag, wiping surfaces and collecting teacups. She didn't seem to be listening to him.

'The part where the esteemed author regales us with the moral superiority of the Irish. Where he uses infanticide to promote his national views.'

'Oh them bits. Well I can't say as I would put much credence in the thoughts of newspapermen meself.' Peakin watched Kate as she bent and stooped, little hints of her figure revealed by the stretching of a hem or a twisting of the waist.

'No, very sensible Kate. Surely infanticide might be just as common, per head of population of course, as it is in England.'

'I wouldn't know. But I can't say as Irish men seem any more likely than English men to keep their pricks to themselves. Can I get you more tea, sir? Or anything else?'

'True indeed, Kate. No thank you, I've had enough tea.'

Peakin stroked his moustache in irritation as she closed the door too loudly. The newspapers seemed to see every story as an opportunity to measure Ireland against her neighbour and ruler. Peakin avoided having an opinion on the future of Ireland, seeing it as contrary to good police work. But his opinion was that an independent Ireland wouldn't become the land of milk and honey in nationalist dreams. All the same problems would be there, with less money to solve them.

He already knew about the latest Fenian arrests but he couldn't resist reading the news anyway, poking at the bruise to see if it still hurt. One man had been hunted up in Liverpool. The court martial trials continued in the Royal Barracks. Stashes of arms were found. Far from suppressed, he thought. Meanwhile this infanticide was dragging on unsolved and he wasn't getting any closer to Sub-inspector.

With no information and a body that could tell him nothing, he wasn't hopeful of finding the culprit. The questioning would have to continue. He drained his tea, put on his too-warm coat and left his rooms, ringing the bell for Kate to clean up as he went.

The sun was already high, glinting cruelly off the little glass and metal it could find in a Dublin street.

Passing a tenement with its half-broken windows fogged by dust was a relief next to the searing shine of polished door knockers.

The heat of his rooms saved him from being shocked by the heat outside — any movement of air felt like a small relief. Peakin closed his mouth against the dust swirling up off the streets and wondered if it carried the germs of disease. He imagined the breeze full of sparks waiting to light up the next fever nest. Dublin failed to keep her poor contained in any one place; in his own respectable court a number of tenements rubbed up against the ubiquitous offices of lawyers.

When he arrived at Exchequer Court, Constable Delaney was at the door.

'There's a gentleman here to see you. Has some evidence he thinks you might want to hear.' The march of suspicious neighbours had begun again. And it was hardly eight o'clock. But he could be optimistic. Maybe someone would provide information of real use.

'Where is he?'

'I showed him to the newspaper room.'

The newspaper room was silent except for a dry wrinkle and snap. Nodding to one or two other officers, he approached the only man he didn't recognise. The man was fully absorbed in the paper he'd been given. Peakin looked him over carefully. He was very relaxed for a man with evidence about a crime. He was dressed with care, and a silk top hat as expensive as Dr Mapother's sat beside him on the table.

He dropped his newspaper and smiled as he sensed the detective approaching. A set of dentures seemed to stretch the groomed and clean-shaven face.

'How do you do? I'm Detective Peakin. I believe you're waiting for me.'

'Yes. I'm afraid I'm an early riser. Habit acquired in the Navy. I'm Zachariah Mills, pleased to make your acquaintance.' The hand was smooth, the nails a little long.

'Mr Mills. Delighted, I'm sure. Constable Delaney tells me that you have information for me? Shall we retire to an office?'

'Of course, I shan't keep you long.'

As they ascended the stairs, Peakin tried to watch the man a little more. There was nothing military in his bearing. He was languid. He'd either spent years reclaiming a poor posture or he was lying for an indiscernible reason. Maybe he thought it would lend his evidence some extra weight. Peakin found a room that was empty except for a couple of constables and he shooed them away. He closed the door behind them.

Mills took in the room.

'No office of your own, eh?'

'I'm afraid only men above the rank of Inspector have offices and even then they have to hire them. They're in places around the city.'

'I see. Well soon enough, I'm sure,' and he smiled his lopsided smile. Peakin was close enough to see the gold that was holding the false teeth in place.

'We're not here to discuss my promotion prospects.'

'Indeed,' said Mills and took a flyer from his pocket and handed it across to Peakin. It outlined a new society 'for the protection of infant life'.

'I don't see how this is evidence?'

Mills laughed again, displaying the same flashes of gold.

'No, no of course not. I am the founder of this little society. It's my contribution, you know. A need that I saw. After years in the service and then another few in America and London, I've finally been able to move back to my home country and I find it sadly changed. It seems chastity is no longer the first quality of an Irish maiden.'

'I'm still in the dark as to what this has to do with my case exactly.'

'Baby farmers.' At this Mills became more animated. He placed his soft hands on the desk and pushed his face towards Peakin. 'They're like the parasites who feed off the products of society's vice. They thrive in it. Their clients are all disgraced women, whores mostly, who wish to avoid the inconvenience of their choices by farming out their children. Sometimes they take the children back when they're old enough to work as thieves. And the whole system just perpetuates itself. But at the bottom, there is the baby farmer. Who has not a care for her charges, who leaves them in filth and feeds them on adulterated milk and hopes that they will live just long enough for her to make a tidy profit while she waits for her next victim.'

'I've heard of nurses, yes. They usually take in a single child. But this baby farming system, as far as I know of it from the papers, usually involves many children. If this was a pervasive problem here then I'm sure I would know more about it.'

'Well, you soon will.' Mills sat back in his chair, evidently feeling he no longer needed to press his point by breathing on Peakin. 'There are a few of them in the lanes around Moore Street and Purdon Street. And one of them has had a part in this crime. They offer to kill a baby slowly by malnutrition or quickly, if the price is good.'

'But do you have any evidence? I can't just go around accusing women of murdering babies.'

'I do. Only last month a madam sent one of her girls to this baby farmer in May Lane I told you about. Kitty Conroy she's called.'

'But how do you know this? Has the society developed its own detective branch? If you wish to submit formal evidence

I'll need to take your name and address, of course.' Peakin moved to open his notebook and discovered that it was his entomological journal. He kept it closed. Hoped that Mills would take this as a sign of his prodigious memory rather than his lack of preparedness.

'My address is 16 Leeson Street and I believe you know my name already. I can tell you how I came by the information. I'm a patron of the Magdalen asylum situated, as you know, on my street. I was a particular friend of the late Reverend Pollock, may he rest in peace. Our governesses are aware of all the goings on in the world that our penitents come from. They had recently accepted a penitent who came to us much distressed after she was brought to this Katherine 'Kitty' Conroy as a solution for her impending child. She was given the impression by Conroy that she could call on her for the birth and then she never need worry about her baby again.'

'And this penitent, is she still in the asylum? Her baby wasn't killed?'

'No, it wasn't. She's still with us. I'm pleased to say that her baby has gone to a very good family and she herself is on a path to recovery. She'll soon be placed in a respectable household to earn an honest wage. She told us that Miss Conroy regularly kills infants, had just killed one for a woman called Elizabeth Mooney. I'm sorry to say that Miss Mooney also spent a time at our establishment but obviously she was beyond reform.'

Eliza? His Eliza? Peakin struggled to contain a gasp of surprise. Would Mills, with his oddly fake accent and very fake teeth, see that Peakin was faking indifference? He tried to think what he should ask. He commanded his heart to stop beating so fast. He picked up the pen on his desk, angled the notebook so that Mills could not see that it contained sketches of insects, used the pretence of writing notes to compose himself. On the page he wrote, *Eliza Conroy Kitty Mooney Wilson Mills kills kills kills.*

'May I speak with her?' Peakin mustered. 'The penitent, I mean? I assume this Miss Mooney has disappeared.' He sucked on the end of his pen, trying to look intent and thoughtful. Mills looked troubled for a moment.

'I'll speak with the head matron. We try to keep our girls out of any relations with the police and away from excitement. This could set back her rehabilitation. Surely you could take the head matron's word as corroboration?'

'It would save a good deal of time to speak with the girl herself.'

'I'll see what I can do.'

After Mills left Exchequer Court, Peakin worried this development over in his mind. There was something repulsive about Mr Mills and his enthusiasm for hunting baby farmers. Something utterly dishonest about his demeanour which made Peakin doubt every word that he said. As if Mr Mills was almost enjoying himself. And yet here was the closest thing to concrete evidence that he had. What if it turned out that this story about Eliza was true? What if Eliza was found, angry and unreformed and hurling accusations? Not that he'd done anything wrong, or anything more wrong than all the other men who sated themselves at the city's brothels. And this penitent of Mr Mills's, what if she had worked at Mrs Wilson's and she recognised Peakin? He imagined the smirks of the other acting sergeants if he was found out, pecking at the details of his tawdry sins like delighted hens. They resented his careful steadfastness and his semblance of book learning, mocked his 'insect habit', begrudged him the freedom of shabby rooms that weren't barracks. Peakin ran a hand through his hair, fiddled with the chain of his watch. For the first time in many years, he was thirsty for a strong drink. He opened his billfold, counted the coins in his pocket and confirmed that this was out of the question.

Chapter Eighteen

Anne

April 1866

Matthias didn't reply to Anne's letter. She went over and over it with Rose. Yes, she'd handed it directly to him. Yes, he'd opened it. No, there was no reply. She didn't realise how much hope she'd been holding out for him until it was gone. The silence was unbearable.

She'd been starving herself but still her stomach stretched. Every time she counted the months her heart pounded in panic. Rose showed her how to stand, shoulders slightly forward, to hide the looseness that she'd added to the waists of all Anne's dresses.

'Honest, you wouldn't notice if you weren't looking. And no one is looking.'

Anne didn't believe that no one was looking. Cook's glances felt searching; she flinched when her aunt put on her spectacles. Aunt Julia was distracted by worries about the proper schooling of her grandchildren, the potential rental of further acres in Galway, the need for replacement servants in Bray. But Anne never knew when her attention might turn. When she might make sharper inquiries about

Anne's impending employment. When she might just notice what was right in front of her face. Anne only relaxed when she was alone with Rose. She kept hoping that capable Rose would find a solution. So far, all Rose had done was to urge Anne to tell her aunt.

'She's not cruel,' Rose said. 'What do you think she'll do to you? It's not your fault.'

'I can't tell her,' Anne replied, and watched Rose shake her head. Rose couldn't see that Aunt Julia wouldn't be sympathetic. This was the distance between them: Rose didn't fear anyone's judgement, while Anne feared everyone's. She pictured the satisfaction her aunt would get from being proven right. Anne was just as indulgent and selfish as she believed. Instead she continued hiding things as well as she could. She hoped that something might happen, an accident on the stairs or an illness or just an answer to her prayers.

'Hard to believe the child is almost five months today,' her aunt said over breakfast. Anne almost choked on her toast before she remembered Ellen's baby. 'Your father wrote to ask after you. He's worried because you told him you'd been ill. He'd like to see you.' Anne nodded and pushed away her plate, the boiled egg uncracked.

'Yes, I've had a little trouble with my stomach. And then the headaches. I worried I might give something to the baby.'

'If you carry on not eating you'll make yourself sick in the end. I'll send Johanna to say you'll call on them tomorrow.'

The visit was short. Anne kept her shawl on and watched the terrifying minutes tick past on the mantelpiece clock. She waited for them to ask a question, to comment on her figure. But her father and Ellen stared at the bassinet where Maryanne sighed and stretched in her sleep. Before she left,

Anne leaned over the baby and touched her tiny hands. She pictured the baby curled inside of her and felt nothing but churning terror. Everything in her said that she would have to run away. What else was there left to do? She had no money of her own. Everything she had was managed by her aunt. The only person who might help her, who might be able to give her what she needed, was the last person she wanted to see. But there was no choice. She would go to see Matthias. He might take pity on her if she begged.

She passed several days working up her courage, walking almost as far as his street before scurrying back to Mountjoy Square, breathless. She chose the luncheon hour when she thought he was more likely to be at home. As she approached the house, she thought it looked cleaner and tidier than she remembered. She thought of his fiancée. It hadn't been hard to discover her name: Martha Clancy. What if she was there, sitting on the deep blue sofa sipping tea? Her teeth were chattering when she knocked on the door. Mrs Tuffy opened it and looked her up and down.

'Is Dr Kelly in?'

'Is he expecting you?'

'I'm afraid not. I was nearby and—'

'Miss Mulhall isn't it? I'll go and see.'

Anne watched her turn down the hall. She didn't close the door so Anne stepped inside and closed it herself. She realised now that she hadn't considered what she would say. Surely Mrs Tuffy would have sent her away if there were other callers. Or would she have? This was a mistake. She began to turn the handle on the door.

'Miss Mulhall? He says that he'll see you now if it's important. He hasn't much time before he has to leave.'

'Yes, that's fine. Thank you.'

Anne followed down the familiar hallway, noticing things she'd not seen the last time. There were small prints, images from Greek mythology that she half recognised. A pair of botanical paintings showing birds of paradise. The bright orange petals looked garish. She was grateful that Mrs Tuffy led her into Matthias's office and not into the little sitting room.

'Anne! This is a surprise. Are you on your own?' The question seemed to be for the servant's benefit. Matthias stood and crossed the room to offer her a chair. If he felt uncomfortable he didn't show it. He left the door open. Mrs Tuffy didn't close it as she retreated. 'And how have you been?' Anne sat down in the chair. Her fingers were clumsy and numb as she tried to smooth her dress.

'Would you mind, Matthias ... I mean,' she gestured towards the door but he didn't move. She sighed. 'I'd prefer if you would close the door.'

Instead of surprised he seemed amused. He closed the door and then sat in the armchair across from her. He crossed his legs at the ankles, knitted his fingers together and waited. She said nothing.

'You're looking well. I'd heard that you were ill. Is that why you're here? I'm sorry that I didn't return your letter. You made it clear a few months ago that you didn't want to see me and I could understand that was for the best. The letter seemed ... out of character. So I decided it was better for us both if I didn't—'

'I need your help. I'm in some difficulty.' She looked around the room, filled with all the signs of a comfortable single life. Surely he wouldn't grudge her some assistance. She couldn't just turn up at her sister's house, disgraced flotsam from Ireland. He would understand if she could explain it the right way.

'My help?'

'I need money, Matthias. I need money so that I can go to England to get help.'

He looked confused now but not yet alarmed. Was it possible that he hadn't understood her earlier letter? That he'd not been able to read between the lines about her predicament?

'But why would you ask me? I'm not sure what you think about doctors, but I thought I made it clear that I don't have much money. And besides, why wouldn't you ask your aunt? Or your father? I'm grateful for those months of friendship, but I'm engaged to be married.'

Anne thought that she might vomit. Tears pooled in her eyes and she wiped at them. She wanted to show anger but she revealed only despair. She loosened her shawl. She felt his eyes on her but there was no intake of breath, no gasp of recognition.

'You see, Matthias. The last time that I saw you—'

'We got carried away in the moment. I know you must have felt regret at what you'd done. What you'd permitted me. But you didn't reply to my letters and so I thought it was best to leave it alone.' He placed his hands on hers, his fingers now only inches away from the catastrophe he'd caused. She took a deep breath and tried to look him in the eye.

'I need to go to England because I'm carrying your child.' He withdrew his hands, leaned away from her. 'I'll need money for the doctor and the passage, and for a place to stay. And if you give me the money then I won't bother you again. I'll stay in England. You won't hear from me.'

'My child? That's not possible.' He laughed. He stood up and walked to the opposite corner of the room. He shook his head. 'My father warned me about this kind of thing. Traps that women set. But I didn't expect it from you.

You cannot come here and convince me to cover for your indiscretions. I knew from the day I met you that you'd been with other men.'

Anne hadn't expected this onslaught of denial, his accusations. She lifted her hand to her cheek as though she'd been slapped. She opened her mouth and closed it. She remembered his weight on her, the knifing pain, the way he'd not been able to meet her eye. She tried to remind herself that everything was ruined anyway. It didn't matter what he thought. All that mattered was that he gave her the money so that she could run away.

'I'm sorry that you think so poorly of me. I need twenty pounds. For the ferry and for the doctor and a place to stay until I can work.'

'This situation is ridiculous. You have no idea. Twenty pounds? Even if your story was true, I don't have twenty pounds. Everything is tied up. My rent is enormous. There are wedding expenses.'

Anne grasped for something that would wound him. Make him take her seriously.

'Do you think the Clancys would like to know about this? What if I were to write to them? Or go and speak to them? If you give me the money they will never need to know.'

There was a sharp intake of breath. That's done it, she thought. She felt disgusted with herself but relieved that it was over now. She heard him shuffling something on his desk and then he was beside her. He leaned over her chair. His breaths were steady. She kept looking at her hands. When he opened his mouth the words sounded like a hiss.

'No, you won't do it. You would never do that. What proof do you have? You'll only sink yourself further. If you're really in the trouble you say you are it's nothing to do with me. I won't be blackmailed. It was a brief attachment, nothing more. I'll remind you that *you* chose to end it. I have nothing to give you. I'm sorry for your trouble but there's nothing I can do.'

Nothing, nothing, nothing. She was nothing. Matthias crossed the room and opened the door wide. He went back and sat behind his desk. The shuffle of papers sounded like a chorus of whispers. Nothing, nothing, nothing. Her vision blurred. She stood and let herself out.

Part III

The tide turned and the river gnashed her liquid teeth against the quay walls, rushing to meet the sea. In the fading light the water grew darker and darker until the only thing you could see were the white feathers of the few birds still bobbing on its surface. Down in the murky depths, the river worried at all the things that had fallen into her. Stones tumbled over half pennies thrown in by people wishing for luck they probably didn't need. If you listened, you could have heard the emptying of drains into the river, each bringing its own special mixture of fouled water to join the stream. The sluice of slaughterhouses and bacon factors mixed with the tenements and the brewery at Wood Quay, the washings of lawyerly piss pots trickled down from the King's Inns.

From Mulligan's Court and Off Lane came the rustling of cheap petticoats, the recitation of choice obscenities and the waft of whiskey-sweetened breath. A gentleman lawyer, having ventured the walk home after a few too many glasses of claret, stumbled across Carlisle Bridge. He fumbled in his pockets. At the sound of a penny dropping and falling into the river, Eliza stepped closer and caught his arm. She plucked at his moustache, exclaimed at his fine appearance, and guided him gently away from home.

Chapter Nineteen

Rose

11th August, 1866

Rose knew the detective was following her on her way to work. He thought he was clever, staying a good distance behind and taking care to stop and look in shop windows. But Rose knew what it felt like to have eyes on her; she'd known it all her life. The grabbing, the calling, but most of all the staring. So she could feel his eyes as well as she could feel fingers that pinched. And then he turned up at the house. Asking about burglaries. And he recognised her. What exactly did he think she'd done? The detective ruffled Mrs Kennedy and disturbed Rose's working life. Denis was the one who had gone into the river and now his sordid discovery came along and upset the calm quiet of Mountjoy Square. She didn't want to talk to Mrs Kennedy about her husband or her home. She wanted to tidy and serve and dust and sweep and polish and forget herself. She'd helped Anne but she wasn't a dishonest person: she couldn't lie if she was asked. Not even for Anne.

'What did you make of all that, Rose?' Mrs Kennedy asked her after Detective Peakin left.

'Don't know, madam. S'pose it's his job to be nosy.'

'Yes, I suppose it is. But I hadn't heard of any burglaries on the square. Or not any ones that seemed out of the ordinary. I didn't like his questions. There was a sense of fishing about. Did you see the way he looked around the house? Like I could be under suspicion for something! Like I might be harbouring someone unsavoury behind the curtains or in the basement.'

'Maybe that's just his manner. To be alert.'

Rose bent to collect the teacups and loaded them onto her tray, taking extra care and hoping she wouldn't decide to ask about Denis. Rose's mother had explained to Mrs Kennedy about the stillbirth, about why Rose couldn't bear the butcher shop. The woman never asked about it. And that was fine with Rose. Mrs Kennedy spoke as Rose went to open the door.

'Still, we don't want him back again. The neighbours will talk. I'll write to some people. He can't just go prowling around the square asking nasty questions. This is how rumours start. I can hear the neighbours now, whispering about how I was visited by the police. Once was enough. Twice could be the beginning of a slide. Fetch Anne for me, will you please?'

'Yes, of course.' Rose bowed her head in agreement and took a deep breath as she pushed out through the door.

Anne could not hide her alarm when Rose explained that her aunt wanted to see her. She sank into her armchair and covered her face with her hands.

'She knows everything. I'm sure of it. The way that Cook looks at me! I pinch myself all the time to see if I will wake.'

'She knows nothing. There is nothing for her to know,' Rose tried what she thought was a reassuring tone. She'd known there would be questions sometime. They would pass.

But even Rose was alarmed when Mrs Kennedy demanded that Anne play a piano concert for the Society for the Protection of Infant Life. 'An opportunity,' she heard Mrs Kennedy calling it. 'You never know who might be listening. Besides, it's very important to be involved in charity work. Your mother would agree.' Anne's face paled at that and even Mrs Kennedy seemed to regret her tone for a moment. Once Anne relented, Mrs Kennedy spent the rest of the afternoon writing angry letters to police officers about the detective while Rose brought her sustaining titbits from the kitchen.

She longed to go upstairs to comfort Anne, to tell Mrs Kennedy that Anne was too ill to play any concert. But this would bring questions and Rose didn't want to answer any questions. Rose found herself jumping at every unexpected sound. For the first time in months, she was glad to go home to Denis.

He was still in the shop when she arrived and began to prepare the dinner. Poor Denis. He had such patience. She could tell that he was growing tired of waiting. He hadn't married her so he could look at her behind the counter or sit next to her at the table. She could read the urgency of his desires in the occasions when she let him kiss her. She told herself that she would try. Tonight she would try just to lie down next to him and let him touch her. He was gentle, really. She was being unfair. She knew what her mother would say. Each time she passed the sideboard she took another sip of gin until the edges of things fuzzed a little.

All through dinner she made an effort as the sun beat in and kept the room far too hot. She wanted to close the curtains but feared he would suggest they retire early. She wanted to open the windows but knew it would bring no relief. Denis told funny stories about the customers they both knew and Rose listened and laughed in the right places.

She said nothing when he followed her up to their bedroom. She felt her skin react to the eyes trained on her. She undressed and climbed under the sheet. Her head began to ache. She hoped Denis had washed. Really washed. Even the touch of the sheets could bring the images. The sound of her own flesh tearing, the terrible sensations of her body trying to expel the baby before he could kill her. There had been blood and fluids everywhere by the time the doctor arrived.

'Rose.'

'Yes, Denis.'

'I love you.'

'I know.'

'Did you want to tell me anything?'

'Like what?'

'I don't know. Anything at all. Tell me what you did today.'

'You don't want to hear about that. There's nothing to tell.' To prove that everything was fine, she turned on her side and kissed him. She let him kiss her back. He placed a hand on the back of her neck, pushed her mouth harder against his own. And then she could smell it. She pulled back and gasped for air. The tears had already started to flow — maybe they'd been there all along. Sweat made her scalp itch and her shift stick. She lay on her back and tried to breathe. Denis watched in silence for a moment. 'It's happening,' she said, 'I'm sorry.'

She closed her eyes. She heard him slide out from under the sheet and cross the floor. He lingered at the door. 'Goodnight, Rose.' She couldn't reply because she wasn't there. She was back in her childbed. She must have cried out because Denis said 'Do you want me to stay?' and all she could do was shake her head. The door handle turned and she was alone with her demons. All alone, she relived the birth, hour by agonising hour. Her sweat turned to blood, the sheets twisted around her like hands. When the visions released her, she cried herself to sleep, not caring if Denis could hear.

Chapter Twenty

Anne

June 1866

Anne resented the awakening of June. There was something unseemly in the way that life was bursting forth from everywhere. She wished for the flowers to wilt and the birds to fall silent. After the disaster of her visit to Matthias she received a parcel with some tablets in it. The note said: *These may be of some use. Take one a day for a week. M.*

She swallowed them full of hope. They made her sick: days of stomach cramps and waking in the night to retch into the chamber pot. For a few hours she thought she might die along with the child she was carrying. She imagined the guilt that Matthias would feel. But her body betrayed her with its strength. Her monthlies did not return. She dreamed of blood flowing from her like a stream and woke slicked with sweat.

Anne slid past the servants, growing anxious and suspicious at the slightest smile. She never lingered in the kitchen, never spoke to the groom. The ever-present shawl made her aunt comment that she was turning into a perfect Connemara peasant. Anne made it clear to everyone that she preferred Rose to look after her. She had no appetite but her stomach bulged anyway and her breasts swelled, her body felt distorted.

If there was a single blessing then that was Rose's sympathy. She bound Anne's stomach and her tender breasts, lied and told her that no one had noticed anything. Anne was grateful for Rose, for the pleasure of her attention. Hers were the only hands that touched Anne now and they were gentle, comforting hands. Rose fussed over her, straightening her clothes and brushing her hair.

Aunt Julia insisted that Rose serve the dinner, claiming that Johanna was sloppy and had bad breath. 'It turns my stomach every time she leans over me to serve the soup,' she whispered, though Anne had never noticed. She just liked having Rose around because everyone liked having Rose around. In the late afternoons, when all her tasks were done, Rose would sit with Anne or they would go for a walk. She clung to these moments of peace.

One afternoon Anne felt especially bereft. She'd just received the inevitable letter of dismissal from the Lynches. She'd delayed her arrival in Athlone more times than they could tolerate. No miracle occurred to end her limbo and now one avenue of escape from her aunt's house was passing by and all she could do was watch it recede into the distance.

The rain began, as though the sky sensed her mood. First, the occasional drop landed in the fire with a hiss. Then the wind picked up and the rain began to streak across the windows, louder and louder, like a caller rapping on the door. She finished her book and went downstairs to find another. When she opened the door to the library, Rose was already there.

'Rose! You must have read my mind, I was just coming in to fetch a book. I was thinking I might find a few old copies of *All the Year Round* in here somewhere.' Rose turned as though startled. She was standing in front of the liquor cabinet.

'Oh! Yes, of course. Well, I did think since it's lashing down …' Anne noticed that Rose held her hands behind her back and her face was flushed.

'Are you quite alright, Rose? Do you need help with something?' Anne thought that Cook had sent her for some Madeira for a cake and she couldn't find it. How would she even know what a bottle of Madeira looked like?

'No, no. Everything is fine, I'll be up to you in two ticks.' She stepped closer. Rose's basket was on the floor just behind her skirt. In the basket was a bottle of gin.

'I'm sure it's not gin that Cook wants, Rose. I heard Aunt Julia ask for Madeira cake. There's no Madeira here, I think it's only some gin and whiskey for when we have gentlemen to dinner.' Rose covered her face with her hands. 'What's wrong? Don't worry, I'll show you where the Madeira is and Cook won't shout.' She dropped her hands and straightened her face.

'No, it's gin I want and it's not for Cook.' Anne noticed she wore the same expression as Johanna did when she expected a scolding.

'Then who is it for?'

'Anne, don't be thick. I'm only after telling you. The gin's for me.'

'For you?' Was Rose a drunk? Anne studied the yellow ringlets and the rosebud lips. Was her nose turning just a little red? Her cheeks? No, she was the same as ever.

'Yes. Now if you'll leave me be, I'll be up. And please don't blow on me to the mistress.' There was a snap to her voice as she turned back to whatever she'd been doing in the drinks cabinet. Stealing, Anne supposed.

Anne didn't know what to say so she just took a book from the nearest shelf without reading the spine and went back to her room. Rose knocked a few minutes later. She sat down on the stool and waited to be told off. The book Anne had taken turned out to be *The Civilization of the Renaissance in Italy*. She couldn't get past the first paragraph, irritated by the author's repeated professions of modesty.

'I won't say anything.'

'And I won't do it again.'

'Well that's settled then. I'm afraid this book won't do. We may have to entertain ourselves in stitching or talking instead.'

The discovery seemed to pry something open in Rose. She didn't want to read or stitch. She wanted to ask what Anne was planning to do.

'You should tell Mrs Kennedy. You're only making things worse for yourself. Making it harder for her to help.'

But Anne saw no signs of the kindness Rose claimed was there.

Aunt Julia sighed and huffed through their meals together, spoke sharply to Anne about her appearance, treated her like one of the servants. The only thing she and her aunt could agree on was their affection for Rose. So Anne was devastated when Aunt Julia announced the annual summer stay in Galway, at the estate her cousin Caroline managed with her husband. She feared leaving Rose, being paraded in front of another set of people who could detect her secret and humiliate her. But then she thought that perhaps this was the push she needed. An old friend of her mother's lived near the estate, someone she'd visited as a child. Maybe she would help her. Or there was always the boat to America. She hugged Rose hard until she laughed and said, 'It's only a few weeks, Anne.' She felt that Rose had almost convinced herself of their deception, had forgotten that there would be a baby at the end of all this lying.

The house was packed and the train was boarded. Anne and Aunt Julia lurched and rattled their way west. The carriage smelled of damp. Ireland stretched flat and green in all directions, dark water the only interruptions. Drovers walked alongside the tracks, flicking their sticks at the flanks of cattle. Every station held its own selection of country beggars, even worse off than the Dublin variety. Here they had to make their rags with sacking or whatever could be got to hand. Anne looked but never saw a single one with shoes, not even broken ones.

As the train pulled away from Athlone, Aunt Julia put her book down.

'I asked Mr Kingsley to get the piano tuned for you. I hope you brought your music.'

'Oh that was kind of you, I didn't want to ask about the piano as there were so many other preparations to make. It didn't seem important.'

'Well, I know it offers some amusement for you. And of course there will be company and it is pleasant to pass an evening in music. Mr Kingsley was most happy to help.' Anne had met the estate manager once when he'd visited her aunt in Dublin. Maybe now he was being viewed as a potential suitor.

'I hope it won't be raining when we arrive,' Anne said, trying to change the subject.

She turned back to the oscillating landscape. From a distance it was as lovely as any painting. Haze hung over fields where cattle lay in little groups like women at a tea party. The countryside was picturesque when you couldn't see the dirt, feel the wet or smell its pungent smells.

Of course it was raining when they arrived. Mr Kingsley met them with two carriages.

'Welcome to the west,' he laughed, throwing a hand up towards the sky. Anne pulled her shawl over her head, careful to keep her middle concealed. Aunt Julia got in beside her. They waited as luggage was tied to the top. Cook and more luggage were loaded into the other carriage. Anne parted the curtains to watch their progress out the window and clumps of dust fell from the velvet folds like mouse pelts.

If Mountjoy Square was experiencing a kind of slow, genteel decline, then the house in Galway was headed rapidly for a dilapidation that even Caroline and Anthony seemed unable to reverse. From the carriage the house appeared the same as it had on visits years ago: a block of forbidding grey stone looming at the end of a bare drive. The windows still scowled at you as you arrived. Inside, the hall was hung with trophy heads. The most prized was a wolf, which Anthony told her was one of the last of its kind ever killed in Ireland. The fur was patchy, as though the animal had mange, and the lips were curled back in an expression of menace that didn't match the eyes, placed too wide apart.

Anne studied the wolf while Mr Kingsley and his helpers carried the cases into the house. Caroline was directing.

'Anne's room is at the top of the landing, the first door on the left. Mother's is the room across the hall from that. And Cook will stay where she usually does, out behind. Above the kitchen.'

'Everything looks just the same.' Anne saw Caroline flinch a little under her mother's scrutiny. If everyone was occupied with their own problems then she could fade into the walls like another stuffed trophy.

Anne ascended the stairs to her room. Out the window the rain battered down. Even the few trees, bent at the waist, seemed to feel the weather as an assault.

Chapter Twenty-One

Peakin

13th August, 1866

The inspector's face was red, but whether from heat or anger Peakin couldn't tell. His voice betrayed nothing other than a kind of bored irritation as he recited the pertinent contents of Mrs Kennedy's letter. Peakin tried to keep his eyes on the inspector's face but they wandered to the window. Through it he could see only more windows on the other side of the street. A city, he thought, was a collection of windows. The windows might be smeared or cracked or freshly cleaned and framed with the best curtains à la mode. They might let in a healthful breeze or the noisome belch of a laneway. No matter, because behind every one was a person who wanted nothing more than to see out of their own window while preventing anyone else from seeing in. To know the worst about everyone else while hiding their own sins.

'Are you listening to me, Peakin? I'll have no more of this. You're a good detective. Diligent. But we must set boundaries on our investigations. We must stay within the realms of the reasonable.' He waved the letter, one side of it crowded with a tidy, dense script. Peakin wondered what

Mrs Kennedy had written. 'Mrs Kennedy has sent letters not only to me, but also to the superintendent and the police commissioner. Her husband, you might have known had you bothered to consult the peerage, was a distinguished officer in the army. Served in the Punjab. Well connected.'

'I'm afraid I used less than my usual measure of discretion. It's only that ... there was a letter suggesting ... and a rumour about—'

'Detective.' The inspector put his arm up as though to shield himself from the horror of gossip. Peakin pictured timid Anne Mulhall, the watchful wariness of Mrs Kennedy.

'You're right. I won't pursue it any further.' He wondered if Dr Pratt would be disappointed.

'Good. I think we're reaching the end of what can be done. Follow up on the information from Mr Mills. Try to find this Elizabeth Mooney. Visit her employer.' He glanced down at some papers on his desk, 'A Mrs Wilson. Mecklenburg Street. If she has no news of Miss Mooney then perhaps the coroner will be satisfied that we have done our utmost.' Peakin felt his stomach twisting and squeezing. Just his lunch, he told himself: insufficient like the breakfast before it. Isobel had been right, he could never have kept her comfortable on less than £2 a week.

'I'll do it straight away.'

'And take Constable Delaney with you.' Peakin's stomach performed another acrobatic contortion.

'Yes, sir.'

Peakin managed to send Mrs Wilson a message to warn her that he would be calling in a professional capacity. He hoped that between the lines of his bland pleasantries she would read, 'I am reliant on your discretion.' It was bad enough that he would have to arrive at the door with a policeman in

uniform. If anyone in the neighbourhood had not already
known his identity it would now be clear. His convenient
arrangement, his neat division of himself into mind and
body, would be disrupted. Perhaps this was the incentive
he needed to give it up. He had to eat more. Respectability
aside, it came down to meat or whores.

'I'm ready now, sir,' Delaney rapped on the door as he
entered. Peakin twitched in irritation.

'Excellent. Let's be on our way.' Delaney's face remained
clean-shaven. He looked absurdly young. Peakin thought
the accent was Louth. He remembered when he'd arrived
in Dublin himself, fresh from famine-ravaged Wicklow.
His parents had made it clear that there was no future in
the farm. They'd given it all up to his brother-in-law who
turned the lot to pasture and kept them in two cold rooms at
the back of the house. With a small stab of guilt he recalled
his mother's most recent letter, unopened on his dressing
table. He was bracing himself for news. Perhaps Isobel had
married someone else.

'Is it very far?' asked Delaney. Peakin wondered if the
lazy sod was hoping to take a cab.

'It's a good walk but it gives us the chance to discuss
our approach. This is a very delicate situation.' Peakin was
seething at the inspector for making him bring this bumbler
along. He wondered yet again what the inspector knew. Mills
hadn't seemed to know of his connection to Eliza but he
couldn't be certain.

'This is my first interview in this kind of ...' Was the
constable actually blushing? Dear God. Not one of those.

'Ah, I see. Well, Mrs Wilson, from what I understand, is
quite a respectable woman in appearance. I don't think there will
be much of anything to find discomfiting.' The man probably
imagined that at noon on a Wednesday there would be women

running up and down the halls with their breasts bared. They'd all be asleep. Or working at other jobs. 'I will ask the questions. It would be useful if you would take notes. Here.' Peakin handed him a blank notebook and a pen hoping that a task might help to blind the man to any oddness at the interview.

'Oh! Thank you. Thank you for your trust in me, detective.'

'We all have to start somewhere, Delaney. Remember we're most concerned with what she knows of this baby farmer, a Miss Katherine 'Kitty' Conroy. She's not going to tell us anything about any of her girls so it's hardly worth pressing.' He dreaded Delaney jumping in to clarify some point about Eliza, Mrs Wilson tossing him a knowing glance. He wiped his palms against his trousers, stopped himself from itching at his moustache.

When they arrived at Mrs Wilson's, Peakin knew she'd received his note because the door was closed. Wet streaked the ground under the windows as if they'd just been washed. He knocked. The maid, a matronly whore known as Mrs Plunkett, opened the door. She rustled like a paper doll in her starch-stiff dress.

'We're looking for Mrs Wilson. Dublin Metropolitan Police. We just need to ask a few questions.' He handed Mrs Plunkett a card and she nodded.

'I'll see if she's in.' They waited on the step. The street had its day clothing on and was quiet. The door opened.

'Mrs Wilson will join you shortly in the parlour,' Mrs Plunkett told them. He wondered how many times she'd practised that phrase.

The parlour was a completely ordinary room with no sign of the business of its owner. There was a round table, spread with a lace-edged cloth and holding a vase of flowers.

Two stuffed chairs and a small settee crowded around the fireplace. Peakin suspected that there had never been any Mr Wilson, but she kept a framed photograph of some man on the mantelpiece among her other knick-knacks.

Peakin took one of the stuffed chairs and suggested that Delaney take the other. He could see Delaney trying to take it all in, looking for clues that would tell him he was sitting inside a brothel. Mrs Wilson entered in a pale grey dress matched to a countenance that was more school mistress than madam.

'Gentlemen. I see you've made yourselves comfortable.' Peakin watched her, waiting for signs of familiarity that Delaney could detect. She was dry and brusque. She perched on the settee. 'Shall I have Mrs Plunkett bring us tea?' Peakin visualised a crumpet, a little pat of butter. Maybe a bit of marmalade. He hoped that no one heard his stomach burble.

'Thank you, that won't be necessary. I'm Detective Peakin and this is Constable Delaney.' Peakin thought he glimpsed the edge of a smile on Mrs Wilson's practised countenance.

'Very pleased to meet you.'

'And you, madam. I mean Mrs Wilson,' Delaney flushed and busied himself with turning pages in the notebook.

'Mrs Wilson. You'll be aware of the recent discovery of a dead infant boy in the River Liffey? The subsequent inquest determined it to be infant murder.'

'I've heard of the case, yes. Very sad indeed. So many hazards to young lives between the whooping cough and now the cholera. We should all thank God every day for our health.' Delaney wrote something down. Peakin wondered what it could possibly be. Mrs Wilson shifted on the edge of her seat as though prepared to flee.

'We are making some routine inquiries. However, a man by the name of Mr Mills has provided some evidence concerning women employed by you.'

'Mr Mills. I believe he is one of the patrons of an asylum for women.'

'Yes, that's the man. He has recently founded a Society for the Protection of Infant Life. They take a great interest in this case.' Peakin noticed Mrs Wilson hold a handkerchief to her face to disguise a sniff of disgust. With alarm, he heard Delaney open his mouth.

'A woman in the asylum has confessed—' Mrs Wilson held up a gloved hand.

'Please, let the detective finish. That way, you'll take much better notes.' Peakin felt a wave of relief. Perhaps they were on the same side after all.

'As Constable Delaney suggested, there's a woman in the asylum who Mr Mills *claims* was previously an employee in this house. I'm afraid he hasn't told us her name. However, she made some accusations about a woman called Katherine Conroy. Do you know her?' Delaney leaned forward in his chair, pen poised, and Peakin thought he would never make a detective. He'd be sent back to B Division where the giant country oafs belonged.

'I've heard of her. She's a nurse. Takes in a few babies in her rooms.'

'Exactly.' Delaney was scribbling away at his paper. 'This penitent, again, we don't know her name, claims that Miss Conroy may have killed the infant. In fact, she goes further, claiming that Miss Conroy routinely provides a service of killing unwanted infants.' Mrs Wilson laughed and Delaney's head snapped up.

'I'm sorry,' she said, 'this is a serious matter but the accusation is absurd. Never mind that it suggests bloodthirstiness on Miss Conroy's part. It simply makes no sense. Why would she kill the babies when she can make far more money in keeping them alive on watery milk and cheap gruel? I'm sure Miss Conroy is no fool.'

'So you think the idea is implausible?' Perhaps he could avoid a mention of Eliza completely. Surely there was no need to pursue any specific allegations if the entire idea was ridiculous.

'I will go further. I think it impossible. Gentlemen, I'm afraid that I have many business matters to attend to myself and I will have to bid you good day. Can you find your way out or should I call for Mrs Plunkett?'

'Mrs Wilson, there's just one other thing—'

'Constable, I believe we have all we need. Thank you for your patience, Mrs Wilson.'

Delaney inhaled, as if preparing to say something, but Peakin shot him a sharp look and so he rose and nodded at Mrs Wilson before pushing open the door into the hall. As they stepped back out onto the street Peakin felt a rising unease. He liked to be the one to end interviews. Was there something else that Mrs Wilson knew? She'd seemed suddenly eager for them to leave. He knew he should be relieved, but she had given them nothing at all.

'We didn't get a chance to ask about Miss Mooney,' Delaney said, revealing an irritating ability to recall details. 'I think we might have pushed a little further, maybe.'

'Constable, we cannot go blundering around, asking every question that occurs to us. We'll find no one will co-operate in future. Mrs Wilson seemed quite certain that this Miss Conroy had nothing to do with it.' Peakin wiped his palms on his trousers while Delaney looked down at his notebook.

'She didn't say that exactly, detective,' Delaney stared at a page, 'what she said was—'

'I heard what she said. In my experience, constable, people rarely do things that are not to their advantage. In particular, they do not take large risks without the promise of large rewards. Mrs Wilson made it plain that there is money in the nursing. It seems to me that killing would carry far too much risk and could not incur sufficient reward.'

'Yes, that was more or less what she suggested.'

'Why don't you head back to Exchequer Court and write up a report for the inspector? It seems you're a thorough note-taker. I'm going to take my tea out.'

'Yes, sir.'

Peakin walked, not knowing his destination. He was hungry but the greasy mists wafting from the eateries only turned his stomach. Besides, he needed to postpone his meal if he wanted to avoid waking at midnight in hunger. Seeking distraction, he paused at the window of Alexander Ogilvy's and decided to enter.

Shelves rose to the ceiling. Some were crammed with fat rolls of plain fabric, reminding Peakin of shrouded corpses. Ogilvy had sprayed perfume to mask the animal scent of the wool, amplified by the heat. So the shop smelled like sheep on their way to the theatre.

On the tables were more fabrics, as well as lace trimmings, bonnet strings and ribbon sashes. Even the black fabrics seemed to have almost infinite variety. So many ways to wear sadness. He wondered idly about the difference between a grenadine and a grosgrain. He supposed it was this kind of knowledge that separated a gentleman from someone merely respectable. He thought of Dr Mapother's easy finery, the way that his clothes shone just enough and not too much.

As he prodded the fabric, Peakin imagined himself in a summer suit for the next entomology expedition. He would look more the part, more scientific naturalist than policeman on a holiday. He thought back to their last outing. At the picnic afterwards, the others had crowded round him to see what he'd collected. Their praise was made less sweet, Peakin felt, by their ongoing surprise at his capacity to identify his catch. He'd grown tired of playing the part of specimen, evidence of their broad-minded acceptance of the working classes.

'Can I help you, sir?' A shop assistant shook him from the daydream.

'Oh, no, thank you. I'll come back another time.'

On his way to Exchequer Court he bought four roast potatoes from the most hygienic-looking seller he could find. He swallowed rather than ate them. When he arrived at his office he found Delaney's report of their interview with Mrs Wilson. He ignored it and returned to the maps, searching for anything he might have missed, something to move the case away and out of Dublin. The maps refused to offer him an escape: the infant must have been dropped from the bridge or, at most, from slightly further west of it. No drain large enough emptied nearby and the tides and flow of the river since the night before its discovery did not suggest that it could have been carried a long way.

Peakin turned to Delaney's report with trepidation but it was plain and clear, stating only the facts of what had been said. There was a single sentence at the end declaring that they hadn't had the opportunity to inquire specifically about Miss Elizabeth Mooney. Even the presence of her name in the report made Peakin squirm. This was ridiculous, because of course her name appeared in his own report to the inspector after the visit of Mr Mills.

Peakin opened a drawer and took out a map of the city he had cut from the back of *Thom's Directory*. He unfolded it, located Richmond Bridge and began to survey the surrounding areas, even though he could conjure every building on the riverbank in his mind. On the southern bank lay Merchant's Quay and the Adam and Eve Chapel. On the northern bank much of King's Inns Quay was taken up by the Four Courts.

Aside from the church, Merchant's Quay was lined with houses, but most of them had been converted into solicitors' offices, paper manufactories, engravers or merchant stores. If he added in Wood Quay he just added in boot manufacturers. Still, if any among them had been working very late they might have seen something. He would send Delaney to ask.

He returned to the map. There was no hiding the fact that Mrs Wilson's and the baby farmer in May Lane were within an easy walk of the river.

He weighed the possibility of visiting the baby farmer. He didn't doubt that he would find Kitty Conroy or that she would turn out to be exactly as described. And what if she mentioned Eliza?

Chapter Twenty-Two

Anne

July 1866

Without Rose to retreat to, Anne trembled through the first few days in Galway like a harp string pulled too taut. She was unnerved by the strange, remote house and the wild, unfamiliar countryside. She had nightmares where she was left behind, shut up like a forgotten dress.

The weather was reliably bad so she spent most of her time inside. Anne felt sorry for her cousin Caroline but relieved at how she drew Aunt Julia's focus. The children were a welcome distraction, an excuse for Anne to avoid company while also appearing to be helpful. Caroline was so unsettled with her mother watching her that she hardly spoke to Anne. Anthony, her husband, spent most of his days visiting tenants or paying bills or hunting. After a week, despite the pressures of dressing herself and binding her expanding stomach, Anne could almost relax.

She began to form a plan. The friend of her mother, a Mrs Cuddehy, lived in a tidy cottage just beyond the edge of the property. Anne's mother was forever befriending people who she felt had intelligence and lacked opportunities. Ellen had also been one of her mother's projects. She knew her mother had probably sent letters, books and small amounts of money to Mrs Cuddehy over the years. Maybe she would feel she owed Anne some small debt? Maybe she could hide her, help her to leave the baby with someone who would care for it. It was an absurd plan, but Anne was absurdly desperate. She wandered closer to the cottage with each afternoon walk.

The estate once extended to at least a thousand acres with hundreds of tenants, or so Aunt Julia claimed. But now only a couple of hundred acres and a few tenants of the better sort remained. Their cabins boasted thatched roofs, more than one room and two chimneys. They kept cattle and sheep rather than trying to pull crops out of the rocky, unwilling soil. There was a hill behind the house and from there Anne could see the sea: a thin grey-blue line drawn under the sky. She wondered if there were boats to America from that sea and thought that maybe Mrs Cuddehy could help her arrange a passage. She possessed a few pieces of jewellery of some value and she took to keeping these in a pocket of her skirt every time she went for a walk.

She might never have gone at all if Aunt Julia hadn't insisted on a dinner party. 'I didn't drag Cook to Galway to butter toast for children,' she complained over breakfast. Caroline relented and, it seemed to Anne, invited the most drab collection of people she could muster as though to ensure there would be no need for a second occasion. The estate manager, Mr Kingsley, arrived with his fiancée. There were two large farmers who spoke of nothing except the price of fodder. They were accompanied by wives who spoke of nothing except the price of fabric. Anne's attention drifted. Afterwards, the women went into the drawing room to play cards while the men remained at the table to smoke. Mr Kingsley's fiancée, a pleasant-faced woman in a lovely green dress, approached Anne.

'The meal was wonderful, thank you.'

'Cook is extraordinary, but there's no need to thank me for anything.'

Anne noticed the woman's slim waist and felt a sudden awareness of her body. She felt like she would burst the seams of her gown. It was unfortunate to be wearing the same shade as Caroline, who looked as thin as ever. Her bindings itched and pressed. Her breaths were shallow.

''I'm sure you must be very tired.' The woman placed her hand on Anne's arm and whispered, 'Because of your condition.'

'My condition?' Anne steadied herself against the nearest chair. Was this the end? Would she be exposed right here?

'Your mother told me. I won't say a word — I know it's very early.'

'My mother?'

'Yes, Mrs Kennedy.' The woman looked confused. Anne took a breath.

'Mrs Kennedy is my aunt.'

'Oh! Forgive me!' She clapped a hand over her mouth. 'I'm so sorry. I mistook you for—'

'My cousin. Would you excuse me? I must go to bed. The meal was very heavy.'

'I'm so stupid. Please forgive me. I've never been here before. Everything is so grand, I got mixed up during the introductions and—'

'There's no need to apologise.'

Everything seemed brighter and louder and yet less distinct. She didn't bother to excuse herself but went straight to her room. The next day she left the house before anyone was up, determined to find Mrs Cuddehy. She was grateful to Mr Kingsley's fiancée for spurring her to action. There was still time. Anne walked and walked, feeling her way through memory. She remembered her mother holding her hand and guiding her, pointing out what she should see.

'Keep your eye on that large oak over there, the one that's bigger than all the rest. That's due west. If you can see that, you won't get lost.'

'But it looks like all the other trees!'

'No, it doesn't. Come now, Anne. See how one branch juts out very low down? And how the crown has a pointed peak? No, every tree is different from every other if you look.'

Anne threw her shawl into the pond in the hopes that any searches would conclude that she'd drowned. As she walked, she worried that the cabin would not be there or that she would get lost. But finally she saw it, the stones looking like a tumbled-down wall except for the chimney and the thatch on top. There was a fenced field next to the house but there was no cow in it. Anne glanced around to reassure herself that there was no other house within sight. She wondered how much conversation she would need to make before she could explain the situation. Or maybe Mrs Cuddehy would know without her saying a word.

Anne knocked at the door, louder and louder. No one came. There was no smoke coming from the chimney. Maybe Mrs Cuddehy had gone to the village. She resolved to wait for her to return. She pushed on the door a little, knowing it wouldn't be locked.

Inside, the earthen floor had been swept clean but there wasn't a stick of furniture. Not a stool, not a bed nor the black pot that had always been on the go. No kettle. Cobwebs filled the corners and there was a rustle and flap of pigeons in the roof. Anne saw a slash of sky where the thatch had rotted and fallen in. The cottage was abandoned. She turned and pulled the door behind her, gulping back tears as she mounted the hillside. As she passed the pond, she noticed her shawl had sunk and disappeared.

Over dinner, Anne couldn't resist asking about Mrs Cuddehy.

'Oh, that's a very sad tale,' Aunt Julia said. 'Beaten to death, poor woman. About a year ago now. And by her own son. He'd gone mad, of course. His sister came up to the house here, raised the alarm. Mr Kingsley fetched the constables and when they arrived at the house, he didn't try to hide what he'd done at all. He kept saying he had "fixed her at last".'

'But what happened to the son? And her daughter?'

'Well Michael was declared innocent by reason of insanity. Spent a few months in an asylum I think. Works as a labourer on the farm now. Lodges with another farmer. His sister's gone so there's no one to cook for him. She sold up the lease and cottage to Mr Kingsley. Went to America.' Aunt Julia sunk her teeth into a second piece of Cook's rhubarb tart.

'But surely murder can't go unpunished? And his own mother! Would he not be seen as a danger to society?' Anne pushed her slice of tart away.

'Well he's never killed anyone else so far as I know.' Never killed anyone else! How could she say such things so calmly when the man had murdered his own mother?

That night she could not get Michael Cuddehy out of her head. She pictured him grasping a log with meaty hands and striking his mother again and again. She pictured the man as a baby, held in his mother's arms. She'd suckled him and loved him and for what? So that he could kill her and destroy Anne's last hope of escape.

Chapter Twenty-Three

Peakin

13th August, 1866 (later in the day)

Detective Peakin found Kitty Conroy's rooms easily enough. They were in a dirty but unremarkable tenement building on a street dotted with many others. He sniffed at the distinct sweet-salty smell of a bacon factor and the accompanying unpleasant odour of pig manure. Peakin thought they must be going all hours in an effort to keep the meat from tainting in the heat. Had Eliza been here, he wondered, begging for Kitty's help? She'd been particular about hygiene, making him wash at a little basin before he lay down.

He knocked twice on the door before pushing it open. It gave way with surprising ease.

'Miss Conroy?' he called into the gloom. There was a different smell in here and Peakin refused to consider what it might be composed of. Kitty Conroy's rooms were on the ground floor. Better than basement, but prone to damp and draughts. Less desirable than the floors above. Peakin knew that he would find the windows at the back sealed up against the fumes of the yard's overflowing privies.

'Miss Conroy?' he called again.

'I do be coming. Mr Mulligan, is it?'

'No, madam, it is Martin Peakin of the Dublin Metropolitan Police.'

A head emerged from behind the door, and a hand on the door itself suggested a reluctance in opening.

'Yes? You'll be finding no trouble in here, sir. Only a few babbies never give a woman even a bit of peace.'

As if summoned, a wail was raised. A second joined it.

'Please let me in, Miss Conroy, I'd like to ask you a few questions.'

The eyes betrayed nothing. Peakin thought she was less suspicious than she ought to have been.

'Alri', but you'll have to sit here while I'm at the feeding.' She opened the door into a forlorn little parlour. A partition that didn't reach the ceiling divided this 'room' from the scullery and a bedroom. The door to each was a grimy cloth. In the parlour were two baskets, their broken straws gnawed by rats. Their inhabitants made thin desperate cries that seemed to have no impact on Conroy. She stood staring at Peakin, one hand on her hip, despite declaring her intention to begin feeding. Peakin, who'd never taken any interest in infants, found himself wanting to lift one and soothe it.

'You get used to it,' said Conroy, reading his glance. 'I can't be pickin' 'em up every time they cry or I'd never get a lick done.' She signalled towards one of two stools in the bare room and Peakin sat.

To have three rooms to yourself would be a luxury, but he could hear the snores of Conroy's tenant coming from behind the partition. Judging from the straw in the corner, someone also slept in this room. She returned with two bottles of milk and Peakin found himself wondering how she kept it cool in this heat. As she lifted the first infant, its cries went silent and it clung to the bottle and sucked. A smell of excrement wafted across the room. Conroy replaced the infant in the basket and lifted the other. This one, evidently too young to hold the bottle itself, she cradled as it sucked thirstily.

'Has someone been complainin' about the noise again? Who was it? Mrs Kealy, I'll wager.'

'No, I'm afraid it's more serious than that. I'm investigating the death of an infant and I've been asked to make an inspection of nurses.'

'All the nurses in the city? Sure you'd be at that for the rest of the year.'

'Where are their mothers? The babies' mothers, I mean?'

'Well they're at work, aren't they?' Conroy addressed him as though he were an idiot. 'Was it Gem Ryan complained?'

'There was no complaint about noise. And what do the mothers work at?'

'All sorts. Laundry if they can get it.'

Peakin wondered how a woman with so little regard for the cleanliness of her offspring could work in laundry.

'And their husbands, what do they work at?'

'I'm sure I've never asked them. What business is it of mine? So long as they pay what they owe. It wasn't that gentleman from the asylum was it? Miller or something like. Sent his uppity little messenger round here to threaten me.' Miss Conroy looked unmoved.

'Threaten you about what?'

Conroy smiled broadly to reveal a selection of teeth in various states of decay. The smile aged her almost a decade.

'Takin' babbies from the wrong sort of women. Givin' the wrong sort of food. I think they's just worried I'm getting their customers. If they come to me they won't go throwin' themselves on the mercy of Mr Miller.'

'Mr Mills, I believe it is.'

'Yeah. Him. Sure he's no better than the workhouse. Worse, more like. You know what they say about him? That he sells them babies. And that when the women die there, he sells their bodies. To the doctors so they can cut them all up for show.'

Peakin found himself at a loss for words. He watched her put the infant to her shoulder and slap its back a few times, as though underscoring her point, before replacing it in the basket. Before he could think of something to say, she disappeared into the scullery corner with the bottle and returned, to Peakin's surprise, with a tea kettle. She stoked the fire and hung the kettle to boil then sat on the second stool across from Peakin. The other baby continued to suck in quiet solitude. Peakin thought he'd never seen anything so sad.

The door opened and a child entered, carrying an empty chamber pot. Peakin thought from her size that she could be no more than six, but it was hard to tell. Her eyes were too large for her face in the way that they are with children who are too thin. She waited for Kitty's instructions.

'Thankee my pet. Fill the water jugs now.'

'Can I eat then?' the child asked. Her voice was flat, and she barely seemed to have noticed Peakin's presence.

'You can. Please God these greedy ones will have left a drop o' milk for our tea.'

The child soon emerged from the kitchen with a large jug. Peakin couldn't imagine how she would bring it in again once it was full. He felt a sudden loathing for Kitty Conroy. His eyes scanned the room as he catalogued every evidence of sanitary indifference. Were poverty and filth inevitable bedfellows? No, they were not. He had seen neat and tidy tenements and this was not one of them.

'May I ask, Miss Conroy, how much do the mothers pay for your services?'

'For a babby? Two shillings a week and I supplies the food and clothing.'

Two shillings a week! For watered-down milk and unwashed nappies! Peakin calculated this would be half the wages of a laundress or a badly paid kitchen maid.

'And how many will you take at once?'

'Depends how many is asking.'

'But surely you could manage no more than two.'

'I've Sarah to help me,' she waved a hand towards the door, indicating the girl who had just left.

'And what else do you do for money?' Peakin had no business asking this, but Miss Conroy didn't seem to notice.

'I've a tenant. And I take in mending. I'm a dacent seamstress. Sarah sells fruit at the Four Courts sometimes.' Nothing untoward there, the same miserable calculations made across the city in rooms like this.

'Oughtn't Sarah to be in school?'

'She goes most days.'

Peakin was tired of talking around the subject.

'Has any of your charges ever died?' Kitty Conroy's features assembled into that blank countenance so familiar to police magistrates.

'Once in a while. Though it be no fault of me own. The poor wee things is often very weak when I get them, and I does me best but there's God's will to reckon with. They all get a Christian burial.'

Now we are getting somewhere, thought Peakin.

'Do you pay for their burials yourself?' Peakin tried to avoid sounding incredulous.

'That is for the mammies. I make sure they get the blessing and left with the priest. Is someone spreading lies about me? There do be some who want me business, detective. If any of them babbies gets sick, they go straight home. It's only rare they die with me.' Peakin stared but her face remained impassible. Like a sheep, he thought. He glanced again at the two little baskets. It was true that the babies seemed healthy enough. Dirty and thin, maybe, but that made them no different from the babies in any other room in the building.

'You'll be aware of the dead infant so recently found in the River Liffey?'

'Very sorry that was. There's always some as can't afford to keep 'em.'

'What do you mean by that?'

'I don't mean nothin' by that except what everyone, even gentlemen such as yourself, already knows. You can't think it was me threw it in there?'

'Well, Miss Conroy, I do thank you for your help,' Peakin said as he rose unsteadily from the stool. I'll get nothing further from her now, he thought. There was no point asking about Eliza just yet. Would Eliza really resort to the services of Kitty or her ilk? She was careful but even careful girls got into trouble. He'd accepted her departure from Mrs Wilson's, made no inquiries. Why hadn't he? He thought miserably that he would have to return here. He wondered how long the room's peculiar odours would cling to his moustache. He felt like going home to wash his face.

'I was just about to offer you a drop o' tea.' She sounded a little disappointed. He couldn't make heads nor tails of the woman. He was sure that she was robbing her clients blind but either she was a very good actress or she really believed she had nothing to hide.

'Thank you, Miss Conroy, but I have had my tea, for the morning anyway. Good day.'

She didn't get up and he let himself out into the hall. A woman was on the steps on her hands and knees engaged in a valiant attempt to push back the tide of filth that promised to engulf them all. He wondered how Sarah was getting on with her jug.

Back at Exchequer Court he wrote up yet another report for the inspector. He thought about what Kitty Conroy had told him about Zachariah Mills but he could hardly credit her view of things. Fiddler was also scribbling madly and he wondered if the content of his report was more promotion-worthy than his own. He was just about to file it and return to his rooms when the inspector walked in.

'Good evening, gentlemen.' Chairs scraped. 'No, no, sit. Just a quick word for Detective Peakin. I've had a note from the coroner. He's happy to close the inquest if there is nothing further to pursue. Is there anything further to pursue?'

Peakin could not decide between relief and disappointment. He looked down at his notebook. He heard the others turning pages but the pens had ceased and he knew they were all listening for his answer. Each of them calculating what it might mean for their own chances of promotion. The inspector leaned back on his heels, waited.

'I think at this point we have pursued all of the usual avenues and then some.'

'And nothing came of this evidence about a baby farmer?' Peakin tried to decide if his conviction that Kitty had done nothing was a scientific piece of deduction or merely personally convenient.

'No, nothing that could lead to an arrest. She showed no inclination to confess. To be frank, her lack of guile surprised me.' And Peakin felt that was true. Kitty didn't appear to be hiding anything, was unruffled by his visit.

'Then you can return at once to your usual beat.'

Chapter Twenty-Four

Rose

August 1866

Rose was glad when Anne and Mrs Kennedy returned. She was glad to be back in the house. The month had dragged. She ran out of gin. Somewhere around the start of July an occasional nightcap turned into a teacupful or two, depending on how exasperated she was with Denis. The weather warmed and they snapped and sniped at each other. Denis always apologised, even when he wasn't in the wrong. In the end she bought her own bottle with some money she'd hidden from Denis. She thought that he suspected about the gin. She almost wished he would accuse her and start a row, but he didn't. He only turned sad eyes on her every evening as she turned her back and left him to make his bed in the sitting room.

In the rising heat, she missed the cold indifference of Mrs Kennedy's house. She missed its stillness and the musty smell of fabric and carpets. She'd never understood why Anne found it depressing. She longed for the feeling of emptiness that the house gave her. Her own home felt full to bursting, with just the two of them and the ghost of their baby there.

On her first day back she stood in the hall and inhaled. Mrs Kennedy demanded that Johanna keep all the windows shut against the cholera and told everyone who would listen about the horrors of 49. Rose bit her tongue. Cholera, she knew, didn't care about closed windows. It crawled up the drains or wandered in with the servants.

The house's machinery slowed with the heat. Even Cook, accustomed to steaming in front of her ovens, coloured like a boiled beet. She had no choice but to stoke the fires and try to cook the meat that was going rancid. Rose helped her chase black clumps of flies around the kitchen. Then she heard Anne's bell and she went upstairs.

'Morning, Anne.' She surveyed her for signs of the month's changes. Should they embrace? The time had made them strange again. She remembered the bottle of gin and almost blushed with shame.

'Good morning, Rose. I'm so happy to see you.' Anne sat up against her pillows. As Rose came closer she could see that her shift was sticking to her. Her cheeks were red and feverish.

'Is everything alright, Anne?'

'I'm not sure. I seem to have had … an accident … in the night. Don't come too close, in case it's cholera. I'm having the most awful cramps in my stomach.'

'Pull back the covers, let me see.' When Anne didn't move, Rose stepped closer. 'It's my job, Anne. Even if I have to lift you out the bed, I'll be cleaning it up, cholera or no cholera.'

Anne pushed herself to the edge of the bed and stood up. She kept a hand gripped on the bed post and pulled down the sheets. A familiar smell brought Rose back to her own childbed. She had to stop herself from retching. Her heart was pounding now. She needed a little drink and then she would be fine.

'Your waters have broken. It was probably all the jolting in the train.' Rose tried to steady her racing thoughts enough to think for both of them. What were they going to do? The baby would come, today or tomorrow. Anne couldn't leave this room. She might need a doctor. She'd have to tell Mrs Kennedy. Who else would help them? Anne was crying. She should have been thinking and planning while Anne was away instead of feeling sorry for herself and fighting with Denis. She didn't know how she could help but she would have to. There was no one else.

'I thought I would have more time,' Anne said. Her voice had just the edge of a childish whine to it. 'To do something. To decide what to do. We counted the weeks.' Rose held her breath, listening for Johanna or Mrs Kennedy in the hall.

'I can help you. I helped me ma deliver a baby once or twice. But I think you should tell Mrs Kennedy.' She gave Anne's shoulder a little squeeze and felt her flinch.

'No.' Anne's voice was steady, demanding Rose's agreement. 'If she finds out I'll go to the workhouse. Promise me you won't tell her.' It was an absurd threat. Rose didn't believe she would make it down the stairs; nor that Mrs Kennedy would be so cruel. But she'd seen women do things she did not think possible while in the throes of labour. In a surge of nausea she remembered the demands she'd made that had gone unheeded, how Denis and her mother had tried to comfort her as she bled and bled. The doctor's face when he'd finally been called. She couldn't let that happen to Anne. But for now she would keep everyone away, she would gather the things she would need.

'I'll tell her you have a fever.'

'She'll think it's the cholera. She'll call Dr Mapother.'

'I'll offer to nurse you. To wait and see. She won't want anyone to think it's in the house.'

'But what'll we do after? When it's come?' Anne clung to the bed post. Her chest moved up and down in pain or panic or both.

'Leave it to me,' Rose said. She would think of something. There was always the possibility of leaving it on the steps of the workhouse. She'd like to leave it right in front of Dr Kelly's door. Screaming and carrying on so the neighbours would come out to have a good peep. But what if it arrived in daylight? She could hardly march unnoticed through the house and streets with a wailing infant, no matter how she bundled it. She helped Anne into a clean shift and changed the bed.

Once she was out in the hallway she took huge gulps of air, tried to steady herself. She found the gin where she'd hidden it and took two great swallows. She thought again about telling Mrs Kennedy. Rich people had ways of solving problems. As she served breakfast, she explained that Anne was poorly.

'I thought she might have taken a turn on the train,' Mrs Kennedy said, showing no evidence of surprise. 'She went quite pale. Terrible rattling. And so crowded. I don't see how anyone believes them to be an improvement on the stage coach.'

'I've only been on one meself, Mrs Kennedy. Just out to Kingstown. It did jolt a bit.'

'That Galway train would shake your teeth loose. My leg is sore again, I was up all night.'

'I'm sorry to hear that.'

'And about Anne,' Mrs Kennedy lowered her voice and leaned towards Rose. 'What do you think it is? Tell me the truth Rose.' She froze. 'Do you think it could be cholera?'

'I don't think so.' She relaxed a little. This was not a lie at least. 'But don't you be worrying. I'll mind her. I'll go to the chemist for a few things.'

'Thank you, Rose.'

Rose tried to hide her alarm at Anne's dishevelment when she returned. Mrs Kennedy had given her plenty of money for the chemist. She bought a few cholera tonics just in case she had to account for the purchases. The bottles shouted all kinds of nonsense about strengthening the body and purging poisons. She sniffed one of them and it made her nose sting. She bought a whole jar of opium lozenges after arguing with the chemist about whether she could be sure they contained opium and not just arrowroot and sugar.

'Anne, I think you should get back in bed,' she said, trying to keep her voice cheerful. She wondered if she'd been so wretched. It seemed impossible that it was over a year ago now. 'I have something for the pain.'

'Alright, Rose,' Anne crawled back under the covers, childlike.

'Here, take this.' Anne swallowed the pill she was given. 'Now lean forward, let me push on your back. It helps with the pain.' Anne relaxed a little, her shoulders dropped.

'Where did you learn how to do that Rose?'

'My mother.'

Rose remembered how the soothing had made her feel even worse: reducing the pain only amplified her thoughts. At some point during the labour she felt the struggle become life or death, as though her baby wanted to enter the world by ripping her apart. Neither her mother nor Denis seemed to notice this change. Only the doctor, when he was called, had known. Only the doctor had wanted to save her life. Rose was relieved when it was all over, when the baby arrived dead and she was still alive. She was sorry, of course. And full of guilt. She knew she would never do it again. She would never let Denis make her pregnant again.

Oh God, she thought, what if this kills Anne? Then it will be my fault that I didn't tell Mrs Kennedy. That I didn't send for a doctor. And what on earth was she going to do with the baby when it arrived and began to scream? Would Anne be able to suckle it, just to keep it quiet? If she could do that, if she could just keep it quiet until dark, then there was a chance that Rose could bring it to the workhouse. Leave it there. She had better go for what was needed. But first she needed just another sip of gin.

When Rose returned with the cloths and the kettle, Anne seemed almost unconscious. The room was filled with the sharp fumes of vomit. Rose had to waste valuable clean cloths on wiping up the floor. Anne came to herself a little as Rose cleaned her mouth, wiped her brow. She looked pale and small and feverish.

'You'll have to go now, tend to your work Rose. Otherwise my aunt will suspect something is wrong. She'll worry and call the doctor.' Rose tried to disguise her fear. How could she have counted the weeks wrong? How could she have been so unprepared? Anne gripped her hand, as if trying to reassure her. The grip tightened as another pain came. 'The best thing you can do is to keep everyone away from me.'

'Yes, of course. But you'll ring the bell if you need anything? You won't be foolish?'

'No, I won't be foolish. And don't you do anything foolish either.' Rose coloured, knowing that Anne had smelt the gin on her breath. She smiled her smallest smile, curtsied. She went out the door and came straight back in.

'You're going to ring when you feel the head pushing, right? It will feel like it's coming out your back passage, like you need the privy. You'll need me then.'

Anne nodded, her eyes closed and her fists balled around two handfuls of bedclothes.

The bell didn't ring, though Rose imagined that it had several times. Cook told her that she looked as jumpy as a cat. Rose kept moving away from her, hoping that she wouldn't get a whiff of her breath. She served Mrs Kennedy lunch and then dinner. She tried to answer her questions about Anne without telling any lies. All the while she had her ears pricked up, listening for a sound upstairs that she would have to explain or for Anne ringing the bell. When she'd cleared the dishes and persuaded Mrs Kennedy that she would spend the night in case Anne needed her, she had to stop herself from running back up the stairs.

Rose saw that Anne had not followed her instruction to ring but there was no time to chide her as she squatted miserably over a heap of cloths next to the bed. Rose held her hand, whispered to her. Later she would have no idea how she'd survived it all. How she'd stopped herself from fainting or the images from taking her over and pulling her down into herself. She was glad for the swig of whiskey she'd taken straight from the bottle in the study, not caring if someone caught her. The smell of blood and sweat and urine and the hidden folds of bodies filled her nose. Her hands were sticky. The baby came out in a sudden rush, slippery with Anne's muck. A boy. Rose cut the cord, wiped him down and he flailed his limbs and began to whimper. Anne's face contorted with panic and Rose thought she might begin to wail herself.

'It's okay, shush shush. Here Anne, if you just suckle him. You need to make one more push to get everything out. Just keep him quiet a little while. I'll take him then, I'll take him away.' Her mind churned through possibilities as she tried to clean up the mess of blood and afterbirth. Where? Where would she take him? There was Kitty of course. A friend from school. She might take him on the promise of payment. It would buy them some time. Anne might give in, speak to Mrs Kennedy. Mrs Kennedy would know what to do, Rose was certain of it. While she thought, she pressed the baby into Anne's arms, tried to help her guide him to the breast. There would be no milk yet, but the comfort would soothe him.

The baby wailed. Anne was holding him too close, pressing him too hard and he couldn't find the breast.

'Let me help you, Anne. At least get back into the bed.'

'No, don't touch me. Don't touch me please.' The baby went quiet.

Rose noticed the stiffness in her limbs from crouching on the floor as she stood up. Anne stayed sitting on the floor, her back against the bed. The room filled with silence. She could hear Anne's breathing, great puffs in through her nose. Something was wrong. What was it? Rose looked at the baby again. His arms stopped flailing, they hung limp. Oh God, what had Anne done?

He rested, pink and silent, in Anne's lap. Rose couldn't see his chest rising and falling. What now what now what now? Anne closed her eyes and didn't move to stop her as she picked him up and swaddled him in the cleanest bit of cloth that remained. She was sure that he was dead and she didn't know what she would do now. Anne was in no fit state to do anything. Rose tucked her back into bed, bundled the mess into the bottom of the wardrobe. Panicked, she hurried out to the privy with the baby.

When she returned Mrs Kennedy and Cook huddled in the hall outside of Anne's room, whispering to one another.

'Is everything alright Rose?' Mrs Kennedy asked.

'I think so, Anne's vomited again and it upset her.' This was at least partly true.

Rose opened the door just wide enough for her to slip in and block their view. She lowered her voice. 'She's gone back to sleep. But I do think she's taken a turn for the better. The purges are further apart and she took some broth.' She could hear her own breathing, Mrs Kennedy shifting her weight on the carpet. Cook leaned over and spoke into Mrs Kennedy's ear.

'Are you very sure Rose? We heard a terrible noise, a wailing. I thought for a moment the banshee had arrived.' Rose heard Cook stifle a snort but Mrs Kennedy's voice was full of worry. 'I must have been half asleep myself, I woke up certain that Anne was dying.' She reached out and put a hand on Rose's hand, as if to prove to herself that Rose wasn't the banshee.

'No, there's no banshee here. I think all you heard was Anne cry out. She doesn't like being sick. I think she's afraid. But I'm sure she's getting better.'

'Well, I won't disturb her sleep, then. Thank you, Rose, I don't know what I would do without you.' And then she turned and walked down the hall. Cook glanced back at Rose but said nothing.

Rose almost wished they had pressed more, had made her tell. The lies lodged like unchewed bread in her throat. Holy Mary mother of God, what would Denis say? He would throw her out. She prayed that Anne would live. She couldn't face Mrs Kennedy if she didn't.

Rose decided that she would carry the body to the river. She cleaned him as best she could, wet a cloth in Mrs Kennedy's holy water font and baptised him. He looked so restful. She checked him several times for breath but felt nothing when she placed a hand in front of his mouth.

'I claim you for Christ, by the sign of his cross,' she recited and she traced a cross on his forehead with the holy water. 'Holy Father forgive me and forgive the child, he done nothing wrong.'

She felt no certainty that the baptism would achieve anything, but the fact that she'd tried gave her some small relief. Forgiveness and acceptance were the only lessons she'd ever valued from the Church.

She made sure the body was tucked firmly into the basket. She considered bringing a candle with her and then decided against it. She would have to feel her way. As she crossed the garden she checked that the windows of the house were dark. The garden gate creaked as she knew it would. She didn't turn back after she stepped into Grenville Lane.

The air was still warm, the heat hadn't broken. The darkness felt thick. Rose wanted to reach out and part it with her hands. The gaslights produced a glow near to them but seemed unable to push away the black. Down Gardiner Street she walked, where a few lit windows made yellow rectangles on the street. As she reached the Custom House she realised that she'd been walking as though she were a stooped old woman and felt the relief in her shoulders as she raised herself up straight. Rose was glad to hear the sounds of men at work and almost forgot that her errand was a secret one. Once or twice she startled when she thought she felt the basket move.

She followed the quay wall along the river, looking for a quiet place for her business. She'd turned towards the city without thinking. As though she were going for an ordinary message. She passed Sackville Bridge. A few policemen on their beat regarded her but she kept her head up, her steps purposeful.

The dome of the Four Courts appeared, visible only because she knew it was there. Across Richmond Bridge was the Church of the Immaculate Conception. Here was the spot. Sorrow replaced fear as she pictured the black water covering the little body, filling it up.

The streets were quiet, just the distant rumble of a cart. The body seemed to stir in her arms as she lifted it, but she dismissed this as folly. Her hands shook as she reached over the side of the bridge.

When the wail began she almost dropped him in fright. Her guilty conscience was playing tricks on her. But when she drew him towards her he flailed with surprising strength. She stood staring at his angry screaming face, unable to believe what she was seeing. Not knowing what else to do, she swaddled him in the sheet and put him to her shoulder. She looped the basket over her arm and began to walk again. Faster and faster, down Arran Quay and up Church Street until she turned down May Lane, towards Kitty Conroy.

Chapter Twenty-Five

Denis

14th August, 1866

When Zachariah Mills first announced his intention to hold a charity event for the society, Denis imagined something rather like the usual Easter or Christmas bazaars where women sold needlework and lace. The Lord Lieutenant would swoop in and buy handfuls of bog ornaments that Denis imagined he later used to build up the fires. Everyone else would parade slowly through the room, admiring homely displays and drinking strong tea.

But Mr Mills had something far grander in mind. Denis had been to the exhibition in 1865 and the 'Crystal Palace' impressed him then. He understood from the newspapers that the structure was smaller than its older sister in London, but the soaring glass ceiling ornamented with coloured flags seemed no less marvellous for that. The exhibition was long over and Denis wondered whether Dublin really needed any palaces. Mr Mills must have some important friends, he thought.

Nothing could convince Rose to attend. He'd suggested that she buy a new dress for the occasion but this was met with scorn.

'Do you think you can buy me company?' she'd snapped. 'Och, Denis I didn't mean nothing. I have me suspicions about Mr Mills and all his charitable works.'

'Why on earth? He's a respectable man who's more generous than most. What is there to be suspicious about?'

'I've heard tell of the sort of institution his Asylum for Women is. Don't pretend you're foolish Denis. You've heard the same things. About every one of them institutions.'

'They're only trying to help people. Nothing is perfect, Rose. It's bound to go wrong sometimes. And where is there for women to go to? When even their families don't want them?'

He was sure Rose was exaggerating about Mr Mills just to wound him. She'd continued slipping further away from him. He didn't know what to do. When he ignored her insults and provocations, she got angrier. When he responded, she stomped and slammed doors on her way to their bedroom. Had she met someone else? Maybe someone who could give her more than he could? Someone in Mrs Kennedy's house? Someone younger or richer or better at conversation? He couldn't sleep after they argued: he lay awake on the settee, reviewing their three years of marriage and trying to figure out how he could start it over. If he could just go back to the time when Rose seemed to love him and figure out what had happened. He thought that her grief at the loss of the child would pass. The anger he didn't understand.

So Rose stayed home and Denis entered the palace alone. He'd worried about the quality of his own suit of clothes, but frugality prevailed. It was his wedding suit: the best he could afford at the time.

The room was steaming. Thousands of panes of glass had been letting in sunlight all day and the sky still wasn't dark. He could see the condensation on them. Like they were in one of those glass boxes of plants, what were they called?

Terrariums, that was it. He took his seat with a few others as a young woman sat down at the piano. Anne Mulhall, the programme had said. The name seemed familiar but he couldn't think from where. Most people were still talking and moving around so it was hard to hear but he liked music so he tried to focus. It made him want to close his eyes, it was so clearly the sound of somewhere else. Waves lapping the shore, or like one of those paintings of the muses dancing with their skirts trailing. In and out, up and down. He felt it in his chest, felt its loss when she stopped.

Mr Mills stood to address the audience. His voice shook Denis from the pleasure of the music as bodily as if Mills had seized him with two hands. He was back in the stuffy greenhouse misted with human breath. He watched Mills, searching his face for signs of the monster Rose had described. One who profited from locking women up and selling their babies. He just didn't see it.

'Good evening all. It is so wonderful to see so many ladies and gentlemen here, ready to offer their support to this worthy cause and to make sure that the crime of infanticide cannot get its grips into this city and country as it has done in our sister isle.'

Mills continued for some minutes, enumerating the many faults of England and describing in lurid detail the underworld of London. To Denis's great surprise, he heard his name. His face grew hot.

'We are lucky to have in this city such concerned citizens as Mr Denis Doyle. A humble butcher who, as you know from the papers, was instrumental in finding the most recent unfortunate victim of the heinous crime of infanticide. If more people conducted themselves like Mr Doyle, if more citizens were on their alert, then we should soon sweep this city of the crime altogether. Please stand up, Mr Doyle, receive your due.' Denis wished that Mills had told him he planned to do this. He felt the eyes of the room upon him as he stood, tried to appear sufficiently humble to satisfy them. A ripple of applause greeted him. He sat.

After the concert, the pianist was back. The crowd ignored her. Released from the tedium of listening to the singers, they rose from their seats to sip and talk. Anne Mulhall seemed not to notice their indifference, intent on her task. When she was finished, Denis approached the piano.

'You play so well,' he said. She put her hands in her lap.

'Thank you.' Denis noticed that sweat gleamed on her forehead.

'I know nothing of music but it must be quite tiring to play like that.'

'I suppose it is. I don't think of it in that way, but yes, I am tired now. It is so dreadfully hot in here. You must excuse me, I have to find my aunt. How nice to meet you.' He hadn't introduced himself and neither had she. He watched her walk away and it struck him that she was in pain. Her gait was uneven, like a horse that was going lame. He saw her greet an older woman that he recognised as Mrs Kennedy. He'd met her once, back when Rose had started working for her. She'd asked him to call on the pretence that a husband might want to meet a wife's employer. Of course, it was Mrs Kennedy who'd wanted to inspect him. The piano player must be the niece who lived with Mrs Kennedy. The one who'd been ill. How strange that Rose hadn't wanted to come and hear her play. He thought of trying to approach her, introduce himself properly this time. He should have asked after her health. He should have said he was Rose's husband. But he watched her fold into the crowd of other people dressed like her and move away.

Chapter Twenty-Six

Anne

August 1866

In the end, he forced his way into the world. He parted Anne's flesh, pushing through her in his eagerness to arrive. For months he'd been an invisible thing, made only of movement and a distortion of her own body. She'd wanted him gone, though she couldn't think of the pills as trying to kill him. Instead, she'd be removing a part of herself that she didn't want. An act of restoration or of reclamation. Her body would be returned to her, to be governed by her mind and according to her own appetites. But he wanted to live as much as Anne did. None of her efforts would dislodge him. He clung to her like she clung to dignity. She would have admired this tenacity, this ferocity of his livingness, if it hadn't been at her expense.

Rose didn't understand her wishes and maybe Anne didn't understand them either. But when he came, when he slid through a slick of her blood and tried to announce himself to the world, Anne decided that he couldn't stay. And so she held him against her, she squeezed him to her as tightly as she could. At first she only wanted him to be silent. She'd kept her secret for so long and she didn't want everything to be undone now. As she pressed, she wanted to make him dissolve back into her, return to her flesh, no longer a separate life of his own. Like some contortion of Genesis: body becomes rib becomes clay.

The last thing she remembered was Rose talking to her, saying something she couldn't hear over the sounds of her own body, the blood inside her pumping and whooshing.

Then Rose went silent, her face turned white.

When Anne woke up it was still dark. She was in her bed with the covers pulled up to her chin but shivering. She could feel blood stiffening the back of her shift. Around her there was nothing but a thick blackness. She was cold and limp. She was sure that she'd been swallowed by the river. She opened her mouth, expecting the grateful water to rush in and push the remaining air from her lungs.

She gasped and opened her eyes. Rose. Rose was knocking. Calling.

'Anne, are you alright? The mistress does be worried. You've the door locked.'

Anne blinked. She saw her wardrobe, doors closed. There was the window, a slice of light between the curtains. Her dressing table looked the same, all the ribbons and hairpins in their neat boxes. She was not at the bottom of the river. But why did its vapours cling to her hair? Why did her sheets smell of its effluvia? Why did her mouth taste like a sewer? She pushed herself from the bed, crossed the floor and unlocked the door.

'Jesus, Mary and Joseph. The state of you.' Anne looked down, studying the streaks of blood and what might have been vomit or urine or something worse. 'Johanna's bringing up the bath. Now let's get that off you. Fit for the fire I think.'

Rose clucked and fussed in her usual way but her mouth was set firm and there were dark crescents of exhaustion under her eyes.

Anne raised her arms to let Rose remove the shift. She put a robe around her and Anne sat facing the window while they waited for the bath to arrive. Thunderous clouds hung in the air, pressing down on the city and wrapping it in heat.

'Everything looks the same.'

'Still no rain. See how the grass has gone brown,' Rose said. She ignored Anne, pretended not to notice her desire to talk about what had happened. Anne didn't have the energy to press her.

'Will you open the window?'

'Are you sure? There's a horse festering in one of them lanes, the knackers haven't collected it. The whole square smells like death.' Rose covered her mouth with her hand. Anne watched her straighten herself out like she was shaking creases from a dress. She said nothing about what Anne had done and what Anne had made her do. She couldn't meet Anne's eyes as she bound her breasts. She pulled too tight, pinching Anne's skin between folds of cloth, but she didn't complain.

Anne wanted to ask, to be sure that he was gone, but the words stuck in her teeth. When she was alone she examined her body, trying to feel what had happened. She squeezed the pouchy skin at her waist until it brought tears to her eyes. Her breasts ached.

Alone in her room, Anne recited her regrets like an incantation. Should have gone somewhere, to one of the homes. Should have let herself be flagellated with the shame of him, allowed Sisters to show her mercy that they didn't believe she deserved. Should have taken him and fled. Swaddled him and gone begging on the road. Should have left him at the workhouse door and fled alone.

She wondered what Rose had told her aunt, why everyone had left her alone. And then she fell back asleep.

Anne woke on the second day convinced that he was still there, still in the room somewhere. She lurched from the bed. She knew she had to find him before her aunt did. Johanna or Cook would smell the death hidden in her mattress or in the bottom of the wardrobe. Where was he? When Rose came in with her breakfast, she'd torn the covers from the bed and the dresses from the wardrobe. She was on her hands and knees, searching.

'What have you lost? Here, let me help you,' Rose said. She put down the tray and joined Anne on the floor. 'Is it a necklace or a collar?' Anne couldn't answer, only sat on the floor and sobbed.

'I thought he was still here,' she said between heaving breaths.

'Oh Anne, I promise that he's gone. He's really gone.'

'What will happen to me now?'

'Nothing will happen. Only wait.' Rose's certainty gave Anne no relief at all.

Rose straightened up the bed and put the dresses back in the wardrobe. After she left, Anne kept searching for the body. She lifted her mattress to be sure, rifled through the wardrobe another time, pulled boxes out from under the bed. She opened her box of mementos, tried to soothe herself with memories of home. No matter how she pressed the letters to her face she couldn't get the scent into her nose. It was full of the stench of her own body and its horrors. She cried so hard that her tears began to blot the pages and blur the words, threatening to erase her mother. She put them away.

On the third day Anne felt that she'd begun to resume her shape from a formless puddle of grief and fear. Aunt Julia came as far as the door. She didn't like illness of any kind and was convinced all infirmities were catching.

'I did tell you all that walking would do harm in the end,' she called to Anne from the safety of the hall. 'And in this heat, as well.' Anne hadn't been out walking for almost a week, but she was grateful that her aunt hadn't noticed and she didn't bother to correct her.

'Yes, Aunt Julia. I'm sure I just need some rest. I'll be more careful from now on.'

When Rose came in to bring her lunch she told Anne that she would have to get up. There could be no more hiding in her room. Anne wanted to roll on the floor and throw a fit. She couldn't leave the room. It was impossible. She would live here now, she thought, one of those sad curiosities that some families kept upstairs.

'The mistress is starting to worry, Anne. I've kept her away as best I can,' Rose said. 'I can bind your chest until the milk stops. No one will notice anything. You're as pale as a shade, you need to get the blood circulating.'

Anne knew that Rose was right and she couldn't think of anything else to do. She forced herself downstairs where she tried to play the piano. Her fingers were clumsy and stiff. 'Perhaps you need a few more days to recover,' her aunt suggested before asking Anne to read to her. Anne pronounced the words without understanding them until her aunt fell asleep. Then she stared out the window, pushing horrific visions from her mind one at a time. During tea she was an actress waiting for the curtain to fall, glancing to the wings for the stage hand who'd disappeared without doing his job. By the time she got back to bed she was exhausted to her very core and slept deeply.

Her body betrayed her by beginning to heal. All the signs of the past months began to disappear from her flesh while the wounds grew deeper in her mind. When she sat in front of the mirror she wondered at how depraved she must be that she did not go mad, but instead began to look quite well. There was no outward sign of the blackness within her. On the fourth day Anne said to Rose, 'I can't bear it, I'll confess to the police. I'm finished with all the secrets.'

'Nonsense, there's nothing to confess. Try to stop worrying. What's past is past.' Rose said. But how could she believe such a thing? Anne had everything to confess. She didn't know how Rose could look at her, dress her, touch her as though she was still the same person.

'I won't tell them about you. I never will,' Anne said. 'They won't even suspect a thing.' Rose looked uncomfortable.

'There's your aunt to think of. She might send me packing and what'll I do without a job or any references?'

'She wouldn't do that,' Anne said, knowing that Rose was right. But Rose had the shop and her husband. She wouldn't be out on the street, would she?

Part IV

If you hovered above the city like a crow, you would see coaches, hackneys, carts, dogs, horses, mules and people flowing around the city in a constant stream. The river cut through the middle of it all, forcing the stream onto the bridges where everyone was pinched together with no regard for station. Children stood along the quay walls, flicking crumbs at the gulls. They didn't watch the gulls snatching them out of the air, diving and swooping and never breaking the river's surface. Instead, they watched the stream of people for a billfold left unprotected, a bulging pocket, a handbag with an especially slight strap.

Kitty told Sarah that the metal bridge was her favourite spot for dipping. The turnstiles creaked, the tollkeeper turned to share a joke, and Sarah ducked the bar onto the bridge. She didn't know the man was fresh from the jeweller's on Grafton Street. He froze just when her fingers curled around the box. People gathered as she tried to twist away, the man gripping her wrist. She dropped it and ran, without turning to see the prize she'd left behind. The box tumbled and opened and the little silver heart on the chain slid out and into the river. She'd been swallowed by a laneway before he looked up from the sight of the locket sinking into the current and joining the silvery fish headed out to sea.

Chapter Twenty-Seven

Peakin

15th August, 1866

'I'm afraid that's it. A disappointment in some ways, a relief in others.' The inspector had at least called him to his office and saved Peakin further embarrassment in front of the men. The coroner and the inspector agreed between them that there was no case to pursue.

Out on the street Peakin reflected unhappily on his own response. He'd inquired, carefully he thought, about the possibility of an assignment to the Fenian conspiracy.

'We have plenty of men on that for the moment, Peakin,' the inspector said, shaking his head with finality.

'Well, perhaps you would consider me should there be something in that line,' Peakin replied, unable to stop himself from shifting on his feet.

'Of course. In the meantime, I suggest that you give the pawnbrokers your full attention. Theft is, after all, a significant crime. It is in such *inconsequential* matters, as they may seem to you, in the resolution of thefts and the *deterrence* of violence, that we endear ourselves to the citizens. Police work is grind rather than glory.'

'Yes, of course.' Peakin tried not to spit the words with the venom he felt. He knew as well as anyone that police work was grind. Hadn't he spent eighteen years grinding his boots to powder against miles of Dublin streets? Years of collaring drunks, sniffing out overflowing privies, fining drivers for beating their horses to death. No, he hadn't joined the force for glory. It was only that the Fenian business had given him a taste of what might be.

Peakin conjured happy memories of the previous summer, the do-or-die excitement over G Division. He'd interviewed informants, conducted raids: real detective work. He'd been part of the raid that closed their newspaper office. Afterwards people treated him differently. True, some of them seemed to disapprove of this interference in politics with the police siding firmly with the Crown. But they seemed a force to be reckoned with and maybe even feared. He for one walked taller.

Now Peakin dragged his body by force of will through the heavy streets. He considered tying his handkerchief over his face but he didn't want anyone to see how the river vapours had begun to turn his stomach. He couldn't eat his breakfast, only cut up the egg and nibbled at the toast. He lived on cups of tea, apples and potatoes. The newspapers ranted on about avoiding raw fruit during a cholera outbreak but it was meat he couldn't face. He was slowly starving, his belt gathering the waist of his trousers like a pleated curtain. He knew his body needed more nourishment but he was also glad to save the coins. He wondered if this lack of appetite was a sign that his health was beginning to fail. But no, he reassured himself, it was just the heat.

He caught up with the newest two of his constables coming from the Coombe. He saw them from a distance and imagined that every thief and dishonest pawnbroker had already memorised their faces. They'd joined the force only six months ago, and as immigrants to the city they still had a less than perfect grasp of its geography. They spoke in a slow country way, using expressions that Dubliners sniffed at. Within a year they would learn to adjust their speech and their gait but for now they stood out like a couple of fat wood pigeons trying to roost in a tree full of rooks. They cooed when everyone else cawed. No one was going to be intimidated into a confession by a wood pigeon.

They paused as he approached, eager faces ready to make a report.

'Continue on your beat, gentlemen. I'll expect your report in the evening.' He was just about to bid them good day when he realised that there was nothing to stop him making a few personal inquiries about Eliza. Not continuing the investigation exactly, but perhaps reassuring himself by trying to locate her. To make sure that she was safe and well, that was all. Now that there would be no need to bring her in for questioning. 'There is another small matter, if you please.'

They leaned forward.

'I require your utmost secrecy. There is a young woman, a Miss Elizabeth Mooney, who has gone missing. She has fallen, the poor creature, but her relatives wish to bring her home. Back to Galway. If possible, they wish to recover her and bury her past.'

The larger one spoke first. He was a great gom of a man and Peakin thought he was a loss to whatever farm he'd fled. His suit, which the police required the men to pay for themselves, was made from a worsted wool so coarse that it looked like sacking. He was out of breath, accustomed neither to the heat nor the constant walking.

'Yes, Sergeant Peakin. We can do that. And where should we inquire?' How could Peakin express to them the delicacy that was required? And what if they did find her, what did he plan to do then? Or worse, what if they found no one but managed to alert half of Dublin that Martin Peakin, Acting Sergeant of G Division of the Dublin Metropolitan Police, was looking for a whore for no other reason than his own sentimentality?

'I cannot emphasise enough how careful you must be. You must not spook her or she will bolt. When you visit brokers simply tell them what I have told you, but ensure that you do not speak openly in front of the customers. Insist on privacy. Explain the delicacy of the situation. The relatives do not wish for anything to appear in the papers. You are not to pursue her, you just turn over any news to me.'

'Understood. And will we tell them that we are searching on your behalf?'

'No. You are to say nothing of the kind. You are asking the questions, you are the detectives. You do not give information, you receive it. Only ask the questions.'

Peakin watched them walk away, and considered that he'd probably made a terrible mistake. He made a few more rounds of the pawnshops, circling past Patrick Fennell's and James McNulty's and Peter Keon's. He didn't enter any of them, he simply walked by the fronts of them and reassured himself they were still there. He had no energy for conversation or for the song and dance of his usual inquiries. He found a few of his informers in their usual haunts: a particular stool in a public house; shoeing horses in a stable; selling plucked hens from a cart. They'd nothing to offer except some complaint about the heat ('These hens do be rotting while they're still alive, and faster once me da has wrung their necks,') or a rumour about the cholera ('Did ya hear of the man arrived from Liverpool? Only home a day before he began to show signs. The whole household succumbed. Turned blue and all, so they said.')

Thus he whiled away the afternoon and returned to the office for the evening's flurry of paperwork. He filed two reports on cases that had been closed, filling them in with an elegant rounded script that he reserved for jobs completed. Then he leafed through the open cases and soon returned to a dejected humour. A review of the state of his finances did not improve things.

He took his tea in a chop house where he disapproved of the greasy sauce that pooled on his plate and amused the owner by asking for a dry chop and a raw carrot. Even the second chop tasted too much of the smell of sheep for his liking and he filled the gaps in his stomach with potatoes and bread (which he also ate dry).

After tea he walked through a few of his favourite rookeries where he spoke to anyone who would greet him and gathered no information about anything. Even criminality slowed in the stultifying air. Who could think of anything but a breeze? Who could want anything more than a cold drink to relieve his thickened tongue? One of his stockings rubbed painfully in his shoe. Every man he passed on the street had darkened patches of sweat under their arms and with horror he realised that he must have them too. He tried to examine himself in a shop window but couldn't see anything. He felt as wilted and greasy as the chop he'd barely managed to eat.

By nine in the evening he found himself turning towards Mrs Wilson's. He approached it in the most indirect way he could think of. Now that he had men making inquiries about Eliza it seemed even more important to be cautious. He took off his hat as he approached the door.

Mrs Wilson could smell a customer and she appeared in the hall within seconds. She paused and looked him over. She seemed to be waiting for him to say something.

'I appreciate your discretion, Mrs Wilson,' he said.

'Always. I hope you haven't any idea of hunting up Miss Mooney.'

'You'll be relieved to know that the case has been closed. Of course, I would personally like to speak with her.' Mrs Wilson snorted and rolled her eyes to the ceiling.

'You think you're some kind of gentleman, don't you? You're not so different as you think, Mr Peakin. In here you're just like any other man. You gave Eliza the same as what the other men did, nothing more and nothing less.'

Peakin had no answer for this that he wanted to say out loud. He climbed the stairs slowly, not wanting to arrive out of breath and sweating even more profusely.

Peggi's door was open. He wondered if she had heard Mrs Wilson's little speech.

'Well now, officer, I wasn't expecting you back so soon,' Peggi said as he put his head in the door.

'Here I am, expected or not,' he replied and closed the door behind him. He began to remove some outer layers of clothing. This time he folded them himself and placed them on her chair.

She always called him officer. Since he wore no uniform he didn't know if she thought he was in the army or the police or had chosen this title for some other reason.

She watched him from a seat next to the open window, a fan moving slowly up and down in her hand. The room was even hotter and more still than the street. Stray pieces of her hair stuck to the back of her neck and the sides of her face. She wore only a thin robe and her shift. The covers on the bed were peeled back, possibly airing the smells of a previous customer. Peakin saw the toe of a stocking peeking out from where the covers touched the floor and wondered if it was Peggi's or someone else's. It was too bright in the room, this time of year was uncomfortable for gentlemen with any modesty.

Peggi read his thoughts and pulled the curtains over the nets. The room fell into a murky dark and immediately felt even warmer. She took off the robe and the shift and hung them carefully on hooks, shaking them out to prevent wrinkling. Then she lay on the bed and waited for him to finish undressing himself. He soon lost patience for folding the clothes and piled them on the floor beside him. The fucking was over almost as soon as it began, the feel of his sweat between their bodies both disgusted and aroused him. He spent no time in touching Peggi or in talking to her but pushed himself inside her and hurried through until he'd spent himself. Then he collapsed into a black sleep on the bed.

He felt her shaking him awake at the same time as he heard a knock on the door. 'You'll have to be moving on, officer. I've a busy night,' she said.

When he opened his eyes she was dressed again in her robe and shift, her hair was refastened and she smelled of soap. How was it that she was the whore but he felt dirty, he wondered, lying in sheets damp with his sweat. The sheets where she'd soon be on her back again with someone else.

As he dressed he was seized by exhaustion. Was this to be his life? A not-quite gentleman with no wife or children who frittered away his salary on whores until he retired with no achievements to speak of or savour? A name in the register book and nothing more?

Chapter Twenty-Eight

Denis

16th August, 1866

Denis didn't like to admit that Zachariah Mills's speech had affected him but the truth was he found himself viewing the city with different eyes. As he walked to Mass he watched women on the street. Young ladies, dressed as prim as can be, let their pimply suitors kiss them with only feigned horror. They leaned their bodies into them, clung to their arms. He saw groups of soldiers on the prowl and women eager to be noticed. Had Dublin gone mad in the heat? The whiff of sordid desires was as thick as the smell rising from manure heaps and unscavenged lanes.

Inside the church the musky sweetness of the incense lost something of its power to soothe him. From his pew he studied his fellow citizens, heads bowed in prayer, and saw not penitents but sinners brimming with lust. The priest recited the liturgy as a kind of lazy hum. The homily was about cleanliness and made no mention of infanticide. Denis wanted to shake him. Surely this was a concern of the Church. He wanted to see the men and women around him shudder in the same revulsion he felt, to recoil in horror at this crime that looked set to go unpunished.

Rose hadn't come with him. She said she would see him for lunch. Over their meal he didn't dare to ask her where she'd been in case she told him. When she went to hang out the washing he went to help her. He sought some comfort in their marriage rituals, reassurance that all was well or would be again.

'If you shove the peg on like that you'll have a crease in the middle of your shirt. Here, let me. You never listen. Hang them from the bottom edge where the shirt will be tucked in.' Rose smiled. She enjoyed telling him he was making a mess of it. He knew she was proud of having a husband who thought to help about the house. For his part he wished again that he could get a servant so that Rose would not have to do any chores. She could take up some other hobby, maybe learn the piano. Or read novels all day as far as he cared. And raise their children, whenever they might get back to having them. He began to peg the next shirt on the line, deliberately starting with the sleeves rather than the hem.

'Like this, Rose?' he called. She snorted and he turned it the right way round to show he was listening. They pegged out his shirts and one of her petticoats, which she wouldn't let him touch even after three years of marriage. Then came the sheets.

With his face hidden as he tried to drape the large sheet over the line, Denis asked, 'Is Mrs Kennedy's niece called Anne Mulhall?'

'She is.' Denis was surprised at the caution in Rose's voice. She continued hanging out the clothes but didn't look at him.

'I saw her playing the piano at the society's gala. She's very talented.'

'Well, I'm no judge of music and last I checked neither are you. What you know about music wouldn't fill a teacup.'

'True, true. She played very well. I spoke to her for a minute.' The yard was silent except for the flap of washing and the slight creak of the line. 'I only realised afterwards that she was your mistress.' Denis waited. Rose took a breath.

'She's not my mistress. Not really. That's Mrs Kennedy.'

'Yes, of course. She's young. I wouldn't say much beyond your age.'

'You planning on setting up a match for her?' She snapped the pillow cases against the breeze and hung them straight, overlapping the corners to save the pegs. 'Or is something bothering you? We're going round the houses.' Denis wasn't sure if anything was bothering him. He felt somehow that Rose had not been forthcoming, but what she might be hiding he wasn't sure. He had finally begun to understand that she had another life in that house. One that she kept from him. Maybe it involved a lover. Whatever it was, it was still pulling her away from him. As though when she was in that house she wasn't his wife at all.

'Why didn't you want to go to the gala and hear her play?' Another sigh.

'I hate those sorts of things, you know that, Denis. Everyone standing around, talking to only their sort. Stewed tea and someone giving speeches. And all in the heat. I don't know how you could stand it.'

'I wanted to help. That baby haunts me. If you had seen it you would understand why,' he continued. 'The way it was mingled with the day's rubbish. Just a wee tiny thing, left alone to rot unburied and unblessed.' Rose touched his hand but she didn't reply. 'Mr Mills hinted last night that the police had a suspect.' Rose withdrew her hand.

'Is that so? I assume he didn't say who it was.'

'Only that inquiries were being made into ... what were his words? "the dark world of baby farming".'

'Hmmph.'

'You don't believe it?'

'Oh they'll turn someone up alright. And nurses is just women trying to get by like anyone else. Mr Mills makes it sound like they're some kind of evil plague.'

'I suppose you think they're just helping women who got themselves in a bit of trouble. Like Mr Mills is doing. Except they're making a tidy bit on it.'

He heard Rose take a deep breath.

'Mr Mills gives a little speech and suddenly you're an expert on baby nurses? Denis you don't know the first thing. What happened to that baby is no concern of yours. Baby farmers, as you call them, are no concern of yours. You're a butcher with a shop. And if Mr Mills is the gentleman he pretends then I'm the Queen's long-lost cousin.'

And those were the last words that Rose spoke to him that day. By four o'clock Denis was tired of cleaning the yard and whitewashing the walls. He'd had enough of the heat and Rose's burning silence. He thought a silence was meant to feel cold but Rose's anger billowed in the air like steam. He still wasn't certain what she was mad about.

He was angry, too, but not at Rose. Not exactly. The dead infant had become more than a poor creature and an unsolved crime. Some mixture of faith and magic bound his fate to the crime and the criminal. To see the child buried, to have the crime solved, to have the murderer confess — he was convinced that he would never have a living child of his own if these things were not done. If he'd known a wise woman in Dublin he would have visited her, he would have tried to bring down a curse on women who threw babies into rivers. What quality of police force, what kind of detective, could not find out the perpetrator of this most base and pathetic crime?

Rose had asked him, 'What if she was raped? The mother. Maybe she is a victim, too. Or she'd had ten childers in ten years and couldn't take no more. Or the babby died and she was too scared to tell anyone.' But he didn't understand how any of these could be considered a reason to throw a baby to the river. A rape was terrible, but it was committed in a moment, it was a kind of succumbing to animal instinct. It was a single mistake, a misjudgement, an unclean thought converted instantly to a deed before it could be mastered. Whereas concealing a pregnancy, feeling the infant move inside you and wishing it were dead, killing the newborn and hiding the body. These things took planning and preparation.

And so, speaking out loud but expecting no reply, he told Rose he was going down to the shop to review the ledger. There, he perched on the edge of a stool and turned the pages without really reading the figures. He sighed and closed the book.

He couldn't bear the silence. He needed company. Without saying anything to Rose, he went out the garden gate and headed over the river.

The sun glared off the surface of the sluggish water so that Denis squinted, distorting his view of the people he passed. They wavered like spirits.

He reached Thomas Maguire's place just after five o'clock, walked around to the laneway behind the row of buildings and pushed on the back gate. It was open as usual. He didn't want to surprise his friend so he made as much noise as possible and began calling out 'Maguire! Are you there! It's only me, Denis!' as he approached the back door. Maguire should be more careful, he thought, glancing around the yard at a number of theft-worthy objects. Upturned wooden barrels lined one wall. On top of one was a small pile of horseshoes and nails. A great number of flour sacks were draped over a line.

He heard motion and Maguire appeared in the back doorway. His face was red and his shirt stuck to him. Denis saw from his own shirt that he was in no better shape. Damn the heat.

'I am glad to see you,' Maguire said. 'I have a fierce thirst on me. Is your leash long enough to reach a public house?'

Denis winced at the allusion to Rose but he said, 'I was thinking the same. The Brazen Head? And you'd better lock your gate.'

'If I lock it the thieves only jump the wall or break it. But I'll bring in the sacks and the horseshoes. I don't think they'd get away with too many barrels, I'll take my chances.' He gathered up the pieces and brought them into the house and the two men left the way Denis had come in. A few hens wandered down the laneway, picking at heaps of rubbish in a search for grubs. Maguire clucked at them and they marched over in their funny regal gait, each foot raised solemnly one after the other. He threw some seeds on the ground.

'Are they your hens?' This seemed an even more egregious lack of care for one's property than leaving barrels in an unlocked yard.

'No, I think they've escaped from somewhere on the street. I like them. They know me now. You saw how they came when I called. Friendly, intelligent creatures really. You should get Rose some hens. For company.' Denis tried to picture Rose throwing seed from her apron, clucking at the birds.

'There's enough manure with keeping the beasts before slaughter. These are getting nice and fat. If they come to your call it will make it easier to break their necks when you want to eat them.'

'Oh I couldn't eat them, they must belong to someone. Besides they have names now and I can buy my own ready plucked.'

When they reached the pub they found it empty and almost unbearably warm inside. They edged their stools close to the back door where a slight ruffle of cooler mouldy air came in from the laneway behind. Denis quickly finished his pint of stout and called for two more. The barmaid moved lethargically to comply. As he finished the second pint, Denis explained his situation to Maguire. Maguire sipped in silence, moving the glass up and down from his mouth and occasionally ruffling his own hair or tugging at his beard. After Denis stopped talking he took some time to consider his response.

'Well, that's not the first thing I'd expected you and Rose to quarrel over. There's no shame in quarrelling with your wife. Rose will give up the silence eventually, there's nothing women love more than to tell men what to do.' He winked at Denis. 'And you'll forget about this case in a few weeks and worry about something else, like that cottage you plan to rent.' There was no comfort in these words for Denis, he felt deflated and exhausted. They moved onto other subjects and he tried to be sociable until the fifth or sixth pint swam in his head and swelled his tongue. He opened his mouth for more convincing words but they didn't come. He rose, slammed the empty glass down and glowered at the barmaid as he lumbered towards the door, trailing an apologising Maguire behind him.

He strode towards the bridge, his friend's steps behind him. Maguire in his own state of intoxication noticed only the drunkenness and not the rage in Denis. When he caught up he was jolly.

'How about a game of cards? I know a place nearby. Only small wagers, a bit of fun. And the most obliging serving ladies.' Denis paused to consider. He might as well stay out and give Rose a reason to be furious. And that is how an hour later he found himself teetering home, very drunk and relieved of his billfold. The latter he did not know yet and the former he was in denial of. He left Maguire with one hand down the front of a girl's dress, having refused offers of similar accommodation.

On the way home he became more and more indignant over Rose's coldness towards him. She was his wife! She owed him certain duties, she couldn't ignore him. How dare she? As his unsteady hand groped for the lock in the door he became determined to confront her. And then he was in their bedroom standing over her and shaking her awake.

'Wake up, Rose and listen to me. You can't treat me this way. I've been patient, I didn't ask for anything. But you don't treat me as a man. A husband. I love you Rose, how dare you keep me away? I'm your husband.'

He reached out and shook her again, wanting some reaction. Not caring if all she did was shout back. But instead she lay there, her face a mask, and waited to see what he would do next. He thought about pulling off her shift, about lying on top of her. About taking what she should give him willingly. But his prick fell limp between his legs, as though his body were ashamed on his behalf.

'I have to tell you something,' she said.

Chapter Twenty-Nine

Peakin

17th August, 1866

Peakin arrived at Exchequer Court on Friday morning feeling very well rested. He wasn't sure, but he thought that perhaps the temperature had dropped one or two degrees. Kate nicked two kippers from the kitchen and served them to him with a conspiratorial wink. He protested but she waved him off, 'A gentleman needs more than porridge. Mrs Malone'll not notice a wee few now and again.' He laughed and called her a clever girl when she slipped the bones into her pocket to hide the evidence. He tried to remember the last time he had laughed and could not. He felt fresh and hopeful. One of the pawnshop searches turned up a substantial lot of silver plate. Not as large as Fiddler's haul, but something nonetheless.

As he entered, he felt himself dissolve into Exchequer Court's familiar hum and clatter. A calm came over him such as he experienced during the first few years of his career. The comfort of regular work and regular pay, the expectation of regular food. Things that he'd learned not to take for granted during the hungry years. He told himself that he could succumb to the larger machine, could lay aside grasping ambition. Advancement would come inevitably. Embrace the grind, as the inspector said. Have faith, as his mother said. He made a round of constables and pawnshops at a brisk pace. He ignored squalor and sought out beauty: a freshly painted sign, the dart of a bluetit's flight from gatepost to gatepost, the sound of a church bell echoing.

When he returned, he was surprised to see Mr Zachariah Mills waiting for him just inside the door.

'Good morning, Mr Mills. What can I do for you?'

'Good morning detective. I have brought a statement for you from the penitent. We had it notarised. I hope this will be sufficient to arrest Miss Conroy on suspicion.'

The satisfaction on the man's face was unbearable. Peakin turned away so that Mills wouldn't see his reaction.

'I see. Well, come with me and I'll enter it into the book.'

The office was empty, all the other men out on their beats. Peakin motioned for Mills to sit and explained that he'd followed up the leads offered by Mr Mills but uncovered nothing. Had visited Miss Conroy and found nothing awry. Had no reports from neighbours, no signs of Eliza Mooney. That the coroner had decided to close the inquest. There was insufficient evidence.

'Well, you don't expect some woman to just come out and confess, do you? I'm no expert in police work, but I wouldn't have thought that was how it normally went.'

Peakin wanted to tell him that he would be surprised just how often people *did* confess, but he only said, 'No, indeed. But so far we have only your word on this matter with the baby farmer.'

'And that is why I am here.' He pushed an envelope towards Peakin. Inside was a piece of paper signed and stamped with such authoritative legal flourishes that they took up as much of the page as the evidence.

'I see. But just to be clear, the woman ...' he glanced at the paper, 'but where is her name?'

'When the penitents enter the asylum they take on new names.'

'But "Number Five" cannot be classed as a name! Will the magistrates take evidence without a Christian name?'

'Oh they will. It is perfectly legal.' Peakin bristled at the man's authoritative tone.

'Assuming that to be true, it is not her baby that was found in the river. She simply states that Miss Kitty Conroy had offered to take care of her baby by making sure she never had to see it again.'

'Yes. The woman offered to murder it. For a fee. And you'll see that she also says that Miss Conroy boasted of having done as much for Eliza Mooney.'

Peakin saw and he was uneasy. He felt outmanoeuvred by this slippery Mr Mills. He knew now the extent of his relief at dropping the case and being able to forget its unfortunate connection to himself. He tasted kipper at the back of his throat. What would happen now? Would he have to arrest the woman? And then there was the matter of Eliza. No one had seen her, but what if she came forward? What if she accused him of something? He failed to suppress a sigh as his innards gurgled.

'You find this tedious.'

'No, Mr Mills. Every case holds the same weight. It is just that I dislike this sort of evidence. Where the witness has not actually seen the crime committed. To me, it is little better than hearsay. I don't doubt "Number Five" heard what she heard. But as you and I know, there is often misunderstanding.' He thought longingly of his microscope, of the certainties it revealed. All the complexities of organisation, of classification, that could be seen by the eye. You needed trust no one else, just your own vision. Lately he'd felt his mental acuity was slipping. He was so tired out that he couldn't make any progress with the parasitic wasps he'd collected over a month ago.

'Well, I think that will be up to the inspector and the superintendent to decide. I have sent them both a copy as well.' And having landed his final punch, Mr Mills rose from the chair. Peakin shook his hand and watched him leave with an easy swish of his coat. He knew that in a few minutes the inspector would be in.

What to do about Kitty Conroy? He didn't like her or her nursing business. But that didn't mean she was a murderer. People like Mills seemed to think everyone of a particular sort was guilty of something criminal. If they were, it was rarely something so heinous as murder. Peakin wasn't one of those namby-pamby improvers who wanted to turn everyone to industry and education. There was enough industry and education already as far as he was concerned.

It all came back to domestic arrangements, he thought. The setting up of households. The tyranny of respectability. Maybe Isobel did him a favour by refusing in the end. He imagined her dismay at the poverty of their circumstances, the difficulty of making the right presentation of oneself on £1 1s 10d per week. She would have become someone who sulked when he was late home or worried about furnishings and schools for children. If only he could remove his own anxiety by explaining things to the inspector, make him see that a man of over forty years could be trusted to live outside of barracks without a wife to care for him.

He was so lost in his own thoughts that he didn't hear the inspector's steps in the hall.

'Peakin,' he said, putting his head around the door and knocking at the same time. 'Dear, oh dear.'

'Good morning. So you've seen the letter from Mr Mills.'

'I have. I hoped it wouldn't come to this. That if the coroner was happy then ...' he shrugged.

'And so what do you make of it?'

'It is legal, that much is true.'

'I don't like it. And there's something unpleasant about Mr Mills.'

The inspector raised his eyebrows.

'The newspapers can't get enough of this case, though. Must be the heat. Nothing else is going on. And Mr Mills has some important friends. I've been keeping them to myself, but I've had a few letters. Very persistent these men.'

'What is this case to them? Why doesn't Mills direct his attention elsewhere?'

'This is to be an opening victory for them. To attract more to their campaign against infanticide. They want someone to be made an example of. They seem to completely misunderstand the nature of crime and deterrence. I think they imagine a hanging. You and I know that if the mother's found, she'll either be taken into the asylum or sent to Australia. They've some notion of exposing a scandal, like the famous baby farmers case in England where those two women were executed. The papers were full of it, even here. Disgusting business.'

'So what do you want me to do?'

'You'll have to arrest the woman. Maybe that will force someone to come forward. Or she will confess. But that will be Mills off our case and the law can take its own course.'

'Alright. I'll do it tomorrow. Do you know anything about Mills?'

'Well, some people seem to think he's the saviour of our defiled women. Christ come to earth to save Mary Magdalene.'

'Miss Conroy suggested that he sells babies out of the asylum. Live ones and dead ones, sells the women's bodies. That he's making money off it all disguised as charity.' The inspector scowled and then smirked.

'That sounds exactly like what a baby farmer might say, doesn't it now? Asylums are probably edging in on her business, offering women a safe place and plenty of food for nothing while she bleeds them dry and feeds their babies watered-down milk. Surely you don't give any credence to this kind of nasty rumour, Peakin?'

'No, no. None at all. It seems utterly implausible. He's hardly riding around in a gold-plated coach.' Peakin scowled and remembered the gold on the man's false teeth. 'Though it's true there's a business in bodies for dissection. Not like the madness we used to see, much less grave robbing, but still there's money to be made.'

'Sounds like a bunch of slum gossip to me. I wouldn't make anything of it. Just get on with closing up the case. If Miss Conroy wants to accuse Mr Mills of anything let her do it in court.'

Peakin nodded and the inspector left. He would arrest Kitty Conroy — he could see no other way. But first there was at least one person he could ask about Mr Mills. One person who might know if there was a market in infants' and women's bodies for dissection.

Chapter Thirty

Peakin

17th August, 1866 (lunchtime)

Dr Mapother's house was tall and thin, with the kind of faded bricks and plain plasterwork that signalled wealth of ancient acquisition. Unlike some of the other houses on the Green, his windows shone with recent washing and street dust had been carefully removed from cracks and crevices so that the granite steps sparkled. Dr Mapother, to Peakin's embarrassment, was at his lunch. A servant led him into a sunny dining room where the walls were covered in hunting scenes. Horses leaping hedgerows, riders crouched on their backs. A horse facing left, dogs pacing at its feet. A horse facing right, a child holding the reins. A group of horses and a group of men in black hats and red jackets. Peakin found rich men's obsession with horses to border on the obscene. They could sometimes be heard opining on the proper heft of haunches and the correct curve of a neck in tones that would not be remiss in a bawdy house among men discussing the women they planned to bed.

Dr Mapother rose from the table to greet him, almost knocking over his plate with an enthusiastic sweep of his arm.

'Detective Peakin, what a pleasure. I'm so glad for you to meet my wife. Mrs Mapother, Detective Peakin. He's been assigned to that infanticide I was telling you about.' Mrs Mapother held her fork as though about to take a bite but simply stared at the food. Peakin tried not to mimic her stare.

'Please, sit, Dr Mapother. I am so sorry that I—'

'Not at all, there is no need to apologise. You are very welcome. Isn't he, Mrs Mapother? You see our son is at college and takes his meals with his classmates. And our daughter is not at home but staying with her cousins. A most welcome diversion. You must eat. James, please bring a plate for the detective.' Peakin wanted to protest further but James had already slipped from the room.

'I had no intention of coming here to trespass on your luncheon.'

'Whatever business you have come about, I'm certain it must be more interesting than the new flowerbeds we were planning.' Mrs Mapother cast her eyes down at her plate in an attempt to disguise her displeasure. She replaced her fork without taking a bite.

'Yes, we are delighted. I have heard much about you from Dr Mapother. Please, do sit down.' She indicated a chair across from her at the table.

Peakin sat and James returned with a tray. Unlike Kate, his movements were swift and precise. If Peakin wasn't watching him, if he wasn't so profoundly uncomfortable as to have all of his senses amplified, he might have imagined that the tray had appeared on the table by magic. Soon a plate of cold beef, seeping a rosy tinge of blood, and smaller dishes of boiled vegetables were arranged in front of him. He didn't know what else to do and so he ate. He took no pleasure in the meat though it was the largest portion he'd eaten in some months. He forced it down, chewing as little as possible, the iron tang coating the insides of his mouth. He would be tasting blood for days.

Dr Mapother chattered throughout the meal almost without stopping. He tried over and over to force Peakin to explain the nature of his visit. But Peakin was steadfast that it was not conversation for a lady's ears.

'Mrs Mapother has heard worse, I'd wager that.'

'She may very well have done so, but I would prefer not to be the bearer of offence to feminine sensibilities.'

'Thank you, Mr Peakin, I do appreciate your consideration,' Mrs Mapother said — one of the few sentences she uttered during lunch, and which her husband seemed not to hear at all. She looked weary, though whether it was from his presence or the constant barrage of her husband's enthusiasm, Peakin couldn't tell.

At long last Dr Mapother suggested that they remove themselves to the library. Peakin wondered how a rich person ever had time for anything other than meals. How could they accumulate so much money when they spent so much time doing nothing other than eating? Did the doctor not have patients to see? A clock somewhere was heard to strike half past two and Peakin grew anxious. He didn't want to have to explain an extended absence to the inspector.

The library made him forget all of his concerns. This was not like the Mechanics' Institute's shelves of shabby novels, third-edition scientific texts and encyclopaedias with cracked spines. No. Each book was carefully bound and stood to attention in crisp, straight rows. Spines were stamped in gold lettering and the shelves were labelled. Peakin noticed with some disappointment that the natural history section was small. Three shelves were devoted to pathological anatomy alone. There were titles in Latin and other languages Peakin didn't know. He resisted the urge to pick up a book and open it, to feel the sharpness of its pages and take in the scent of ink. He dreamed of having such a room himself, but he would fill it with every entomological book he could find. Imagine being able to consult every volume of *The Entomologist's Monthly Magazine* right on his own shelf?

In his reverie he almost forgot his mission. If he could sniff out even the hint of a scandal attaching to Mr Mills it was just possible that the inspector would become reluctant to pursue Miss Conroy. Just a little delay, he thought, and then he might uncover something else. Another avenue of investigation that didn't threaten to expose his own habits, his past with Eliza. They could try the workhouses further away, for example. Perhaps the woman fled for the countryside after disposing of the baby. He just needed enough to cast doubt on the evidence of Mr Mills and his penitent.

'Now what was it that you wanted to ask me so desperately that you had no thought to interrupting a meal? I know you, Peakin, you are alert to details and you wouldn't have arrived at lunch if you'd given it much thought. And please don't apologise again.'

'I'm terribly sorry. It's just as you say, I didn't think. Or at least not about the fact that you might be eating. You see, it is this infanticide case.'

'I knew it! You were unhappy with the lung flotation test. We could have a most invigorating debate on it, you know. The *Dublin Journal of Medical Science* might be interested in your views.'

'No, it's nothing to do with the lungs.' What was the right way to ask? Peakin felt sluggish, as though the process of digesting so much meat was at the expense of sufficient oxygen to his brain. He wished now that he'd taken the proffered tea. 'Have you heard of the Society for the Protection of Infant Life?'

'Oh yes, that business. I saw the notice. Zachariah invited me to the gala, of course, but I declined. We gave a donation.'

'Very good of you. Well, it's just that I heard some unpleasant things about another one of Mr Mills's charitable works.'

'Really? What could that have been?'

'Let's say that you wanted to undertake a study of the female anatomy. Of the pathology of birth, for example. You would need bodies to dissect would you not?'

'Well, I should think so. I mean, before routine dissection, supposed experts believed the vaginal canal was just a kind of oversized male member contained within a woman's torso and that the ovaries were simply an inferior variety of testes.' Mapother laughed.

Peakin found himself lost in the soup of words. He tried again.

'And if you wanted a body to dissect, let's say of an unfortunate woman who died in childbirth or, worse again, while pregnant, where would you get such a thing?'

'Ah. Very tricky. We rely on prisons and workhouses almost exclusively. You would be a very lucky man to come upon such a specimen.'

Peakin fancied himself a man ruled by intellect over emotion but he felt a coldness towards Dr Mapother when he heard these words. He'd long since abandoned any religious practice, but the way that Dr Mapother could speak about bodies disturbed something deep inside Peakin. He dismissed it as a lingering remnant of a childhood spent at Mass. If he'd chosen to examine the feelings he would have had to admit that they comprised a great pool of grief and guilt into which he had poured all of his memories of the hungry 40s. The horror of his neighbours, people he knew, turned into spectres, corpses of children made food for crows and dogs. He didn't want to revisit those scenes. To probe the misery and relief he felt at his own fortunate survival.

Peakin sensed that Dr Mapother was waiting so he continued with his questions.

'I presume you haven't heard of anyone coming across such a specimen of late? Or a specimen of a woman who had recently given birth?'

'You know I've thought about putting on a series of anatomical lectures for detectives such as yourself. It would be most useful, I think, in your line. Coroners, too.'

'No, it's nothing like that. I was only wondering if perhaps the woman who committed this infanticide didn't survive herself. And that would be something of a tidy end to this case. Perhaps if a body was found of a woman who'd recently given birth.'

'Hmm. Mmm. This is a needle in a haystack type of search you're conducting. I don't think you'll get any satisfaction. First of all, the woman would have had to have died somewhere in Dublin and her body to have been recovered and given for dissection without a postmortem or a coroner becoming involved. Seems unlikely. Besides, I'd know if it had happened because I know everyone interested in pathological anatomy in this city.'

'Ah, I see. Well that makes sense of course.' Peakin scrambled to think of another way in. He searched the spines of Dr Mapother's books as though a solution would present itself. 'There are rumours, you must know, of a kind of collusion between those who have access to such persons ... bodies ... and those who desire to dissect them. Gossip, but I did wonder ...'

'Ah now we're getting to the nub. Yes some men are more able, on occasion, to find these specimens. There are rumours, as you say, as to how. I have nothing to say on that. I do have a splendid recent example I could show you. A fully intact *gravid uterus*. Dr Budetbrook sent me the draft of his paper with the drawings. It's splendidly done. Here, I've left it somewhere on my desk.'

Peakin watched Dr Mapother move around the piles of books and paper on his desk. He felt that Dr Mapother was being a little coy. Perhaps it was all above board, the workhouse and prisons and the usual places. But he was quite sure that neither of the workhouse matrons had told him that a pregnant woman had died in their care. Perhaps it hadn't seemed relevant because he'd been searching for a living woman who had killed her baby rather than trying to find dirt to sling at Mr Mills.

'Ah! Here it is. The drawings are quite beautiful, really. Whatever else I might say about Dr Budetbrook, he has a skill with the pen. He always draws his own figures. Come, have a look.'

Peakin stepped closer to the desk. Dr Mapother spread out two large sheets of paper. He could see why it was easy for a doctor to refer to a person as a specimen. The head and most of the limbs were left out of the illustration, cut off by the edges of the page. The woman was unidentifiable: she might as well have been a series of geological strata or the inside of a seed pod. Peakin leaned over them, not sure what he was looking for.

'Are they recent?'

'Yes, I told you he's just sent them to me. He must have done them a week ago. There's no date but it does say that the body was donated by the Asylum for Women in Leeson Street in exchange for the cost of burial. I seem to recall he said a death from fever but I can't see the explanation here in the figure text. You know as well as anyone that those women are often in a terrible state when they resort to charity. Why do you ask? You're not looking for a pregnant woman, but one who already gave birth.'

'Idle curiosity.'

Peakin squinted again at the image. And then he saw it. An unmistakeable mark on her thigh that for some reason this Budetbrook had chosen to reproduce faithfully. He hadn't drawn her face but he couldn't resist the birthmark, the one Peakin had always told her resembled a moth.

Chapter Thirty-One

Peakin

17th August, 1866 (afternoon)

After his visit to Dr Mapother, Peakin felt himself groping as if in a fog. The decisive precision of his movements had been dulled, first by the heat and now by this knowledge that he couldn't categorise. He felt pains everywhere: dull, non-specific aches and unpleasant throbbings. His eyelids twitched. He longed to close his eyes and sleep until Mrs Malone pounded on his door. Instead, he must sit at the desk at Exchequer Court, and decide what to do. The other detectives were absorbed in their work as usual but he was certain that they stared. Waiting patiently for signs of his inevitable demise.

The room was full of the quiet ticking of pocket watches and it seemed that his heart fluttered in time to all of them at once. How much longer could he carry on like this? He kneaded his brow. The words of Isobel's final letter, sent three months ago now, spooled out through his mind. *My dearest Martin, I think it would be for the best ... please forgive ... perhaps another woman more suited ...* When he pushed this thought away he saw Eliza, hair pinned, standing in front of the silhouette shop. Her head cocked to one side, hand on hip as she tapped her foot and demanded why he had wanted to take her out at all if he wouldn't spend a shilling on her. He couldn't stop the flush rising on his face, whether for shame or guilt or something else he could not say. The sight of her on that page — he couldn't reconcile it with the warmth of her body under his hands, living flesh that had pressed against his own. Now she was reduced to lines. Lines and a corpse somewhere. Lines that seemed to prove that Miss Kitty Conroy was innocent of the accusations made against her. If Eliza had died without giving birth, then the baby in the river was not her baby and Miss Conroy had not killed him, either deliberately or by neglect. Yet if he were to present his evidence, to try to prove that Miss Conroy was innocent, he would implicate himself and ruin his career. Isobel would never change her mind and marry him. He would not be promoted. Reputation aside, would anyone even believe that he could recognise a whore by a mark on her thigh? He'd been so certain when he'd seen it, he'd had to place his hand in his pocket to stop himself from reaching to touch the page. Even if he was willing to say what he saw, would it be enough to stop Kitty from being convicted and sentenced to death?

Unable to decide on any other course of action, Peakin delayed his visit to Miss Conroy as long as possible. He read the statement of 'Number Five' over and over again. His last desperate hope was that the magistrate would throw the evidence out, refuse to remand Miss Conroy.

Miss Conroy's door was closed tight this time, as though the woman was expecting him. He allowed himself to hope that she'd fled. After a few minutes he heard movement. Footsteps, possibly a baby's cry. But the door didn't open. He tried again. And then, as a last resort, he called out.

'Miss Conroy. It's Detective Peakin with the Dublin Metropolitan Police. Open up at once.'

A man opened the door.

'You're makin' a racket could raise Jesus. Whaddaya want?'

'I'm here for Miss Kitty Conroy. I spoke to her last week.'

'You're out of luck. She's not in.' He opened the door wider onto the same squalor that Peakin had sat in before. The baby baskets were gone. The fire was out. The smell was different. Not exactly cleaner, but less redolent of faeces and sour milk. Maybe she had fled after all. Sensed the danger. Was guilty of something, even if not this particular thing.

'Where is she?' Peakin asked. The man showed his teeth and shrugged his shoulders. He was younger than Kitty and Peakin wondered was he just a boarder or something else. His hair was neat but his breath was rancid and he smelled like he'd been sleeping in his clothes. Peakin held his ground.

'Yiz can wai' if ya want. She could be back or she might have bogged off somewhere else for all I know.' The man turned his back and went back behind the curtain, waving his hand to indicate that Peakin should sit on one of the stools.

'What about Sarah?' Peakin called after him. 'Is she here?'

'She's in school isn't she? No more questions. I'm not under arrest. You can wait for Kitty or you can be off.' Peakin heard a rustling of straw bedding and what could have been the disturbing of another sleeper or a large rat. These sounds were soon followed by snores.

He sat. The stool was short and he was uncomfortable with his knees so high in the air. He took out his watch and wondered how long he should wait. Where were the babies? Maybe the woman *was* actually the monster that Mills made her out to be. But what if she wasn't? What if people came forward to accuse Miss Conroy anyway? What if she hadn't done it but she was convicted and transported, or worse, was hanged? And all along he held a piece of evidence that could save her. Although, would a judge take his evidence? That he recognised a woman from a mark he'd seen in a medical drawing? They would insist on disinterring her to verify the identity. Mrs Wilson might be called in. The papers would have a fine time with that story. Well, he told himself, this baby farming business is cruel even if it isn't criminal. It's almost as bad as blackmail, hiding a baby no one wants for money. It wasn't such a big step to killing them for money. He dreaded when the door would open and the woman would return and he would have no choice. He didn't have to wait long.

'John! John how many times do I be tellin' ya not to leave the door hangin'?' She burst through the open door, clearly on a mission to box someone's ear. She saw Peakin and stopped short. 'You again. What do you want? I told ya all I know.' Peakin rose from the stool with great effort.

'I'm afraid I'm here to bring you to the police station to answer some further questions. A woman has provided a statement accusing you of offering to kill babies for a price. And specifically of having killed Eliza Mooney's baby about two weeks ago.' Peakin almost wished she would run. He watched emotions chase one another across her face. Anger. Fear. Sadness. Back to anger.

'Are you arrestin' me on the word of some little tart that didn't keep her skirts down? I didn't never take no baby for no Eliza Mooney.'

'I'm afraid the witness has provided considerable detail. But you are of course entitled to make your own statement. And that is why I am here to take you with me.' He didn't say the word 'arrest' — it might be like saying 'hup' to your horse. Miss Conroy stood with her hand on the door, still part of the way into the hall. Peakin heard a sudden stillness, as if everyone in the building was listening to hear the outcome. To his surprise, Miss Conroy burst into tears. At first Peakin thought this was an effort to win sympathy, but there was no control in the crying.

'But Sarah, who'll mind Sarah?' She choked out between sobs. With her mouth twisted and her eyes red she seemed younger. She rubbed one hand in the other as though trying to comfort herself. Her shoulders slumped and she dropped the basket she was carrying. An apple rolled out across the floor. Peakin picked it up and handed it back to her. It smelled overripe.

'You can bring Sarah with you if there is no one to mind her.'

'To gaol! And she just a little innocent girl! I'll be doing no such thing.' The anger was back. Peakin felt relieved. 'John!' She shouted now. Peakin couldn't understand why the man hadn't emerged. The racket must have woken him. The curtain stirred.

'Kitty. What is so desperate you do be disturbin' me rest? If you have to go with the gentleman I can mind Sarah.'

'She can't stay here with only men to mind her. You bring her over to me ma's tonight. You hear me? Don't tell her where I am. Make something up.'

'I hear you. Now, can I get me rest or are you gonna go on shouting the house down?'

'What about the babies?' Peakin asked.

'Well, it's lucky they's gone off to homes and I'm between nursing jobs. Because that'd be some mess to sort out. This will do enough damage to me business as it is.' Peakin wondered what she had done with them. It seemed far too convenient that they should have disappeared. Hope rose a little in his chest. Perhaps there was something nasty here after all. Maybe she'd expected him and tried to prepare. Or the babies had died of neglect.

'If you're as innocent as you say, it may be sorted out quick enough.'

'Let me leave a note for Sarah.' Peakin nodded. Miss Conroy disappeared behind the curtain and Peakin could hear angry whispering for a few moments. A rustle of paper and more angry whispering. When Miss Conroy emerged she had a bonnet on and her face showed resignation to whatever would befall her. He'd been so distracted by his doubts about the arrest he hadn't thought about how he would bring her to the station. As if reading his mind she said, 'Don't think you can clamp my arm. I can walk there on me own two feet please and thank you very much. No one can say I had to be dragged.'

Peakin nodded. He thought they would make a fine pair of strollers on their way to Grangegorman. He chose his route along the quays rather than round the Circular Road, thinking it might be a little quicker. When they passed Richmond Bridge, Miss Conroy studied it with curiosity. 'So this is where that baby landed up. Sure it's where them mud pickers come because the water does be low, no wonder it was found.'

Peakin didn't often find himself at Richmond Female Penitentiary. The building was made of stones of different sizes and shapes so that it resembled a cloth that was patched too many times. The effect was not gay but dreary. Inside the door, the prison resembled most others. Same grim corridors, same scent of unwashed skin and bodily fluids, and something else. Peakin sniffed. It was sour milk.

An officious matron in a starched white pinafore signed Miss Conroy into the register. Another woman led her away. Kitty didn't turn back to Peakin. 'I just need you to sign the register here, please,' the matron said with some impatience. Peakin signed.

The next day in front of the magistrate Miss Kitty Conroy was a study in indifference. Her face blank, her shoulders squared, she waited.

'Miss Katherine Conroy. You are charged with the murder of an infant boy, in the week preceding the 1st of August in the year of our Lord 1866. You are accused on the grounds of being a known baby farmer, soliciting clients for whom you offer to dispose of their unwanted children for a fee. It is claimed by the accusers that a woman named Eliza Mooney did, on finding herself with child, avail of your services before fleeing the country for England.'

'It's Mrs Conroy, sir,' Kitty sniffed.

'I beg your pardon. And where is Mr Conroy? Can he account for your actions in the week preceding the discovery of the body?'

'I'd wager Mr Conroy hasn't seen much 'cept the inside of his wooden box these past three years if he hasn't yet made it up to God in heaven.'

'And I must apologise again. I am sorry for your loss. I'm afraid this is a bad start to proceedings. Is there anyone else who could say where you were during the days but especially the nights of the first week of August?'

'Sarah, my daughter. She is with me every night.'

'And what age is she?'

'She's ten.' Peakin's eyes opened wider. He hadn't imagined the child to be more than six.

'I'm afraid that won't do. We'll need the testimony of an adult. What about your lodgers? Mr Peakin said you had a lodger.'

'John works at night down the docks. I only take lodgers with night work. We can take it in turns in the bed and there's no funny business.'

Peakin's eyelid twitching had worsened and was now accompanied by a kind of burrowing pain in one temple. His insides seemed to wrestle with each other. He prayed that Mrs Conroy would not look at him. Her face showed nothing. He thought that the city's poor were often like this. They accepted a situation they couldn't control; they awaited their fate. It was a little bit noble, he thought, and also a little sheep-like. A woman of the better sort might have tried to plead, would have surely wept, but Mrs Conroy just sat there, knowing she was condemned. There was a kind of bravery in that, he conceded. The evidence against Mrs Conroy was read into the record. The magistrate seemed to share his concerns about the evidence. He shuffled his papers for what seemed like a long time and Peakin allowed himself to hope. But then he announced: 'Mrs Conroy, you are to be remanded in custody on suspicion of infant murder. You will reside in Richmond Female Penitentiary until the trial unless you can raise bail of £10. Do you have anything to say?'

'I say it weren't me. I don't do that kind of thing, you've got me mistaken for someone else.'

'To be clear, you claim that you did not in fact receive payment in exchange for killing the infant of a Miss Elizabeth Mooney? Do you know Miss Mooney?'

'Sure, I know her. She came to see me, she'd gotten herself in some bother.'

'What kind of bother?'

'The same kind that every whore gets in, sooner or later. She asked me for pills to bring back the bleeding. Said she'd been threatened, that she'd have to get out if she couldn't clear it up.'

'And did you provide them?'

'No. I already told you. That's not me business. I'm a nurse, I don't know about herbs or tonics. Not any more than any other woman knows what you could take. But you're as likely to be killed as cured, I told her.'

'And did you see Miss Mooney again?'

'No, sir. She went into that asylum and that's the last I knew.'

'Thank you, Mrs Conroy. I'm afraid that it is your word against a gentleman's for the moment.'

The whole time Mrs Conroy hadn't even glanced at Peakin but she met his eyes now. Far from sheep-like, her gaze was fiery hate. Peakin turned away, remembering the smell of her rooms and the thin little babies in their baskets.

Part V

After Carlisle Bridge the river had space to breathe. Released from the grip of quay walls, she spread her waters across the widening mouth and gulped in the saline freshness of the sea. She lapped at the sides of ships as they slipped to and fro along the invisible lines of commerce that tied Dublin to Liverpool and Calcutta and Sydney. All along the quays sat women with baskets, scattered like boulders. They watched the animals being loaded, bellowing and bleating. They watched the people coming home and going away. From their baskets they sold eggs and fish and potatoes and apples and flowers, clutching them in fingers like knotted rope. Sometimes they dropped their rubbish into the river just to watch it float away.

Chapter Thirty-Two

Peakin

18th August, 1866

Peakin felt the fierce stare of Kitty Conroy wherever he went. He held no idealised view of police work as the implementation of a higher moral order. He carried with him the weight of many small, daily injustices. A hungry thief confined to gaol where he would be fed while his children starved. A woman ruined for palming a few coins that her employer ought to have paid her in the first place. A drover given hard labour for prodding a cow too vigorously while the man who ate the cow suffered nothing worse than indigestion. This he accepted as a duck accepts that water is wet. But could he let Kitty hang for a crime that he was certain she did not commit? For hang she would, if she was convicted.

His intestines became unreliable, food ran through him. He felt his own forehead with the back of his hand, wondered if he might be coming down with cholera. All routine and order was disturbed by this confounded case that he didn't want. Perhaps he should ask the inspector for a few days of sick leave. Allow someone else to close the case. He turned the drawing of Eliza over and over in his mind. He knew it was her, it had to be her. It explained her disappearance. And then there was the mark on her leg. But the drawing was even more dead somehow than a corpse might have been. He could not reconcile it with his Eliza. The sounds and solidness and colours of her were gone, she existed only as black lines on a flat, white page. Yes, there was something wrong with him. His mouth was too dry and his eyes were too moist. He would have to eat more carefully.

At first he thought that Kitty might be guilty of something anyway, something bad enough to assuage his conscience. His interviews with the neighbours in her tenement were not revealing.

'She keeps herself to herself,' said Mrs O'Regan, who lived on the same floor. 'Don't bother no one. I do sometimes wonder about them babies in there mostly in the dark without their mammies, but that's no business of mine.'

No amount of questioning would bring anyone to say much about the women who brought their babies to Mrs Conroy, aside from what they thought were subtle allusions to their line of work. Mrs O'Regan confirmed that she'd heard three different babies a week or so ago. 'A racket, it was. Always one of them wailing. I don't know how John could stand it.'

Once again he sat in the airless office in Exchequer Court, feeling the accumulation of perspiration and watching his pen drip tiny spots of ink onto the page where he ought to have been writing a report. When a constable opened the office door and announced that a woman was there to see him, Peakin anticipated further horror. Eliza's mother come to find her, perhaps. Or maybe Dr Mapother, noticing Peakin's reaction to the diagram, had alerted Dr Budetbrook, who had alerted Mr Mills who had sent someone to accuse Peakin of something.

He gathered up his things and looked for somewhere private to speak with her. A few doors down was a room with a table in it so large you had to sort of shimmy around the edges. The table was low and uneven, surrounded by four chairs in various states of ruin. Peakin liked this room because the tilt of the table, the fragile seats of the chairs, made witnesses feel unsteady. They hurried to make their point and leave.

Peakin waited for the woman on the landing, studying her as she climbed the stairs towards him. She was well dressed although not showy. She was not old enough to be Eliza's mother. Something about her steps suggested the prim demeanour of a young spinster. His bowels gurgled in complaint as he considered that she might be a matron from Mr Mills's Asylum for Women. She looked up from her feet and he recognised her. Why on earth was she here?

At the door to the room, they made their introductions and he pointed her to the chair least likely to collapse. She sat on the edge of it, holding her hands together in her lap. Peakin knew from experience that no matter how you sat in it, you could not get up quickly without risking a loss of balance. He saw her reach the same understanding and shift her weight in an effort to steady herself. Peakin chose the most stable chair for himself but he'd forgotten that the stuffed seat was burst and the wiry stuffing prickled his rear so that he found himself almost as uncomfortable as his guest. They sat there, listening to the furniture creak, neither eager to begin.

'Now, what is it that you wanted to see me about?' Peakin asked.

The woman pushed her shoulders back and lifted her chin.

'The infanticide. The baby that was found in the river. I understand that a woman has been arrested.' She was nervous. Peakin studied his pen, creasing a fresh opening in his notebook. She waited.

'Please, begin.' He watched her face, comparing her to what he remembered from his visit to Mountjoy Square. Pretty but not remarkable. A bit pallid but with her hair done in the fashionable way. Long fingers that moved to grip the chair's arms but nails bitten to the quick. Attractive eyes, eyelashes a bit too light, dark circles beneath them.

'I have some information about it. About ... the ... infanticide.' She put the hands back in her lap again. Scanned her eyes across the table. More gossip, perhaps. Or maybe she'd known Kitty Conroy from some kind of charity work? A society for orphaned children, perhaps.

'Let's start with the basics. There's no hurry. Where do you live? What is your occupation?'

'Oh, yes, of course. I live at 27 Mountjoy Square. The home of Mrs Julia Kennedy. I don't suppose I have an occupation as such.'

'I believe we met there once before. I visited on some other business relating to burglaries on the square. I think I disturbed your piano practice.'

She smiled a thin smile. Peakin thought now he could see her better, he knew Dr Pratt was wrong. This woman wasn't the type. Pratt was sore at his loss, jealous of whoever she'd chosen instead. But she knew Mrs Doyle. Mrs Doyle might be some grim version of a handy woman. Killing the babies instead of delivering them. Yes, it seemed just the kind of side job that a butcher's wife would get up to. And probably plenty of money in it too. At least you had to admire the enterprising nature of some women. She was now worrying a bit of lace on her dress between her fingers. She seemed almost to be in physical pain.

'Can I offer you a drink?'

'No, thank you very much, detective. No, I am ready to begin now. It's rather a long story.'

'Well, I'm in no hurry and it's best if you don't leave anything out.' Peakin tried to look as though he had relaxed into his chair, mastered the urge to scratch his arse.

'I want to say that I'm certain Mrs Conroy had nothing do with it. She is innocent and you should release her from prison.' Peakin swallowed. This woman knew something about him after all. About Eliza. But what could it possibly be? He watched the door, wondering if one of the other sergeants might come in. The inspector could come looking for him, eager to tie up the loose ends and send the case on its merry way towards the court.

Anne Mulhall seemed to shrink as she told her story. As he listened, he wondered at how the rich kept their female children so cosseted. So much innocence wasn't a gift, it was dangerous. Miss Mulhall's story was tragic and yet she could release him.

She confessed to everything: concealing her pregnancy, killing the baby, throwing him into the river. Here, in a sensible muslin dress, was his salvation: no miscarriage of justice for Mrs Conroy. And he stood to gain a reward. A promotion, or at least the admiration of his superiors. His reputation would remain unquestioned. All at the expense of this woman who would lose everything. She reminded him of Isobel. He couldn't imagine Isobel doing any of these things but here was Anne Mulhall, a woman not so different from Isobel, explaining that she had done them. She didn't even dab at her eyes. She was dignified in her misery. He hated that he could be so affected by her appearance, by the studied modesty passed from mother to daughter like silver crochet hooks and a grammatical way of speaking. Even more, he hated the idea that some gentleman, who no doubt appeared just as respectable, stood to get away with it. Peakin imagined that across the city, in sculleries and back hallways and bedrooms, many respectable gentlemen were getting away with all sorts. Soft hands unfastened fine wool trousers and, with a few quick thrusts, sent house maids and laundresses running to a Kitty Conroy or a Mrs Wilson.

'Can you tell me more about the man who ...' Peakin paused. How could he say this delicately? 'Who else is responsible for your ... situation?'

'Is that really necessary? I have nothing to say about anyone else. Let them make their own confession.'

'Forgive me for saying so, but there is more than one crime here. There is the infanticide, of course. And concealment of birth. And then what happened initially, the act so to speak. It was against your will? Or were you seduced? When you discovered your situation, did the young man help you in any way?'

'No, he did not. No one helped me.' She was lying, Peakin could see that. But he wasn't sure about what. Had she been seduced or willingly fallen? If the young man hadn't helped her, then who? A servant? Her aunt? No, not the aunt. People like Mrs Kennedy usually found a solution for this kind of problem, a solution that moved the problem out from under their roof.

'Would you tell me his name, please? The man's name?'

'I don't see why ...'

'I will have to question him as well.'

'Oh.'

Peakin wondered for a moment if identifying him would bring her further shame. Perhaps it was a member of the household. Someone beneath her station. But things were bad enough for her, wouldn't she want the beau to shoulder something of the blame?

'Dr Matthias Kelly.'

'Thank you. And he was aware of ... that you were ... *enceinte*?' Peakin was exhausted by the effort of keeping his questions at a suitable level of specificity and respectability. He was grateful that she was keeping her composure. She never met his eyes but moved her gaze between her hands and a far corner of the room.

'I informed him. He did not believe me. I hoped for some assistance from him, perhaps to leave Dublin.' Once she'd released this piece of information from her grip, she let everything else go more easily. She added details to her story. She was still concealing something, someone. He didn't believe that she'd disposed of the body herself. He might have to question the household again. He dreaded the conversation when Dr Pratt discovered he'd been right. He'd be pleased as punch and Peakin would find this disgusting. Although a doctor had spoiled her anyway. That didn't surprise him. He imagined half of Mrs Wilson's customers were doctors.

'Excuse me, Detective Peakin,' Anne disturbed his thoughts. He took his hand from his moustache and studied his notes.

'Yes, well, you have given me all you can, I think.' Peakin considered his choices. He could arrest her now, take her straight to prison. Release Kitty. Mrs Conroy. Everything would fall neatly into place, the trial could happen soon.

Case closed. No further sleepless nights worrying. But he needed time to think. To make sure this was the right thing to do. He couldn't afford another mistake with this case. First the one arrest and then another. What would it look like? The girl seemed unlikely to flee. Of course, if she did he would be in a pickle. But if she'd been able to flee she would have done it long before now. He could see that she was exhausted. Resigned.

'Go home. Please do not try to run away, that will make things worse for you. Do not talk about this to anyone. Do you understand?' Anne nodded. 'I will take things from here. I will most likely arrest you tomorrow.'

Chapter Thirty-Three

Rose

20th August, 1866

Rose decided to move back home to her parents after Denis came into their bedroom, sideways with drink, and thought about trying something. Demanding his marital rights. Up until then she'd felt sorry about dodging him, slipping away. She felt his menace as he stood over her and couldn't cope with his apologies after. Not enough and too much at the same time. Then everything came to a head when she told him what she'd done. He couldn't believe her lying and sneaking around to protect Anne. 'Did you not think there should be consequences for her actions?' he asked, almost shouting. All the unsaid things were said, the accusations made out loud instead of in their heads. Rose said she would go back home for a while and Denis agreed that would be for the best. Just until they both could think straight again.

She missed him. She was accustomed to his small kindnesses, to the little ways he tried to make things easier on her. She missed the smell of his soap after a bath and his solid company at the table. But the safety she felt in that home with Denis had been leaking away since the stillbirth and one moment of drunken anger drained the basin. She didn't know how to fill it up again.

It felt strange to be back in her parents' flat, the home where she'd lived without thought for any other. She'd visited her parents every week since she married Denis but it wasn't the same. She didn't open the cupboards and help herself, she sat at the table like a guest and waited to be offered things. Familiar spaces had been made strange. The three rooms that seemed more than enough for her whole life now felt cramped. She sat in the guest chair and, since she had no need to fetch anything for anyone, looked around her. She tried to remember the story behind each of the objects on the oversized mantelpiece. Her baptismal candle, a flowered jug given to her mother by an employer, a tail brush from when her father drove a cab and treated the horse like it was his own.

There was a map of Dublin on the wall that she'd never seen before. Just one cut out of the back of a *Thom's Directory*, but her mother felt some need to nail it up. On the map the streets were white spaces, while the buildings were shaded as little rectangles and squares. If she squinted it looked like a bit of crochet work, an unfinished doily maybe. And there was the river, a seam running through the middle of it all.

'Where did that map come from?' she asked her mother.

'That? Been there for years. Your da put it up.'

'Are you sure? I never seen it before.'

'And the teacher was always tellin' us you'd a keen memory. But I suppose the familiar things is the things we ignore and take for granted.' She gave Rose one of her special looks and Rose knew she wasn't talking about the map. They didn't speak about Denis hardly at all.

At night, she listened to her parents snoring on the other side of the partition and remembered how she used to wonder about other noises. She'd imitated them for her friends once in school. She could still summon the hot flush of embarrassment as Lily Know-it-all explained. From then on she slept with her head under her pillow and wondered instead why she had no siblings.

'You're up early.'

Rose started at her mother's voice and almost knocked over the cup of tea she was holding, rubbing her finger over the chipped rim.

'I need to go home,' Rose said. Her mother's eyes brightened with hope. 'Just to get a few things.' Mrs Treacy didn't even try to suppress the sigh. Rose had fled with almost nothing, had forgotten her shawl and a second shift, the book she'd been reading. Maybe she wanted Denis to notice her haste. To regret the things he'd said. Now she wanted to see the rooms again and make her decision. She needed to know if she was leaving him for good.

'Well, you best be getting on, then. Before Denis has opened the shop.'

'I was thinking to arrive after he'd opened the shop.' Rose watched her mother taking the measure of this, trying to decide whether sneaking into the house without speaking to Denis was the sign of a growing rift or a future reconciliation.

'Shall I go with you, petal? Help you to carry things.' Her mother hadn't called her 'petal' since she was going to school. She could hardly bear it, the sadness her mother felt at Rose's failure to make good on the promises of her marriage. Meat and money enough to go around. What had her mother said? 'He's a good man and respectable. He can provide for you, now and to the grave. He won't go to the drink or the whores.' What more did she want?

'No, Mam. I'll go on me own.'

Rose finished the cold tea, rinsed the cup and hung it on the hook. She stood next to the door for a moment, thinking about what it might mean to stay here. To end her marriage and just to mind her parents in their old age. As she descended the stairs, she heard other tenants stirring in their rooms. Rose liked the relative quiet of life above the shop. There was no wait in a freezing cold yard for a turn at the privy or to fill your water jugs. No doors banged unexpectedly, no one sang too loudly as they stumbled home the worse for wear. She worried about her parents and how they would manage with the water and the privies as they got older. The other tenants would help them, of course, muttering all the while about the uppity daughter who lived above a shop.

As she walked, she thought about Kitty. She wondered if the detective would discover that they knew one another and if this would drag Rose into something. She thought of Kitty the last time she'd seen her, when Rose had gone to warn her about Mr Mills and his little society. When Rose had gone to tell her that Mrs Kennedy had found a home for the baby. Poor Kitty who didn't ask questions and wanted only to please Rose. She'd always been thin, but now her face was gaunt and her hands looked like the hands of an old woman. Rose had brought a few sausages from the shop and Kitty wanted Rose to stay and share them. Rose couldn't imagine working up an appetite in that dark room with its hot, sour smell. So she patted Sarah's head, slipped her a few pennies, and got out as fast as she could.

She planned to walk around the block to arrive at the stairs to the flat, avoiding the possibility of Denis noticing her through the window. He would hear her on the stairs and know that she didn't want to speak to him. But all her mother's reproaches rang in her ears. She put the key back into her pocket and opened the door to the shop.

Denis was behind the counter absorbed in the paper spread out before him. He looked up and his face registered genuine surprise.

'Hello,' she said. And then, too quickly, 'I've just come to fetch a few things.'

'Are you in any kind of trouble I should know about?'

Rose was confused. They'd taken care of the trouble. What could he mean?

'No.'

'Are you sure? Have you seen the paper? Have you been to Mrs Kennedy's today?'

'No. She let me have a few days off. Things have been quiet and I spent a few days with me ma.'

'Did the woman not find you? Anne Mulhall? I sent her to your ma's when she came knocking.'

'I don't know what you're trying to say. I've been only at home or running messages. I've not been out gallivanting or making calls.'

'So Miss Mulhall didn't find you. So you don't know.'

'What don't I know?' Why was Denis being so coy? She should have spoken to Anne before she took her leave. She should have told her about her baby, that it was still alive. She'd tried to do it every day, but she could never follow through. She was afraid of what Anne might do. She'd wanted to kill the baby. Rose had seen the way she squeezed it. She wasn't sure the truth would make things easier on her now. She'd tell her eventually, of course she would.

'She's been arrested. You'll be glad, I suppose, to see that Kitty's been released. Anne's gone and confessed. Before you left, you told me ... you told me that the baby was alive.'

Red blotches marked his face and she could see him squeeze his hands and release them. Rose couldn't quite understand what he was saying. What had Anne done?

'The baby is alive. Anne's baby.'

'Then why did she tell the police that she killed him? Why did she say that baby in the river was hers? Rose did you lie to me?'

'I didn't lie to you, Denis. I haven't done nothing except to try to help me friend.'

'Don't be silly, Rose. She's not your friend. Just like Mrs Kennedy was never your mother's friend. She's not one of us. And anyway she's got herself into some kind of trouble that no one, not even a friend, could get her out of. And either you lied to me and the baby is dead or you lied to her and the baby is alive.' She could see that the more he spoke the more certain he became of his anger.

'What has she said? Tell me what the newspaper says.' Rose tried to imagine the possibilities of what Anne might have done while she'd been away. What could have made her go to the police? She remembered all the times she'd almost told her everything and decided against it. She'd been so certain she knew what was best. She could hardly breathe.

'Here, read it yourself,' Denis pushed the paper towards her. 'Take it upstairs and read it before you pack up your things if you want.' She moved behind the counter but she didn't pick it up. She picked up the bundle of wrapping papers and squared them, rewound a length of string. 'And you say I'm the one always sticking my hand in where it don't belong.'

'Not that I think you need to know, but it was my idea. To put it in the river. I thought he was dead.' She could hear his steady breathing, the way he always ran his fingers over the things in his pockets when he was anxious. She heard the sound of the key to the back gate, the rustle of a piece of paper on which he'd written lists of his stocks or things to remember. *Two steaks. Seven lamb's livers. Deliver to Rutland Square.* And so on.

'It was you?'

'Well, it wasn't me of course because that wasn't her baby in the river. I don't know whose baby that is. Some other unfortunate woman. But if he'd died, then yes. I would've thrown it in. To help her. She couldn't have done it herself.'

There was a long pause then. Rose thought of going up but he had something else to say and she thought that she owed him the grace of listening.

'You know why I saw the baby? Why I stopped on that bridge? It reminds me of when we were courting. We crossed it one night and there was a view down the river. Smooth and brown, like a road. I had this feeling like everything was ahead of us. A smooth brown road.' He sighed, looked down at his boots. 'I knew you should never have taken that job in the house.'

Rose didn't know what to say so she turned and went up the back stairs. She gathered her things into a little bundle and looked around the house. She saw the white baby booties on the mantel, the ones that Denis treated like a holy relic. She put them in her pocket.

Chapter Thirty-Four

Peakin

20th August, 1866

Peakin returned to Richmond Female Penitentiary to deliver Anne Mulhall. Mrs Conroy had already been released. He was glad he hadn't been the one to do it. He wondered if the constable had endured a tongue lashing or if she'd remained silent in blazing rage. He expected he would hear from Mr Mills. Now that he knew it was all a lie, Peakin pictured Mills coercing and wheedling the penitent into signing the statement that she probably couldn't read. He wondered how Eliza had died. He hated to imagine her scared or in pain. Whatever Mrs Wilson might say, he liked to think he had a more refined sensibility. He'd had no thought to rescue Eliza but neither had he planned on losing her. And now, in more honest moments, he admitted he was grieving her. He recalled again the time he took her out, her childish joy at being bought a slice of cake. The memory made him feel ashamed. Not of Eliza. No, he was ashamed because she'd noticed his discomfort, his desire to appear respectable. He saw the knowledge arrive on her face, the understanding that he wouldn't take her out again. The acceptance. He wished now that she'd been angry. That she'd mocked him.

He studied the chipped wooden panels and soot-coated windows of the cab and tried not to stare at Anne, who was finally overcome by silent weeping. Her palm was wet with wiping tears as he helped her out of the carriage. He offered her his handkerchief but she wouldn't take it so he used it to clean his own hands.

He did his part quickly and fled. He felt sorry for her. But the judge would have sympathy. Her aunt would hire her a lawyer and the lawyer would say that she didn't know what she was doing, hadn't meant to kill the poor thing, was overcome. She'd be transported. She could make a life, smaller perhaps than the one she'd been prepared for; marry even and have children. Eliza would be lucky if she had a cross to mark her grave. She'd been sick and alone, thrown herself on the mercy of Mr Mills and his asylum and received thin gruel and condescension. The final indignity of dissection. If only she'd come to him! But what would he have done?

He decided he would treat himself to a proper meal. His stomach still wasn't right. When he arrived at the Castle Hotel he was surprised and not delighted to find that there was an entertainment on. *An acrobatic troupe from far Araby*, the flyers declared. Two men and a woman in fitted ornate costumes and tights were contorting themselves on a makeshift stage. There were circles of kohl around their eyes to emphasise their exotic origins, though they were probably from Mullingar. Some members of the audience whistled and howled as one man lay on his stomach and wrapped his legs behind his back and up to his ears. The female acrobat then climbed onto his knees and bent backwards until her hands clasped his toes. Peakin scowled and sat at a table as far away from the stage as possible.

'Two chops, boiled potatoes, cabbage and a pint of stout. The chops are to be cooked all the way through. No blood. No butter.'

The barmaid nodded.

'You heard me: no blood and no butter?'

'Keep yer pants on. I got it, dry chops for a dry shite.' She smiled at her joke and he ignored her.

He looked around the room but all he noticed were women about Anne's age. About Eliza's age. Some were whores looking for a different class of customer. Their dresses were almost fashionable but low necklines and showy colours gave them away. A few street sellers, aged an extra decade by standing out in all weathers, had been allowed to circulate the crowd with bags of salted nuts and Turkish delight. Only the shopkeepers' wives sat. They perched next to their husbands in respectable married bliss, dresses straining over thickening waists.

The plate landed with a slap.

'Now try not to enjoy it,' the barmaid winked and pinched his knee.

'Thank you, I'll do my best.' He dropped the coins into her hand.

The meal was just as flavourless as he'd hoped it would be. Instead of the acrobats on stage, Peakin observed a group of men at the next table as they groped at the barmaids.

'Just one kiss!' one of them shouted at a retreating figure as he tried to use her skirt to pull her back. She shook him off without dropping her tray.

The men wore expensive suits and yet he thought they looked like the monkeys he'd once seen in the zoological gardens. Well-dressed hair and tidy moustaches couldn't disguise the way that lust and entitlement distorted their faces. The monkeys openly masturbated in their cage, whereas these men grabbed at women's hands and tried to pull them between their legs.

'We can't stay here all night,' one of them remarked to the others.

'No fun at all. Will we go to Mother Condron's?'

'I know another place. A little extra but it's clean. And Peggi will let you put it in anywhere.' They all laughed and crashed their glasses together. He couldn't be certain they were referring to Mrs Wilson's or to his Peggi. The city must have a hundred whores named Peggi. He felt his chop settle heavily into his stomach. For all he knew, one of these men might have been a regular customer of Eliza's. Might have been Anne's lover. A group of doctors maybe. A bunch of well-off, well-bred, well-educated cads. He pushed his plate away and rose, holding his pint. He tripped and fell, pouring its contents over Mr Put-it-in-anywhere. The man jumped up, streaks of beer running down the front of his trousers.

'Hey! Watch yourself! I'll make you wash them you fucking cunt!' He swayed and blocked Peakin's exit.

'I'm terribly sorry. You see I have a limp and I must have lost my balance. Served in Calcutta. Injured in the Sepoy Revolt. But we gave 'em hell in the end.' Peakin clapped a hand on the man's shoulder and walked past, dramatically dragging one leg behind him. His hands clutched his hat so hard that when he got up to his rooms he noticed that he'd creased the brim.

The next day he was in a gloomy mood over breakfast and let his porridge grow cold so that it stuck to his spoon in great lumps and coated the inside of his mouth. There was a fair bit of milk in it this morning but it reminded him of the smell of the women's penitentiary. He sniffed the milk jug and took his tea black. He didn't even have the energy to converse with Kate and let her perform her haphazard dusting in silence.

At Exchequer Court he chose a desk away from the window so that he wouldn't stare out of it. Instead he stared at his notebook, knowing that he ought to be preparing the case against Anne. He had another report to write on the pawnshop beat that he should have submitted yesterday. He leaned his chin on his palm and thought of the men at the Castle Hotel. Looking for an obliging woman they could stick their cocks into and not bothered if all of Dublin knew. And yet they'd become, if they weren't already, professionals. He could tell by the cut of their suits, the quality of the material. The air of comfort and satisfaction they exuded. No doubt they read papers at scientific societies that would never accept Peakin as a member, earning £500 per annum while he struggled along on £50. He smiled at the memory of his beer pooling in the man's lap, the red rage breaking out on his face. And yet here Peakin was, letting someone just like them get away with it. He dearly wanted to make life unpleasant for Dr Matthias J. Kelly. It seemed to Peakin that Eliza would have appreciated it, would have laughed with him over a gentleman getting his comeuppance. But how?

Before he could speculate further, a constable entered and announced that Mrs Kennedy had arrived. She wanted to provide bail and bring Anne home until the trial.

'I was directed to you, sir. I understand the bail is set at £10. I am prepared to hand over the sum at once. I would have come yesterday if I'd been alerted soon enough. I don't want it to be said I'm a woman who leaves her blood relative sitting in prison.'

'We'll need to go before the magistrate to arrange it. Anne will be glad, I'm sure.'

'I wonder if you could tell me, from your own experience, what is likely to be the outcome of the trial.' Mrs Kennedy was still standing above him, having declined the seat he offered on her arrival.

'In cases like this there is often considerable sympathy for the woman. I couldn't say for sure, but I imagine that transportation may be the sentence. Or, if she were to appear of unsound mind, a stay in the asylum. That is usually over within a year and the woman considered recuperated.'

'Is that so? Well, she seems of perfectly sound mind to me. I suppose those are both choices superior to prison or hanging. And what about the man?'

Peakin fingered his moustache and wondered what she would expect him to say.

'What do you mean?'

'I presume he will claim to know nothing, that she was a woman without virtue and that any number of other lovers might have brought her low. Yes, I have enough experience of the vicissitudes of courtship to anticipate the line he will take.'

'I fear you're correct. I don't see any reason to expect different from Dr Kelly. He's engaged to someone else.'

She seemed deflated by his agreement and took the seat with a heavy sigh.

'If this new society had its way she'd be hanged,' she said.

'So you've encountered Mr Mills.'

'Oh I've given him money and had him for dinner. I persuaded Anne to play at his grand gala. The truth is that I wanted to frighten her a little. I didn't realise how much I'd terrified her, of course. Right under my nose. I should never have given her so much freedom. If her mother was alive, I couldn't face her. Still, I suppose we must all be humbled occasionally. Reminds us of the virtues of humility.'

'You'll be asked to act as a witness for the trial. Are you prepared to do that?'

'Of course. It's only right that everyone should see me for the fool I have been.'

'If you don't mind me saying, Mrs Kennedy, you would be far from the first to be deceived. Women are very good at disguising a pregnancy. Fathers, mothers and even fellow servants sharing a bed have failed to notice the signs.' Peakin thought of Dr Pratt. 'A man may notice the changes in a woman who slighted him because he is watching her for evidence that she loves another. You were trying to protect Anne's virtue so you couldn't imagine that it had already been stolen.'

Mrs Kennedy's pressed lips suggested she was unmoved.

'Is that so? You seem to have it all figured out. To know what I might have been thinking.'

'I apologise, Mrs Kennedy, I have some other business to attend to. Would it be quite alright if we were to go before the magistrate right now?'

Mrs Kennedy agreed and insisted that Peakin join her in her carriage for the short ride. As he stooped to enter after her, he tried not to reveal his admiration for the beauty of the vehicle. Inside was like a sitting room reduced to miniature. Whatever wasn't brass or wood was leather or velvet. In the heat it was stuffy but still felt like a buffer against the cruder world outside. He tried to sit so that his knees would not touch Mrs Kennedy's even if they jolted.

'I see you admire the carriage. A Clarence. My late husband had it made to very exact specifications when our children were younger. Many would consider it old fashioned and rather oversized for a woman living alone, but I am used to it. I should probably get a little Brougham instead.'

'It is a very grand vehicle. What do you intend to do with Miss Mulhall when you bring her home?'

'She'll eat and sleep and stay in the house until the trial I suppose. I never imagined that I would have to endure this kind of humiliation when I took her in. But I'm partly to blame. I accept the ostracism that will come. People will grow tired of shunning me and my dining room eventually. I fear for Anne, though. I don't know how she will bear it. Although she has already borne more than I expected her capable of. And if you don't mind me saying, I'd wish Dr

Matthias Kelly to meet with some humiliation and ostracism. I hope that his fiancée and her family have a terrible shock when everything is revealed at the trial.'

'I agree with you completely. But he may find a way not to be named at all. He could make my superiors quite squeamish with the right sort of letters.'

'Detective Peakin, may I make a suggestion?' And she leaned in close to him and whispered so that the driver couldn't hear. She had a pleasant scent, like the waft of polish and wood inside an expensive shop. Peakin listened without saying a word until they arrived at the police court.

Chapter Thirty-Five

Anne

21st August, 1866

Anne had spent only one day in the prison cell, but one day was quite enough to develop in her mind a lively picture of her future. She'd floated through the previous day on a cloud of self-satisfaction. She'd confessed and she felt better. Rose had been wrong. Anne should have confessed long before, not waited until another woman was in danger. But now she'd done the right thing and she was confident that some reward awaited her. Prison could be endured and then she might be transported as the detective had explained. She would have to make her own way in the world, in a strange country. She didn't fear this as she should have. She welcomed the thought of a solitary life of danger and punishment she was certain she deserved.

The cell was lime-washed and seemed almost clean except for Anne's companion. The woman had clearly worn the same clothes for years and was unacquainted with soap. The little room filled with a rank smell of sweat, urine and stale whiskey. Anne regretted selecting one of her better frocks that she thought would make her seem demure. She was convinced that the matron had chosen this particular cell mate as a kind of rebuke. At least the prisoner was so inebriated that Anne couldn't be expected to make conversation. She sat up twice during the night and seemed to be raving. Anne lay on her straw and tried to focus on how she would present her case so as to avoid implicating Rose. She pictured herself as a holy martyr now, patiently bearing her cross. The task distracted her from the rustling of rats and the screams and wails of a lunatic prisoner.

The night passed and a matron went up and down the hallway. Anne was brought to breakfast and to Mass. The dining hall smelled of cabbage, though there was only stirabout on offer. In the chapel she sniffed at the holy incense like it was a fine perfume. By afternoon, after more tedious hours in the company of her own thoughts and a myriad of distressing noise and odours, her enthusiasm for self-flagellation began to dim. She'd imagined her aunt's house as some kind of prison. How naïve she'd been. Her chest tightened at the dawning realisation that she had no control of any kind — no autonomy — in here. She was a body to be moved around as the matrons pleased.

A key scratched in the lock and the head matron appeared in the door. She beckoned Anne to follow and her heart lifted a little.

But then the matron turned and said, 'Here's the constable come for you.' She handed Anne off to him with a small but perceptible shove.

'Constable Delaney, miss. I'm to take you to see the magistrate. A Mrs Kennedy has posted your bail.' Anne deflated. Back into the arms of her aunt.

The constable helped her into a hackney that carried them across the river. From the open carriage she watched the water twirling all the unwanted things that floated on its surface, swirling them round and round.

In the heat of the dingy police court Aunt Julia stood next to Detective Peakin. Anne couldn't meet her eye. Her heart shuddered and she took deep draughts of the courtroom's sweaty, smoky air. The room seemed too bright, there was no shadow she could step into. Anne had somehow believed that her confession to the detective would save her from a confrontation with her aunt. She could feel every seam in her dress, every rib in her stays squeezing her chest. The magistrate puffed his round, red cheeks in and out as he read the papers in front of him. His wig lay beside him on the desk and his robes were thrown back as far as they would go. His hair was dark and curly, almost feminine, so that he seemed in disarray.

'I am satisfied with the conditions of bail. I've received the £10. Mrs Kennedy, do you understand that you are undertaking to guarantee that Miss Mulhall will appear in court on the designated date of her trial? And that if she does not you will forfeit the sum?'

'I do.' There was the familiar voice, softer than Anne had expected.

'And Miss Mulhall, do you understand that if you violate the conditions of the bail then you will be charged with further crimes?'

'I understand.'

'Then you may turn Miss Mulhall over to the offices of her aunt,' the magistrate waved a pudgy hand at the man holding Anne's arm. 'The trial has been set for next week.'

They said nothing as they walked to the waiting carriage. Aunt Julia allowed Anne to help her up onto the step and inside. Anne felt how light her aunt was. For the first time she saw a frail old woman and not a fierce gaoler. Anne wanted her to scream and slap her face. Instead, she sagged in her seat.

In the carriage they sat facing one another and yet each avoided looking into the other's eyes.

'I'm sorry,' Anne tried. 'I never intended ...' Never intended what? Never intended to kill the baby? To disguise the pregnancy? To get pregnant? To fall for a man like Matthias?

The carriage bounced and rattled as they skirted the wall of the park. Dust rose up from the parched street. Aunt Julia sighed.

'When your mother died and your father asked me to take you into my house I didn't think twice. I loved your mother. She knew I didn't approve of her marriage. We'd become distant. I thought I could do this one thing for her. I wished I'd done more for her. I never expected her to die so suddenly.'

'Well, no one did. Father didn't, certainly. Though he was not overly attentive at the best of times.'

'Your father. I let your father ruin everything. It was petty of me. I was so angry with your mother, for what she'd done.'

'What she'd done?' Aunt Julia looked on the verge of tears and very tired.

'Not because of the pregnancy. Because she thought the solution was to marry your father. I wanted her to go away somewhere. To give up the child. Anything but marry your father.'

'To give me up?' Anne whispered as all the pieces fell into different places than she'd put them. The pregnancy, the marriage, the estrangement. She'd made up a story in her head that was all wrong.

'Well, your mother didn't want to give you up and she didn't want to give your father up either. I can understand the choices now, of course. But at the time I thought she was foolish and your father would make her miserable and poor.'

'He didn't. Make her miserable. They were very happy. Or at least that's what I thought. But since he married Ellen I don't know ...' Aunt Julia placed her hand on top of Anne's.

'I never liked him, I've made no secret of it. And your mother sacrificed everything to marry him. I was left with all of the property when our brother died. I felt bad about it. I offered to help, to pay for schooling or whatever was required. I want you to know that your mother wasn't sorry. She didn't regret marrying your father. I believe they loved one another. Don't let Ellen rob you of your memories. A man finds single life harder than a woman does.'

Not knowing what to say, Anne turned back to the window. The driver had decided to avoid the quays and so the view was of more walls. The gate of the barracks passed and then squat little redbrick houses appeared on either side. Their dull repetition was broken on occasion by a colourful door or a shop disgorging its wares onto the footpath.

Aunt Julia gave a forced little laugh. 'I shouldn't have agreed to take you into my house. I couldn't provide what a mother would. I didn't protect you as I should have.' Her voice was soft but the words cut. Anne leaned back against the seat and closed her eyes.

When they arrived at Mountjoy Square the house felt homely for the first time. Anne went up to her room, running her hand along the banister with affection. The wallpaper that had seemed dreary now appeared welcoming, its faded patches like familiar faces. In her room she noticed the way the half-closed curtain glowed pink with the sunlight behind it. She sat in the armchair, trying to soak in the sight of things that she'd been so eager to throw away. Rose opened the door without knocking. Anne had missed her, too. She felt a surge of warm affection and began to stand to embrace her. Rose put her hand out as if to keep Anne in the chair.

'I've something to tell you.'

'Aren't you glad to see me home? It's only for a little while, maybe a few days. But we might enjoy them now that the lying is over. I wonder if Aunt Julia would let you join us for meals. She's very fond of you.'

'Anne. You've made a mistake. I've been sick over it. Why didn't you tell me you planned to confess?'

'You have nothing to worry about, Rose. I didn't mention your name. So long as you deny everything I think you'll be fine. That detective is soft, really. He has a way of looking very shrewd but he can't make me say anything. I don't think he even really wants to. I'll just repeat the same statements I made to him. But I don't want to talk about it now. I want to pretend that I'm not doomed rather than counting down the days. Please, Rose.'

'Anne I do be trying to tell you. It's all a mistake. That baby. It wasn't yours.'

'Of course, it must have been. How many babies ... how many similar situations could there be? I mean, let's not adopt Mr Mills's hysterical tone.'

Rose looked at Anne with genuine anguish. For a moment Anne worried that Rose was ill. Or that the strain of all the secrets, of all the things she'd had to do, was beginning to take its toll. Anne had a sudden picture of Rose gone mad, her curls limp around a blank countenance. A gin bottle at her lips. What good had her friendship done Rose? Anne's ears grew warm. Rose twisted the ribbon of her apron and looked at the floor.

'Your baby is alive. He isn't dead. I didn't put him in the river. A frail little thing I thought but he flailed and screamed and I couldn't just drop him in. Maybe I should have ... I should have ... but I couldn't. I didn't know what else to do. I'm sorry. I never imagined that you'd confess. I tried to tell you a few times. I couldn't tell you.'

The words made no sense.

'But I don't understand. You told me ... you took him ... I thought that I ...'

'I know. I can't forgive myself. You must have been pure tortured thinking that you killed him. I don't know what I was thinking. I just thought it might be worse if you knew. Oh, Anne, can you forgive me?'

Anne's thoughts swarmed, buzzed and flew through her head like bees. Relief, she supposed, to know that she wasn't a murderess after all. But panic too. She thought she'd faced all the trials but here was another one she'd not expected. He was still out there, he could be returned to her and then what would she do? All the colour was gone from Rose's face. Anne offered her the chair and went to lie on her bed.

Rose took her time explaining things. After he'd woken, she said, she took the baby to Kitty. Kitty was the only nurse that she could think of and Rose had known her in school. She paid her for a week out of money she'd been saving from her work in Aunt Julia's house. She thought for certain that he would die within the week, he'd seemed so sickly. But Kitty was remarkably good with babies and she'd kept him well. Then when Denis found the baby in the river, the Society for the Protection of Infant Life had started sniffing around baby farmers. Kitty got a fright. Rose approached Aunt Julia and told her that a woman she knew was in a bit of trouble and did she know any charity that would take the baby. Anne was breathless with the scale of Rose's deception. She'd never lied exactly, but she'd concealed everything.

'But whose baby was it? The one Mr Doyle found in the river?'

'I don't know, Anne. Maybe Kitty's as bad as Mr Mills says. I've been sick over it.'

'And my aunt helped you? She helped you to find a home for my baby?'

'She did. Do you want to know who took him?'

Did she want to know? What did she want to know? What difference would anything make now at all? She sat up on the bed and stared at Rose, who still looked miserable. Her face was all blotched. Her hands were streaked with red where she'd been worrying the ribbon, wrapping it around her fist so tightly that it left marks on her skin.

'Why did you lie?'

'Well, I didn't exactly ... I thought I was doing good. I thought it would only upset you more. I thought I was fixing things. I wanted to fix things for you. It didn't seem fair to me. With all you'd been through.'

'Is he alright?'

'He is. Mrs Kennedy tells me they're a very nice—'

'Does my aunt know the baby was mine?'

'She didn't at first. But when I heard ... when you were arrested ... I had to tell her. I'm sorry.'

'It's fine, Rose, I'm not angry.'

The words seemed to release her, even if she hadn't at first been certain they were true. She couldn't be angry with Rose. Rose had done her best. She'd tried to protect her, she'd saved the child. Anne had been convinced that her confession would allow her to start untangling her mistakes. She'd saved Kitty, a stranger, from suffering but she hadn't thought of how people she cared for would suffer – Rose, and even her aunt. The only person who was not suffering was Matthias. The thought of him, snug in his little blue sitting room being fussed over by Mrs Tuffy, made her furious. The anger was uncontrolled, directionless. There was nothing that she could do.

'You don't know the state I've been in. I thought I might walk into the river and be done with myself,' Rose said. 'I didn't know what to do. I wanted to go to the police but Mrs Kennedy told me not to. That I'd only make more of a mess. I wish I could start again. I'd do everything another way. Denis is taking his time to forgive me and I don't think I want him to. My mother doesn't know anything and she's just waiting for me to have another baby.'

Anne realised that she'd hardly asked Rose anything about herself. She imagined a friendship but all she'd done was place her burdens on Rose and accepted no burdens in return. They were not so different really. Walled in by what other people expected of them, wanted from them. A plan began to grow in Anne's mind. But she would have to speak to her aunt. She'd shown more kindness than Anne had expected, as though all the strains of the past few days had cracked her open. She might just be prepared to help.

Chapter Thirty-Six

Peakin

22nd August, 1866

Peakin was surprised to receive a note inviting him to Mountjoy Square. In the carriage on the way to collect Anne, Mrs Kennedy had suggested that in exchange for his careful treatment of Anne, for his pursuit of fairness, he might receive some kind of monetary reward. He insisted that he treated every case with care and there was no need, nor any room, for special treatment. He hadn't wanted to argue for the fairness of the system but he hadn't had to anyway. She'd interrupted him to say that Anne might endure the inevitable if only the man had to face some kind of consequences. Could Peakin make it well known that he was suspected of being the father of the infant? Could he blacken his name just a little in the course of the trial?

Peakin admired Mrs Kennedy's desire to see Dr Matthias Kelly squirm a bit. He saw this as evidence of love. He would have enjoyed making a gentleman doctor the subject of whisperings and newspaper editorials. But he couldn't promise her any such thing for any amount of money. As Acting Sergeant he had to do what his superiors wanted.

The inspector would decide what evidence was presented. Of course, Anne might make any accusations she wished, but they'd most likely be dismissed as the ravings of a loose and angry woman. Easily brushed aside.

The square showed no outward signs that it was harbouring a criminal. The clump of drivers were back, shifting foot to foot like their horses. A group of children were playing at climbing the fence and Peakin was surprised that no one from the houses came out to shake a stick at them. He looked up at the houses and saw set after set of closed curtains. Their inhabitants gone to the seaside, the lakeside, the countryside. Anywhere in search of a breeze.

Peakin was ushered into a different room than last time. The room glowed an almost cheerful colour, made up of green light reflected off the lawn and faded yellow wallpaper. At the table sat Mrs Kennedy and Anne Mulhall. Mrs Kennedy spoke first.

'Come and sit with us, please, Mr Peakin. You may place your hat on the table.'

Her voice was less imperious, though she was dressed in her usual manner. Anne rested her hands on a pile of folded papers. She looked up at him and smiled. Peakin pulled out a chair and felt a sudden longing for domestic comforts. Simple things, less grand than this room: four chairs round a table of dining height, a settee without stains, curtains that lacked moth holes. A room that smelled of sun-warmed wood and paper dust and the fading notes of breakfast rather than slops from the yard and boiled vegetables and river fug.

'How can I be of service?'

'Anne, shall I explain?'

'Yes please, Aunt Julia.'

'When we spoke in the carriage the other day I wasn't aware of some important facts.' Anne picked up one of the papers and unfolded it, smoothed it against the table, and then passed it to Peakin.

'Do you want me to read it?' Peakin glanced at the page. In a slanted script the letter was addressed to *My darling Anne*. He scanned to the bottom and saw it had been signed *Your dearest M*. Presumably M for Matthias.

'You might read them in your own good time. You'll see that they are quite incriminating as far as Dr Kelly is concerned.'

'But are any of them signed?' Realisation dawned. Anne and Mrs Kennedy now hoped to drag the good doctor through the mud using his own words. He admired their determination. He glanced at them and saw the resemblance. Two mouths set in two lines of patient resolve. Two pairs of hands placed in laps. 'Hmmm. Well, if they aren't signed, it is a difficulty. Just an initial won't serve. He'll simply deny everything and heap further accusations upon Miss Mulhall. In truth they might make things worse.'

'We considered that. There might be another way to make some use of them.' Two heads leaned towards him and two sets of eyes fixed on him in hope.

Half an hour later he found himself on the street again. His stomach was comfortably full of scones and milky tea into which he'd had the audacity to stir two spoons of sugar. He couldn't remember the last time he'd been so satisfied by a meal. He knew it was part of the persuasion but he didn't care. Even his shoes had begun to feel loose. When he removed his stockings at night, it seemed like there was too much space between each toe. And then there was the matter of the £10 now tucked into his billfold. It was a substantial sum but was it enough to insure him against the risk he was about to take? He would surely lose his chance at promotion. It might be five years before he had another. And yet he felt that this act of charity would clear his conscience. The idea of owing his promotion to this case ... well he felt it would make him no better than Dr Kelly. No better than Mr Mills. A beneficiary of female misery. There was nothing respectable, nothing gentlemanly, about that. He'd have to be careful how he spent the money. Perhaps he could say he'd received a small inheritance from a distant relative? An aunt he hadn't known. He smiled at his own joke.

And then suddenly he was there, standing in front of Dr Kelly's house. Well, here we go, he thought.

He knocked. A grey-haired servant opened the door and, before she could speak, Peakin placed his calling card into her hand. He congratulated himself once again on his cleverness in getting cards made up that gave his name and nothing more. A respectable suit and a pretty calling card could get you into many an unsuspecting home. The maid ushered him into the darkened hallway and took the card away with her. Peakin looked around him. The house was owned by a bachelor — no woman would have tolerated the drab darkness of this hall, Peakin thought. Nothing wrong with its smart brick front, but inside the floor was covered in rugs and the patterned wallpaper contained a shade of burgundy a little too close to dried blood for Peakin's liking. There were gaslight fittings on the walls and they'd stained the paper as they were wont to do if no one cleaned around them. The hall table was elaborately carved and decorated in gold leaf with a piece of shining black marble for the top. On it stood a vase that held a few lilies, their heavy scent amplified by the heat. If I'd been dropped here and opened my eyes I would strongly suspect this was a card house, thought Peakin. Or something worse. He wondered if that was the desired effect or simply reflected the tastes of the previous resident. The servant reappeared.

'Dr Kelly will see you in his study, Mr Peakin. It is at the back of the house. Please follow me.' Down the hall they plunged. You would hardly know that the sun shone on the street, Peakin thought, it's evening in here all day long. The servant opened a door on the left and Peakin stepped into the study as though from a cave into the daylight. He blinked. The usual mahogany furniture, books more visible than wallpaper. The two windows revealed a plain green square of a yard with a tangle of trees that no one had bothered to train or trim.

Dr Matthias Kelly rose from his desk, where a war had broken out between different piles of papers with unfortunate casualties scattered every which way.

'Mr Peakin. I'm afraid I do not know you nor the nature of your visit. As you can see, I am hard at work here. A paper for the Royal Irish Academy. So please state your business sir and don't beat about the bush.'

'Don't worry, I will take little of your time. I am a detective with the Dublin Metropolitan Police. I am here about an infanticide.' Peakin noted that Dr Kelly's face registered nothing. Instead, he appeared intrigued.

'Do you need a doctor to conduct a postmortem? I imagine I could slip away for an hour ...'

'No, that procedure has been performed by Dr Mapother, but thank you kindly. No, the matter is more personal to you.'

'Personal to me?'

'Do you know a young woman by the name of Anne Mulhall?'

'I did. Some time ago. We haven't spoken in almost a year.'

'Then you may not have heard that she's been arrested. I have taken a lengthy statement from her. She has admitted to infanticide and concealment of birth.' Peakin let the words hang in the air as he examined the doctor's bookshelves. Two different encyclopaedias. A number of titles in French. A shelf full of anatomy books in which he picked out William Hunter's *Anatomy of the Human Gravid Uterus*. Almost no natural history. Just an old edition of Cuvier that looked like it had never been opened and some Lamarck that was surely out of fashion. Where was Darwin or Agassiz? Where was his intellectual curiosity? Dr Kelly continued shifting papers around, closing books and stacking them. Then the silence got the better of him as Peakin knew it would.

'I think I know what this is about. In fact, I was thinking of going to the police myself. She told me some tall tale and tried to blackmail me only a few months ago.'

'Ah. So you *have* seen her of late. You must have forgotten.'

'I suppose it was so ridiculous that it didn't seem important. It's sad, really. You see, I made a friend of her over a year ago and I think she'd begun to expect a proposal. To preserve honour all around I thought it was best not see her for a while. And as I am now soon to be married to someone else I think she has become jealous, the poor thing.' He smiled, which was obviously intended to disarm the listener. Peakin returned the smile, happy to appear disarmed. This was going to be easier than he'd even imagined.

'This attachment you mention. This would explain the letters that you wrote to her, I imagine. I think they suggest a rather more intimate involvement than you have made out. I understand why you would want to conceal this involvement, of course. I mean, it could make things most uncomfortable for your fiancée and her family. A Miss Clancy, I believe? Timber merchants, I think, the Clancys.'

Dr Kelly's face groped for the appropriate expression and landed on something between repulsion and indignation.

'If you believe that I would be foolish enough to write things in signed letters that ...'

'Ah, there you have me. They are not signed. Or at least not fully signed. But it would seem quite possible to match them up with a different sample of your handwriting, such as this, for example.' Peakin stepped towards the desk and lifted up a letter. There was absolutely no chance that the inspector or the judge would accept matching handwriting as evidence but he gambled that Dr Kelly did not know that. 'One letter alone might not be enough, but there is quite a collection. And there's the matter of sending the pills. Even if nothing comes of it in court, well the newspapermen will enjoy it. You know how they are.'

'This is outrageous. Are you here to arrest me? I deny everything and I think you will find that if you insist on pursuing these ridiculous charges it is you who will be humiliated and humbled.'

'I have a different suggestion and I've come here to speak to you as a gentleman, not a detective.' He ignored the sneer on Dr Kelly's face. 'Miss Mulhall herself doesn't wish to press any charges and wishes to avoid the many humiliations of a trial. But in truth, she probably has less to lose than you do. How would Miss Clancy's parents feel if they found their daughter's betrothed was accused of fathering a child and then abandoning the mother? They would find someone else to provide their family with the hoped-for social cachet. There are many men who could take your place.'

'But you cannot say I abandoned her! I knew nothing of the child. I must have written her a dozen letters. She never replied. I admit there was a moment of passion, but she shared in it. She permitted me liberties, detective, such as a lady with any concern for her reputation ...' he went to continue but Peakin waved a hand in dismissal.

'I don't think this would be a useful line of argument for you. Is it not a gentleman's duty to protect a woman? Is it not even more incumbent upon you, as a creature in possession of higher levels of reason? There are other ways to satisfy the body's needs, Dr Kelly. Hear me out at least.' Dr Kelly looked like he might burst his skin in outrage. He picked up a pipe from the desk and stuffed it with tobacco, not caring for the shreds that landed on the desk and floor. He lit it and sat down in the chair.

'I'm listening. But I'll make no promises. And if I don't like what I hear, you can be certain that I will go immediately to the police commissioner myself and report you for any and all improprieties. I think you'll find that a doctor's word carries plenty of weight against a junior officer such as yourself.'

'I'm here to offer you an escape. An opportunity to continue your life unperturbed by this case. Miss Mulhall wishes to leave the country and start again. I ask only for a contribution towards the cost of tidying this matter away. You may consider this a saving from what it would cost to engage a lawyer and to lose the beneficial match you have made for yourself. If you give me £50 for Miss Mulhall then I am prepared to give you back your letters to burn as you wish.'

'Fifty pounds! You must be joking. How do I know you're not planning to take some for yourself?'

Peakin allowed the doctor to rant and rage. To accuse Peakin of villainous extortion. In truth Peakin worried about whether this would work. He didn't think Dr Kelly would really go to Exchequer Court and accuse him of all the things he was now spitting at him. It was too risky for the doctor, would draw too much attention to him. On the other hand, he might just refuse. And then he would have to return the £10 that had pleasantly fattened his billfold. He would have to disappoint Mrs Kennedy and Miss Mulhall.

He would have to watch her be convicted and he would have that weighing on his conscience. Everything hung on Dr Kelly's egotism, his devotion to his reputation and to his new future with Miss Clancy.

Dr Kelly sat down at his desk and put his head in his hands. A few pieces of paper fell off and gently glided to the ground.

'I am not a wealthy man, Peakin. This will ruin me! It's almost all my rent for the year.'

His rent for the year! It was almost Peakin's salary for the year. He wished he'd asked for more.

'Fifty pounds is the amount.' Let him appear humble before Miss Clancy and her family, there would be no harm in that.

Dr Kelly opened a drawer in his desk and withdrew a book of promissory notes for the bank. He sighed long and elaborately. Peakin held his breath. The doctor began to write one out, sloppily, as though he hoped that it might be less valuable if covered in a flurry of ink splats. He rang the bell and the aged maid servant appeared.

'Mrs Tuffy, take this note which is for Mr Peakin but is to pay for the return of some lost property. Some important papers which he will give to you at his office. You are in charge of the note until he has handed over the papers.' He placed the note into a sealed envelope and handed it to the woman.

'There. It's done.' He didn't rise to shake hands or say goodbye but resumed whatever he was writing at his desk. Peakin's eyes swept the green room one last time before he returned down the dark hallway with the servant. Mrs Tuffy opened the front door and they faced into the light and heat together.

They went first to his rooms, where Mrs Tuffy waited in the common drawing room under the watchful eye of Kate while Peakin collected the packet of letters that he had sealed elaborately into a large envelope. Then they went to the bank. Throughout this exchange the servant said no more than necessary and her face betrayed no emotion. Peakin placed the notes carefully in his billfold and lodged it, now bulging, in a pocket of his suit near to his chest before returning to Exchequer Court.

Chapter Thirty-Seven

Denis

24th August, 1866

The night before the trial, Denis couldn't sleep. Rose hadn't come back and somehow the presence of her few remaining things made the rooms feel even emptier. Two old dresses hung in the wardrobe like discarded skins, stretched and shaped by her body. He recognised the curve of her elbow in the sleeve and pictured the white of her throat above the edge of the bodice. He got out of bed to feel the fabric of them between his fingers, to search them with his nose for any of her scent. But Rose was particular about washing her clothes and all he could smell was soap. Denis told himself that as soon as this trial was over, this final ordeal, then he could try in earnest to convince her to return home. He'd seen Mrs Treacy on the street and she reassured him that Rose was well. She was returning to herself. He lay in bed picturing their reconciliation.

In the morning he pulled on his wedding suit for the second time in a month. The detective had told him that he might not be called on at all: the judge could accept the evidence of the inquest. Nonetheless, he was to be present

and prepared. He wanted to see how it ended. He felt sorry
for the woman and grateful that she hadn't brought Rose into
the trial. Even admired her bravery in confessing when the
police arrested Kitty. He wondered what she was planning to
say. Would Mrs Kennedy's word convince the judge that the
baby in the river wasn't Anne's? And shouldn't she pay some
kind of price for hiding her condition, for wanting to kill
the child? And what of the baby he'd found? Would anyone
be brought to justice? Women couldn't be allowed to kill
their babies or abandon them to die. Acts of brutality that
threatened to send society backwards into a dark age.

Denis wasn't prepared for what happened next. At the appointed
hour, the court assembled. Judge and jury, witnesses. Mrs
Kennedy was there along with most of her household. Denis
was alone, sneaking glances around the room, hoping to see
Rose. She wasn't there and neither was Anne.

Mrs Kennedy looked flustered. She fanned herself and
wiped her brow repeatedly. The judge tried to make a start.

'Mrs Kennedy, when you undertook to provide bail for
your niece it was made entirely clear what your responsibilities
were, was it not?' he said.

'It was, your honour.'

'Your responsibilities were to deliver the suspect to the
court for the trial. To ensure that the suspect did not escape.
Miss Anne Mulhall has been accused of a very serious crime.
In fact, we may say the *most* serious crime that our laws
recognise. A murder. She is also accused of concealment of
birth. Without a trial she cannot be established as guilty or
innocent. She is a fugitive from the law. And you have lost
the bail money, of course.'

'I understand this, your honour. I had no reason to
believe that she would leave. If she made plans, she hid them

well. She has few relatives in Ireland, aside from myself. She may as well be estranged from her father. And she was in such distress that I considered that doing some harm to herself was far more likely. I sent my most trusted servant, my cook, to sleep in the room beside hers because of this worry.'

'Do you have any idea where she may have gone? If we find that you are hiding something there will be serious consequences.' The judge's wig shook as he drew out the word 'consequences' for emphasis.

'My only thought is that she went to a cousin in Athlone. The train from Galway stops there and she mentioned this cousin to me. A niece of her father's, I think. Someone she saw as a child often. She suggested some wish to see her again. The name is Grogan.'

'Thank you, Mrs Kennedy. The trial will adjourn now while inquiries are made.'

The court was in chaos, no one certain how to proceed. Newspapermen slunk around the room, hoping to overhear something important. The lawyers huddled together. Yet Denis was hardly aware of the buzzing conversations going on around him. Where was Rose? Why wasn't she here? The rest of Mrs Kennedy's servants seemed to be here. He had a dull, hollowed-out feeling like he'd eaten a very green apple. He needed to check on Rose. Even if she didn't want to speak to him. Just to make sure she was all right.

Denis spotted Detective Peakin, who had formed a huddle with Mr Mills. As he approached, he overheard Mr Mills speaking in nasally tones of disapproval: 'A fine mess you've made of this now detective. Well, the society will advocate that bail be set high enough in future to avoid such an embarrassment to the police.'

'It is unfortunate. One would have thought that Mrs Kennedy could be trusted to keep an eye on her. On the other hand, you were quite keen to see Mrs Conroy punished, though it appears she was entirely innocent. I imagine that the inspector might be interested to know that a young woman who dies at your asylum in mysterious circumstances does not merit a postmortem or a search for relatives but finds herself in the hands of an anatomist. I would think that could be a source of embarrassment to a charitable institution.'

Denis didn't understand what the detective was talking about but Mr Mills looked both alarmed and furious, and as he decided what to say, Denis took the opportunity to speak.

'Excuse me, gentlemen, I'm very sorry to interrupt.' Denis turned to Peakin. 'I've a few things to take care of. Do you think I might return home, detective? I don't want to cause further inconvenience so I'll stay if I'm needed.'

'I think it would perfectly fine for you to go, Mr Doyle. It seems there will be no trial today.' Mr Mills scowled at them both, as though Denis was responsible for how things turned out. As though he hadn't been the one who'd found the body in the first place and thus provided the key evidence that had started all of this. Everything he'd done seemed in vain. He'd thought that Anne would come here and tell the truth and then the police could try to find the real murderer. But instead she'd slunk away. Had she been guilty after all? No, he couldn't believe that Rose would lie about that. But now they might never know who killed the baby he found. No one would be punished, the story unfinished.

As he walked away, he heard Mr Mills declaring that he would close down every baby farming business in the city. Across the room, Mrs Kennedy sat taking small sips from a glass of water. They nodded at one another.

When he got out onto the street he felt an urge to run to Mrs Treacy's house, as though he'd had a premonition that something awful had befallen Rose. If she was ill then Mrs Treacy would have sent word, would have come to the shop. He felt himself walking faster, his breath coming in rhythmic gulps and his arms pumping. At Sackville Bridge he stopped to catch his breath, turned his face to the river in search of a breeze. He didn't want to arrive a sweating mess of worry and bother.

Up Sackville Street and onto Abbey Street and down their lane. Washing hung from windows like loose teeth. The door to the tenement was open as usual. Children scuttled up and down the stairs, fetching things for an adult or engaged in some game with one another. Each floor provided a different set of sounds; a choir of voices shouting or calling or humming, the chants of children's games, a bow across a fiddle, the barking of a dog, the splashing of slops, the whistling of a kettle. He reached the Treacys' door and stood outside for a moment. He'd barely even rested his fist against the door when it was flung open and his mother-in-law stood in front of him.

Her face was like a crumpled rag out of which peered two reddened eyes.

'Oh. I was hoping … never mind. Come in. You'd better come in. I'll put the kettle on.'

Denis already knew but he didn't ask any questions because he thought that maybe, if he waited long enough, the thing he knew would become untrue. Mrs Treacy disappeared into the scullery and he could hear her splashing water into the kettle. She prodded at the fire to raise it and hung the kettle to boil. She seemed even less eager to tell him where Rose was than he was to ask her. She didn't meet his eye as she waited for the water, but busied herself with the teapot and two cups. She poured a drop of milk into each one and sat down to wait. They both jumped when the kettle wailed. She filled the teapot and brought it to sit next to him at the table.

'I'm looking for Rose,' Denis said, unable to wait any longer. Mrs Treacy sighed and leaned back in her chair, two hands on her teacup.

'She left a note. Here, you can read it.' She reached into her apron and drew forth a small square of good paper, damp and creased. As he read, the hollowed-out feeling returned. He put the paper down and did not try to stop his tears. They dropped in such profusion that he watched several land in his tea with a splash, making little spheres on the surface that disappeared as soon as they arrived. He sipped it anyway, wanting to feel the hot liquid scald his throat and the china handle press into his palm as though these sensations would comfort him.

Chapter Thirty-Eight

Anne

24th August, 1866

The quayside was a loud tangle of people and animals, a blur of sound and smell more overwhelming than Sackville Street in the evening rush. Steamships belched out black clouds that curled and dissipated among the masts of the sailing ships. As Anne watched the scramble she realised that she was afraid. The ships were terrifyingly large but also too fragile for battle against the sea. They huffed restfully on the calm river, wooden decks creaking. Once underway, a wrongly tended furnace might turn everything to flame and billowing smoke. She'd seen the pictures of desperate passengers and upended hulls. Anne thought that it would be a fitting punishment for her actions. She looked around at her fellow passengers for evidence that they were also doomed. Was God planning to smite a little girl with serious eyes and matted black hair? Or the man holding fast to his tiny mottled dog? She was afraid of the journey but it was only a distraction from her fear of arrival and everything it would mean.

Now she wished she'd left the very first day she could. She'd lingered on in the boarding house, stewing in its fug of boiled turnips and dirty linens while she thought about changing her mind. She went to Carolin and Egan's almost daily but didn't buy a ticket for the *Zephyr* or the *Foyle* or the *Lady Wodehouse*. Each day that ticked past was another day she risked discovery. She thought about going somewhere else, Belfast even, but the only connection she had was the reference her aunt had given her for a London schoolmaster. And there was her sister, of course. If Anne could face her. She couldn't even buy a steamer ticket, so how would she find rooms to rent or gainful employment? She had risked sending a note to Rose who'd come storming down to the boarding house, marched her to the steam packet office and waited until the ticket was in her hand. Just her presence made Anne feel braver, and now she was supposed to be here to say goodbye.

'Excuse me, is this the London steamer?' Anne turned to the nearest respectable-looking woman. She looked puzzled.

'Sure, doesn't it say so on the sign up there?'

'Oh yes, I see. It's such a crush down here, isn't it? I haven't been away before.'

'Is that so? Well, enjoy the journey,' the woman replied, turning away and ending the conversation.

Anne scanned the crowd for Rose or someone else to talk to. There were great numbers of poor people, all cheekbones and elbows and broken shoes. A few beggars worked the crowd and she kept a hand on her case while the other crushed her ticket. Occasionally, she let the ticket hand brush against her skirt to reassure herself that the money she'd sewn into the lining was still there. She kept her eyes on the ship, waiting for the signal to board. Anne pictured Rose sitting in the courtroom, making a show of comforting her aunt as the judge reprimanded her for Anne's absence. Had it worked? There was no way of knowing unless Rose came. The truth was Anne wanted her to come to England, but she didn't dare to ask. After she'd been discarded by her father and Matthias, she couldn't endure the possibility that Rose would refuse. And of course it would be cruel of her to suggest it, to encourage Rose to leave her husband and her parents. Once she got to England she could write. Maybe Rose would visit.

Beasts were being loaded into the hold of the Liverpool steamer ahead. The sheep were tossed like bales of wool and then the passengers began to mount the gangways. Women in steerage quickly staked claim to portions of the deck and prepared themselves to hunker down, pulling their shawls over their heads. Families scrambled to assemble into orderly packs with everyone accounted for. Still no sign of boarding her ship. Still time for Rose to come.

Anne heard a woman's voice above the crowd, searching for a sister or daughter.

'Someone's calling you, I think,' said an older man as he patted Anne's arm and pointed. There was Rose, waving and shouting her new name. She'd already forgotten that she was no longer Anne (the almost murderer and fugitive) but Mary (the piano teacher).

Rose struggled through the crowd with an enormous carpet bag over one arm.

'I've made it,' she said, huffing out her cheeks and clutching the bag. 'Jesus, I thought I'd miss you and then I don't know what I would've done.'

'Is everything alright? Did my aunt send you with this? It wasn't necessary. I hate to think you've walked all the way here with it. I have all I need.'

'This? This is for me.'

'But where are you going?'

'To London you fool. Unless you'd rather I didn't.'

Anne hoped that her face showed more pleasure than shock. Rose watched with her usual half smile.

'But what about—'

'I'm not going back. This will be easier on him anyway. Let's talk about something else.' Rose leaned in closer and gave the family beside them a warning look. She pulled the bag tight to her chest. 'Please tell me you've your notes secured somewhere. I don't like the look of this crowd.'

Anne could tell from the determined line of her mouth that she didn't plan on saying anything more about her decision and she didn't want to be asked. Meanwhile Anne felt excited for the first time. Rose's presence turned exile into some kind of adventure. There would be plenty of time to ask her about Mr Doyle. To persuade her to go back because of course she couldn't stay with Anne in London forever. Could she?

Finally they were stepping on board. They stayed on the deck as the ship began to shudder and lurch and the ropes were thrown. As they steamed up the river they looked back towards the city. How beautiful it looked at a distance. The rows of houses neat and tidy in the sun, the straight lines of the quays and the hills hovering green above it all. Anne wondered what Rose was thinking as she watched her home shrinking into the distance. She measured the weight of what she was leaving behind: a son and a half-sister who would never know her, a father who might miss her. Her aunt.

'What do you think it will be like?' Anne asked.

'London? I guess like Dublin only bigger. Or like Dublin stretched so that the grand streets are more grand and the filthy ones even worse.'

'I can't stop picturing myself slowly losing my teeth in some horrible hovel in St Giles, surrounded by decrepit buildings and the sounds of chamber pots being slopped into the street. I think I read too many Dickens novels.'

Rose put her head back and laughed. And then she squeezed Anne's hand.

'We'll be alri'. You'll see. We'll find the most dull, respectable boarding house in all of London and get ourselves some dull, respectable occupations.'

Rose put her hand into a pocket of her skirt and pulled out two little white knitted booties. With no explanation, she dropped them in the water and together they watched them swirl in the wake of the boat as though they were headed back to Dublin.

Historical Note

This book is a work of fiction, the characters and plot are invented. There was never any detective Martin Peakin, although there was an Inspector Ryan of G Division. Denis Doyle was a real butcher on North Earl Street but I don't know the name of his wife and I don't think he ever found a baby in the Liffey. The real Dr Mapother, who served as Medical Officer of Health for Dublin, has lent my Dr Mapother his name. Nonetheless, I have relied on historical research to build my characters and this picture of nineteenth-century Dublin.

Elaine Farrell's 'A Most Diabolical Deed': Infanticide and Irish Society, 1850–1900 (Manchester University Press, 2013) gave me a sense of the kinds of women who committed infanticide and what they experienced if they were caught. Infanticide in the Irish Crown Files at Assizes, 1883–1900 (Irish Manuscripts Commission, 2012), also by Farrell, documents all known cases in the court files over about two decades and details of some of these cases appear in the book.

Ireland's first Magdalene asylum was founded on Leeson Street but Mr Mills's asylum is fictitious. Maria Luddy's work, especially Prostitution and Irish Society, 1800–1940 (Cambridge University Press, 2007), is an essential starting point for anyone interested in the history of Irish women surviving on the margins.

Ciaran O'Neill's work on Irish elites flavoured my view of Aunt Julia and her world, especially Catholics of

Consequence: Transnational Education, Social Mobility, and the Irish Catholic Elite, 1850–1900 (Oxford University Press, 2014), as did his chapter on the Irish bourgeois in *The Cambridge History of Ireland, vol III, 1730–1880* (Cambridge University Press, 2018). Ciaran and I wrote about the affair between James Christopher Fitzgerald Kenny and Mary Louise McMahon ('Love, consent and the Victorian sexual script', *Journal of the History of Sexuality,* 2020). The article used Kenny's diary, which is held by Trinity College Dublin. The characters of Anne and Matthias owe something to Mary and James.

My view of dirty Victorian Dublin was shaped by Jacinta Prunty's *Dublin Slums, 1800–1925: A Study in Urban Geography* (Irish Academic Press, 1997) and Mary Daly's *Dublin, the Deposed Capital: A Social and Economic History, 1860–1914* (Cork University Press, 1984). David Dickson's *Dublin: The Making of a Capital City* (Harvard University Press, 2014) was invaluable. Ruth McManus's study of lodging houses looks at a later period but was still helpful ('Dublin's lodger phenomenon in the early twentieth century', *Irish Economic and Social History,* 2018) while Ciarán McCabe's work on charwomen shaped Rose and her mother ('Charwomen and Dublin's secondary labour force in the late nineteenth and early twentieth centuries', *Social History,* 2020).

Georgina Laragy answered a lot of questions about inquests from her research on suicide (*Suicide in Ireland, 1823–1918,* forthcoming from Liverpool University Press). Ciara Henderson generously provided her expertise about stillbirth and its rituals in the nineteenth century.

Brian Griffin's PhD thesis ('The Irish police, 1836–1914: a social history', Loyola University Chicago, 1991) helped me piece together the life of Peakin. I also used Anastasia Dukovna's *A History of the Dublin Metropolitan Police and its Colonial*

Legacy (Palgrave Macmillan, 2016) and Barry Kennerk's *The Peeler's Notebook: Policing Victorian Dublin: Mad Dogs, Duels And Dynamite* (The Mercier Press, 2019).

Finally, I have used innumerable nineteenth-century documents conserved, catalogued and made accessible by librarians and archivists. Without them there would be no history and no historical fiction. They deserve more money.

Acknowledgements

Thank you to my agent, Imogen Morrell, who loved this book from the start and kept faith in it when I'd lost mine.

Thank you to Aoife K. Walsh at New Island for taking a risk on me and this story. Thanks also to Des Doyle, Djinn von Noorden, Mariel Deegan, Cassia Gaden Gilmartin and Elizabeth Goldrick (all at New Island) for their hard work and love of books. Thank you to Luke Bird for the beautiful cover. Thank you to Susan McKeever for her editorial work.

Thanks to Catherine Cleary and Aoibheann Sweeney, first readers of my first fiction. Thanks to Niamh Boyce for her love of Peakin. Thanks to writers-in-arms from The Novelry (Jane Mansour, Cate Guthleben and Shannon Cowan) for reading an early draft. Jane has been the best virtual writing buddy. The following people read drafts and their encouragement kept me going: Rachel Ryan, Damien Owens, Martin Fanning, Darran McCann, Mary Shine, Laura McKenna, Georgina Laragy and Ciaran O'Neill. All errors are my own.

My creative life has benefitted from excellent company. Thanks to Historians Anonymous (Aoife Breathnach, Niamh Cullen, Carrie Griffin, Olivia Fitzsimons and David Toms) and 'The Lakers' who I met at the Tyrone Guthrie Centre one May (Thomas Brezing, Janet Moran, Patsy Murphy, Lianne O'Hara, Fiona O'Rourke and Una Sealy). Thank you to the Tyrone Guthrie Centre and Eimear O'Connor for the wonderful welcoming environment where I got so much done. Thank you to the Stinging Fly Summer School gang (Kelly Dignan, Tam Eastley, Lynne Kinlon, Maya Kulukundis, Angélica Libre, Niall McKenna, John McLeod, Jeannie Sutton, and Sam Furlong Tighe).

My parents, Burt and Lydia, and my two siblings, Ian and Lizzie, seemed totally unsurprised when I got a publisher. I take this as a vote of confidence. I'm flattered that my children, Aidan and Cian, are so proud of me. They might be more proud if this was a graphic novel. Maybe someday.

Finally, my husband Martin foolishly encouraged me to write this book. He read the very first draft and several more besides. He listened to me whine and complain and wallow in self-pity at every stage of the process and for some reason he hasn't divorced me. Thank you, Martin.